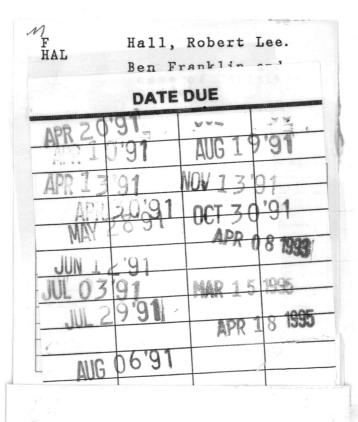

DATE DUE

APR 20'91		
APR 10'91	AUG 19'91	
APR 13'91	NOV 13'91	
APR 20'91	OCT 30'91	
MAY 28'91	APR 08 1993	
JUN 12'91		
JUL 03'91	MAR 15 1995	
JUL 29'91	APR 18 1995	
AUG 06'91		

Benjamin Franklin and a Case of Christmas Murder

By Robert Lee Hall:

Exit Sherlock Holmes
Murder at San Simeon
Benjamin Franklin Takes the Case

Benjamin Franklin and a Case of Christmas Murder

By
ROBERT LEE HALL

St. Martin's Press
New York

BENJAMIN FRANKLIN AND A CASE OF CHRISTMAS MURDER. Copyright © 1990 by Robert Lee Hall. All rights reserved. Printed in the United States of America. No part of this book may be used or reproduced in any manner whatsoever without written permission except in the case of brief quotations embodied in critical articles or reviews. For information, address St. Martin's Press, 175 Fifth Avenue, New York, N.Y. 10010.

Production Editor: David Stanford Burr

Library of Congress Cataloging-in-Publication Data

Hall, Robert Lee.
    Benjamin Franklin and a case of Christmas murder / Robert Lee Hall.
        p.   cm.
    "A Thomas Dunne book."
    ISBN 0-312-05383-5
    1. Franklin, Benjamin, 1706-1790—Fiction. I. Title.
PS3558.A3739B45   1991
813'.54—dc20   90-49305
                                                  CIP

First Edition: January 1991

10 9 8 7 6 5 4 3 2 1

For dear Mady

Preface

In 1795 Nicolas Handy, then an old man, sat down to chronicle for his only son his adventures with the famous writer, statesman and inventor, Benjamin Franklin.

For nearly two centuries these stories were lost.

Then in 1987 my aunt Ivy Goodale died, leaving me all she owned. Among her effects I discovered the first manuscript my great-great-great-great-great-great grandfather wrote. Recently published as *Benjamin Franklin Takes the Case*, it proves that another profession must be added to the number of ventures at which the great man was so adept: that of detective.

Of course detective is a modern term, but that is what Franklin clearly was.

Other manuscripts have come to light. They show that in the midst of pursuing political and scientific aims Franklin also solved mysteries, bringing murderers, thieves, and extortionists to justice.

He even pulled the shroud from a ghost.

And so, after two hundred years, I am pleased to offer the second adventure of Benjamin Franklin, detective.

—Robert Lee Hall

❧ 1 ❧

IN WHICH a merry time of year is marred by a puzzle easily solved—though another soon takes its place. . . .

The day before Christmas dawned upon mystery. It seemed of little consequence, yet it so unsettled Mrs. Margaret Stevenson that the lace fringes of her white housewife's cap trembled.

"Dear Nick," moaned she coming upon me upstairs in Mr. Benjamin Franklin's workshop behind the room he let from her in Craven Street, "have you spied the tailor's pattern card which I placed with great care upon the hallstand by the front door just this morning? Placed with particular care, I say! Yet it is gone. O, where might it be?" She peered about. "There were upon it a good dozen samples of broadcloth, from which I meant to choose one for a fine new coat for Mr. Franklin. Do not you think he wants a fine new coat? I detest his plain brown stuff! And now the card has vanished. Have you seen it, child? Prithee, say you have."

"I have not seen it, ma'am," replied I.

"Dear, dear!" The distraught woman tapped the mole by the side of her nose. "Well, and I believe you, yet it is ill luck on such a day, the day before Christmas, with so much to be done. Polly!" wailed she to her daughter, bustling from the

1

room and shutting the door, and I heard her call twice again upon the stairs: "Polly! Polly!"

As for me, Nicolas Handy, though I did not like to see Mrs. Stevenson so distressed I gave little thought to the card. The good woman's household was to her as a kingdom to a queen, with each domain to be kept in strict subjugation. Yet some rebellious bits of broadcloth could make little matter; they presaged no general uprising. Besides, at twelve years old I was pleased to be let alone with my experiments, insignificant compared to Mr. Franklin's great work on electricity, translated into many tongues, yet sufficient to fascinate an untutored boy who had been whisked from adversity to this cheery house in Craven Street not three months since. So, sitting at Mr. Franklin's pitted workbench, surrounded by his tools and apparati—his Armonica, his measuring devices, the fossil bone of a mammoth on a shelf, his Philadelphia Machine, as he called his electrical battery which might kill a man as well as lightning—I once more rubbed with a soft cloth the long glass tube, then moved the tube near the curls of metal which lay upon the bench. I was delighted to see these curls leap to the glass like mites in a bed and cling to it as if the glass were their dear mother. Yet after a time some of these seemed to weary and fall free, and I was equally delighted, as I moved the glass near them once more, to observe them this time start and jig away, like bedbugs striving to escape pinching fingers. I understood the reason: Mr. Franklin had oft spoke of the positive and negative charge; but it was not cause but effect which bade me play again and again.

Yet this lost interest, and I drifted to the casement window looking out upon Mrs. Stevenson's tidy back yard, with its small rear stables. Snow. It lay everywhere, on gardens and rooftops, gleaming white. All London spoke of it, for though Christmastide was used to deliver some warmth and pleasant

2

days before Old Winter set in, this December was bitter cold, and some upstream reaches of the Thames were said to be locked in ice. This too Mrs. Stevenson called ill luck. I peered south, at the great river flowing not an hundred yards distant. The customary forest of shipmasts from all parts of the world cut the sky eastward, where lay the great docks, and wherries and lighters plied their busy trade. Chunks of ice could be seen bobbing and floating. Would the Thames freeze? Might there be another Great Frost Fair, like the one seventeen years ago, in 1740, when a town of booths sprang up upon the ice, and coaches vied for hire between Westminster and the Temple? Mrs. Stevenson remembered it well. "But a young wife then," she had sighed at supper just yesterday, "Mr. Stevenson living, and Polly but a babe," at which Mr. Franklin sent across the table his warm, kindly smile.

Mr. Franklin! How much I owed him!

Yet I could not think on that now, for Mrs. Stevenson's voice rose once more, bidding me to aid in the quelling of some new rebel.

I hurried belowstairs, to the kitchen, from which the good landlady's call issued. Mr. Franklin had come on business from America to these domestic comforts six months ago. Ever and again I thanked God he had chosen this haven, for had he not I should not have enjoyed Mrs. Stevenson's benevolent rule. True, her greatest enemy was dust (she loved a shining copper kettle better than gold), and her diligence in sweeping and scouring and bringing matters to order had caused her chief lodger more than once to protest that she looked after him better than he wished. But her heart was good; Mr. Franklin never gave thought to removing. "A

3

right heart exceeds all," pronounced he whenever she looked to sweep him up as well as dust.

Having come from a household in which a broom had been used more to beat me than to sweep, I loved Mrs. Stevenson.

"Come, chop these boiled lemons, Nick," commanded she as I stepped into queen's privy chamber, the flagstoned kitchen, warm with heat from the brick hearth and smelling of oranges and cloves. "Afterward you must pare and core these pippins."

"Yes, ma'am," said I, taking up the knife.

Polly Stevenson sat at a small corner table piled with greenery. "O, I want Nick better than you, mother," said she, "for this kissing bough must be made today. Your mince pies may wait 'til tomorrow."

"Tomorrow!" Mrs. Stevenson huffed above her bowl of stoned raisins. "My pies shall hear nothing of tomorrow! How can you say so, child?" Her eyes narrowed. "A kissing bough? For kissing whom?"

"Why . . . anyone," answered the daughter mildly.

Her mother smiled. "Might 'anyone' be named . . . Franklin?"

Polly did not reply, but I saw two spots of color flame in her cheeks. Her name was Mary, but she was called Polly, a pretty, spritely girl of eighteen, with honey-colored hair. Mr. Franklin's handsome son William had accompanied him to London, to study law at the Inner Temple. The merry gleam in Mrs. Stevenson's eye said she believed (as did Mr. Franklin) that some *amour* might arise between his son and her daughter, so thrown together in these precincts. For my part I thought William liked Polly better than she him, and I guessed she would far rather kiss the father than the son, but I kept my counsel and chopped lemons as I was bid and listened to Mrs. Stevenson hum as she tossed currants and

4

candied rind and suet and eggs into her pudding, beating all up briskly with rum and cream. I was content; peeling pippins was no work to me, a labor near bliss after the print shop of Ebeneezer Inch, where I had spent my young life. In that black, angry place I had had no knowledge of Christmas save as a season when Mrs. Inch took extra joy in abusing me, so I was pleased to do anything which might help Mrs. Stevenson.

"And where is Mr. Franklin this morning?" asked she, her lodger never far from her thoughts.

"I saw him early, from a window," replied Polly, tying apples to evergreens.

The ever-working woman sighed. "About his business for Pennsylvania, I suppose. The poor man is much bedeviled. I hope he does not take it hard."

"He was on no such business when I saw him. He was in the back yard."

Mrs. Stevenson ceased stirring. "Doing what, pray?"

Polly laughed. "Playing in the snow, it seemed."

"In such cold?" Our landlady clucked her tongue. "The gentleman will not keep watch over his health. Do not I chide him to do so? Will he obey? O, I admire him, yet he is a boy, a willful boy." Frowning, she beat her pudding hard. "Can it be some fairy stole my tailor's card?"

"Sir, you must bundle up more warmly," chid Mrs. Stevenson when Mr. Franklin came through the front door near three, puffing frosty breath.

His cheeks were red with cold, but I could see from the crinkled look behind his small, round spectacles that he well read his landlady's temper. Bending near, he patted her hand. "Dear lady, do I not wear my coat and my greatcoat, and a scarf about my neck and my beaver hat upon my head? What

5

more might I do but wrap me up like a mummy of Egypt and die breath-starved? Surely you would not wish me such a death?"

"O, no sir, but—"

He began to whirl her about, capering:

> Come and it like you,
> Dance with us now!
> And I without tarrying,
> Shall burst into caroling. . . .

"O, sir, sir," shrieked Mrs. Stevenson, "you take my wind, you truly do!"

His son, Mr. William Franklin, came in too, with a disapproving stare. "Father, remember, you are past fifty!"

Mr. Franklin's brows raised. "May a man not jig past fifty? Well, well. . . ." He let go Mrs. Stevenson, who swayed and laughed and dabbed with her white apron at cheeks and brow.

"Lord, I have not danced so in many a year!" laughed she.

"Yet you do it handsomely."

"O, sir . . . !"

"And do not fear I shall freeze, for even in such a December London has warm nooks where a man may go." (These were the clubs of Fleet Street and the Strand, Mr. Franklin's favorite being the Honest Whigs, which met at the George and Vulture or sometimes London Tavern near St. Paul's.) "The conversation of ingenious men gives me no small pleasure." He pulled off his round beaver hat. "And you, Nick, hearty and well?" and he touseled my hair, as brown as his—though his, pulled back from his broad, balding brow with a plain black ribbon, showed some few strands of gray.

6

"Quite well, sir," said I with the rush of affection I always felt when he returned.

Polly had joined us. "For my part, Mr. Franklin," said she, "I think you dance as well as many men of twenty and are fresher in mind than some men of such an age whom I might name."At this William flushed red, which she pretended not to note. "Yet to play in the snow like a child goes beyond bounds." She swayed coyly. "Or was it not Mr. Benjamin Franklin whom I saw in our back yard at eight?"

"Oho, observed, was I? Clever girl. And how goes Mr. Newton's *Principia*?"

"Very hard."

"Yet you persevere?"

"As you bid me."

"Excellent!—'twill sharpen your mind."

Mrs. Stevenson huffed. "'Tis not a book for a marriageable girl!"

"I own, I agree," put in William, puffing his chest.

A look of danger flared in Polly's green eyes. "You have too low an opinion of our sex. Queen Elizabeth, I suppose, ought better to have practiced needlework than statecraft?"

The young man smiled haughtily upon her. "You are not a queen, Miss Stevenson."

She stamped her foot. "And you, sir, are no philosopher!"

"Lord, Lord!" cried Mrs. Stevenson.

Mr. Franklin merely pulled his lip.

With some small trembling about his jaw William Franklin made curt bows. "I have much studying to be done." He stiffly mounted the stairs.

Mr. Franklin looked sadly after him. "An old young man will be a young old man," murmured he, shaking his head. "Well, he will come round."

Mrs. Stevenson tapped her mole. "I remember me, sir—

7

did you spy a tailor's pattern card on the hallstand before you departed this morning? I am most distressed to've lost it."

The gentleman colored. "Lost? A pattern card, you say?"

"I do."

"With . . . um . . . some cloth of sev'ral colors?"

"Why, both dark and light."

"On this very stand?"

Her eyes grew round. "You know of it, then?"

He contritely bowed his head. "I am a thieving knave, madam, and must beg your pardon; for, seeing opportunity, I stole the defenseless card." He peeped at her over the tops of his spectacles. "With ev'ry intention of returning it, you must believe."

"But why, sir?"

He beamed. "Because the sun shone bright, Mrs. Stevenson. Because the sun shone bright." He took her elbow. "Shall you see? Shall we all?"

"Look you," commanded the gentleman, when he had led us downstairs and out the kitchen door into the back yard, covered in snow which the soot from London coal fires had had no time to bemire.

"At what?" demanded the wary woman.

"At what I have planted." He pointed to a smooth drift of snow banked against the stables, where bits of cloth lay in a row. "My experiment was this. Seeing that the sun came out after so many days of gray, I took a number of the little square pieces of broadcloth from your tailor's card, of various colors: black, deep blue, green, purple, red, yellow, white and other colors or shades of colors. These I laid out upon the snow. See? The black, being warmed most by the sun, is sunk so low as to be below the stroke of the sun's rays; the dark blue almost as low, the lighter blue not quite so much as the dark,

8

the other colors less as they are lighter. The white remains on the surface of the snow, not having entered it at all."

"But what sense in this?" wailed Mrs. Stevenson.

"You ask aright, for what signifies philosophy that does not apply to some use? May we not learn from hence that black clothes are not so fit to wear in a hot, sunny climate as white ones?"

Mrs. Stevenson sniffed. "O, sir, might we not have learned this same in some other season, some other way?" She retrieved her bits of cloth. "'Tis a cold. Let us indoors." In the kitchen she halted us by the pudding bowl. "Each take up the spoon and stir three turns. 'Tis ill luck if we do not." We did as bid. "And now—" Into the bowl she tossed a threepenny piece, a ring, a thimble. These she beat in. "We shall see tomorrow who gets 'em."

"Ill luck to him who does?" asked Mr. Franklin, smiling.

"You scoff, sir," replied she, waggling her finger, "but a man's life may take dire turns by the ignoring of such customs."

"Ah, Nick," groaned Mr. Franklin as he and I mounted the stairs, he leaning heavily on his bamboo stick, "in truth my capering cost me some pain, for Mrs. Gout has once more settled amongst my toes, though I would not have our good landlady learn so for fear she should shut me indoors 'til spring, and glad to keep the key." We went to his bedchamber, a large front room with a bow window looking out upon Craven Street. He had been right to take advantage of the sun, for beyond the small square panes the sky now rapidly darkened. Seacoal burned in the grate. There were, too, the comfortable chair by the fire, the table by it with its *London Chronicle*, printed by Mr. Franklin's friend, William Strahan, the large featherbed, the desk and stool, the dresser with the

9

small paintings of his daughter Sally and his beloved son Francis, who had died at four of the smallpox. There were many books as well, in the tall bookcase by his bed.

Mr. Franklin had been sent by the Pennsylvania Assembly to wrest concessions of governance and taxation from Thomas and Richard Penn. "How goes your business, sir?" asked I, helping him off with his coat.

At my question his countenance grew as cloudy as the sky. "Pah! Obstinate Penns!" grumbled he, dropping into his chair so I might tug off his damp boots. "I do not wish to speak of 'em. I take joy in the season, Nick. Christmas time. That man must be a misanthrope indeed in whose breast jovial feeling is not aroused, in whose mind generous thoughts are not awakened. I would have nothing spoil it." He poked at his spectacles. "And yet it cannot bring joy to all men, though they seem to have little reason for gloom." Going to the window, he stared out. "I was just now at the White Lion, with Roderick Fairbrass." He turned. "Have I heretofore spoke of Roddy, Nick?"

Mr. Franklin had made many friends (and some enemies) in his six months in London, so I was not surprised to hear a new name. "I believe not, sir," said I as I placed his boots by the fire.

"A merchant. An importer of sugar from Jamaica, with three thousand a year, and a fine terrace house in Soho Square; too, a handsome wife and four children—in short ev'ry reason for joy. When first I met him some months ago he seemed a happy man, yet this afternoon I hardly knew him for his sad looks and the reek of spirits on his breath. And yet I hear his business fares well, his family prospers. What changes a man? Ill luck? That is what our Mrs. Stevenson would say. O, I cannot abide superstition! The world is full of reason, Nick, deep hid though it may be; a wise man seeks it

10

out." He brightened. "Speaking of wisdom, what have you learnt today?"

Eagerly I told him. Mr. Franklin had taken my education upon himself and each morn set me some new tasks. I had a Latin grammar, and a ciphering book. This morning I had read Mr. Francis Bacon's "Of Studies," which we now dissected. From his chair the gentleman then related some conversation at the White Lion, which contained much political matter and gossip of the city. It had been agreed I should serve as his amanuensis, keeping record of thoughts and expressions which might escape him should they not immediately be set down; so, using the shorthand of his invention which he had taught me (and from which much of what I now tell is taken), I wrote what he related in one of the small blank-paged volumes which Mr. Tisdale, the printer, had bound for me. Evening drew on outside the bow window. Mrs. Stevenson brought up a warm concoction of rum and water. Lighting a lamp, Mr. Franklin settled with his glass by the fire with a volume of Rowe's *Shakespeare*, reading *Hamlet*, whilst at his desk I scribbled imitations of Mr. Addison's *Spectator*, from which Mr. Franklin himself, when young, had learnt style.

How happy was I in this home, coal fire burning, Mr. Franklin reading nearby, Mrs. Stevenson in her kitchen, all unbuffeted by cruelty or want.

Near six there came a rap upon the door. "Mr. Franklin," sounded the landlady's voice.

"What is it?" called he.

She entered wearing a pale look of dismay. "A young woman to see you, sir, in the front parlor. It is most urgent, she says, and I could not say her nay, for she claims to have seen a ghost."

I felt a chill.

11

"But who may she be?" asked Mr. Franklin, rising.

Mrs. Stevenson twisted her apron in her hands. "Why Miss Cassandra Fairbrass, sir, daughter of Roderick Fairbrass, whom she says you know."

❧ 2 ❧

*IN WHICH a tale of strange portent is
succeeded by much cheer, though I go to
my bedchamber trembling. . . .*

Quite right to say I shall see her," said Mr. Franklin
mildly, though I glimpsed some spark in his gray-
brown eyes. "Pray, go down and tell her I shall be
with her soon." The gentleman wore his maroon dressing
gown. "My coat, Nicholas," said he abruptly when Mrs.
Stevenson was departed. I fetched this from the wardrobe,
unable to help thinking of that time two months ago when
Mrs. Martha Clay had arrived equally unexpectedly seeking
Mr. Benjamin Franklin's aid, and of how this had led to
mystery, danger, and the discovery of much that touched my
small life.

Slipping into his coat, the gentleman stepped to the bow
window. "The lamp, Nick," said he, by which I saw he meant
me to extinguish it. This I did (in some bewilderment),
leaving only the soft glow of coal fire to pick out his shadowed
form by the casement. He beckoned me near, and we peered
out. It was near six P.M., light from several houses all that
illumined Craven Street. Some mummers wove below in the
darkness, jingling their bells, but naught else moved. A sedan
chair waited by Number 7, its two carriers bundled and

shivering in the staves, and I pitied them their frigid vigil on Christmas Eve. A small, closed carriage stood opposite, the man in its box wrapped in black, his breath a wavering plume. "See that carriage, Nick?" inquired Mr. Franklin.

"I do, sir," replied I.

"What can it wait for?"

"I do not know."

He tapped his jaw. "And yet I believed, when Peter drove me from Roddy Fairbrass at the White Lion this afternoon, that I saw some such carriage behind me. Do I imagine things? Have the enemies I have made turned me to a cautious fool? Well, I meant only to see how Miss Fairbrass arrived. Is't not strange she should come mere hours after my sad interview with her father?" He stepped from the window. "There will be reason behind it, we shall see." He went to the door. "Accompany me, Nick. Damn Mrs. Gout! And bring your journal. A story waits to be writ."

The front parlor was chill, no flames leaping in the grate. Polly had hung her kissing bough from the center of the ceiling: a circle of red apples amidst greenery, and this lent some cheer. Mr. Franklin went at once to the front window to draw the curtain. Mrs. Stevenson stood uncertainly in the door. "We must keep out the cold, must we not, dear lady?" asked he, though I saw him peer out furtively before he closed the cloth. "You may leave us, if you please."

Though the good woman looked eager to hear all, she made a quick curtsey and withdrew. Closing the door, Mr. Franklin turned to his guest.

"Miss Fairbrass?" said he.

A thin, auburn-haired young woman stood in obvious agitation near the sofa. Perhaps twenty, she was dressed well, in a long, green-striped satin dress, on her head a simple silk

14

kerchief over a lace-edged cap. She held gray gloves tightly in long-fingered hands. "Cassandra Fairbrass," said she in a dry, quavering voice. "My father is Roderick Fairbrass. You know him, I believe."

"Indeed, we had conversation this afternoon, at the White Lion. Your father is a fine man. Beg pardon, but . . . you have been hanging mistletoe, have you not? Or was't holly?"

She started. "Holly. How did you know?"

"Both may prick the fingers, and yours are pricked." I noted some small cuts upon the young woman's hands which I should not have seen had Mr. Franklin not first spied them. "Do not wonder at my guessing," said he in a dismissing way. "'Tis the season to hang holly."

Her gaze fixed upon him. "Martha Clay was right. You observe keenly."

"You know Martha Clay?"

"She is the reason I am come—she and the knowledge that you are my father's friend. Mrs. Clay sews for our family—she is an excellent seamstress. She talked to me once of how at some peril you discovered who had murdered her brother. She spoke well of you, Mr. Franklin. I hoped in my distress I might apply to you, though it is not about murder I am come."

"A ghost, Mrs. Stevenson said."

"Truly!"

There was much fervor in this exclamation: tremor in the voice and a flaring light in Cassandra Fairbrass's pale blue eyes, as if the knowledge thrilled as well as affrighted her, yet Mr. Franklin showed so little response she might as well have talked of buckled shoes.

"Pray, sit you down," bid he.

"Thank you." As the young woman perched on the sofa, her doubtful gaze fell upon me.

"Tut, this is my young friend, Nicolas Handy," said Mr.

15

Franklin. "He will make some small jottings, which no other eyes save mine shall see. All you may speak to me you may say before Nick, in perfect trust."

"I take your word."

With a small grimace to show the gout yet pained him, Mr. Franklin sat in the chair opposite her, I on a low stool near his side. This gave me opportunity to examine our visitor further. She was not pretty, yet she had a fine-drawn face, with a thin, sharp nose and high cheekbones; a broad brow, a long jaw, large, restless eyes. She was pale as alabaster, with hectic spots in the paleness, as if she suffered from fever. Dots of freckles lay across her nose. Her hands were clenched tight in her lap.

Mr. Franklin sat at ease in his plain brown coat, a look of pleasant inquiry on his round face. "Now. Tell all," urged he softly.

She took breath. "How to begin? I am the eldest of four children. My brother James is a year younger than I. Emily is aged seven, Timothy five."

"No other relations?"

"My father's bachelor brother, in the West Indies. Our family lives in Soho Square, as I believe you know. It is a fine brick house, though we did not always live so. Yet Papa's business has prospered in recent years, and we have been happy, learning to go about in society. Mama has been happy. Dear Papa has been happy too—or," her voice broke, "he seemed so until recent months. O, Mr. Franklin, some cloud has shadowed his sun, and he has been much down! Poor man, he struggles to wear the cheerful face of old, yet 'tis a mask, and something tears at him inside." Here she drew forth a lace handkerchief and dabbed at the corners of her eyes. "And then came the ghost."

"Ah!"

16

She shuddered. "My bedchamber is on the second story, as is my brother's and Papa and Mama's, along a corridor which traverses the house. I am a light sleeper—ever have been; strange fancies make me wakeful. The door to my chamber is thick oak, yet in my sleeplessness I began to believe I heard sounds beyond it, someone moving, though no one had heretofore been in habit of rising at night."

"May you describe these sounds?"

"Muffled footsteps. A voice, perhaps, once or twice."

"A single voice?"

"I cannot say."

"Could you distinguish particular words?"

"No. This happened some nights succeeding, but I hesitated to step out to see what might be."

"Pray, why?"

"Something about the sounds affrighted me."

"Did you speak to your family of this?"

"No." A flush came into her high, pale cheeks, "I would have been pooh-poohed, especially by my brother—'More fancies,' he would say—and I did not wish to make myself his target. I inquired in a roundabout way if anyone had stirred, but all said no. The sounds persisted. At last I took courage and one night, after the clocks had chimed three, crept to my door. The sounds were indeed louder. Putting hand to latch, I softly pressed. I was fearful, Mr. Franklin, for I did not know what might be. The door opened but a crack—and there I saw it! Lamps light Soho Square. Their pale glow seeped through the window at the end of the corridor, and there in flowing white, just turning to drift downstairs, was the ghost! In an instant it was vanished—but I saw it, Mr. Franklin, as sure as I draw breath! A ghost, I tell you, a ghost!"

In the course of her narrative Cassandra Fairbrass had

gradually leant forward, her jaw thrust out, her large eyes wild. I myself stared, my pencil poised above my little book as if my arm had froze.

"Indeed," came Mr. Franklin's musing voice. He had not moved, nor had his expression of unruffled interest altered. "What followed?"

"You believe me, sir?"

"A figure in flowing white . . . the evidence of your eyes—why, I believe you perfectly."

What past mocking disbelief had caused Cassandra Fairbrass to keep such a story from her family? No matter. Mr. Franklin's sturdy credence made her trust, and she went on: "Again I said nothing to Papa or anyone. I did not wish to worry my mother, nor Papa in his state. My brother James would only call me ninny. So, wakeful, I listened in the deepest part of night to these continuing sounds, biting my lip and crouched upon my bed. I feared to peer out, as I had before, and yet there came a time when I must look again, must see the spirit to assure myself I had not been mad. And so, finding courage, I again crept to my door and turned the latch and softly opened. It was there!—nearer this time, moving away, and again it turned upon the stairs to vanish down. I shut my door. I would have cried out but for the terror in my throat. I fell upon my bed and sobbed.

"I determined to follow it, Mr. Franklin. No one else heard, it seemed. Or saw. Had it come for me? Was I meant to learn some secret? I must know.

"And so, the very next night, I turned my latch once more and stepped into the corridor. The spirit had just passed my door; it was near. I called out to it, reached out. It turned—and . . . O, the horror, Mr. Franklin, for *it had the face of my father!*" At this the young woman seemed to see again what she had seen, for her eyes stared, the hectic spots turned white as ivory in her cheeks, and she shook as from a blast of wind.

Mr. Franklin grasped her fingers, chaffing them. "There, Miss Fairbrass. Such a sight might discomfit the bravest man."

"Yes . . . yes . . . !" Withdrawing her hands, she sank back. "I cried out. I whirled from this vision to run I knew not where—and to my amazement fell into Papa's very arms. His and Mama's bedchamber is just across the hall. He wore his nightclothes. He had heard my call and rushed out. 'Child, child,' cried he, 'what is't?' I turned to point—but the spirit was vanished. 'Below! It has gone below!' said I. 'What has?' asked he, at which I told him of the ghost, urging him to the stairs, though nothing appeared upon 'em save black shadow. He looked at me strangely, as if I were mad; yet he showed great, loving concern—dear Papa!—and took up a lamp so we might go below as I bid. We searched, ev'ry room, ev'ry closet—pantry and cupboards as well—but found nothing save frigid chill and two servants sleepily stirring, waked by our search. All doors proved locked; Papa insisted on seeing to 'em too, as if that might assure me. All windows were bolted as well, though that made no matter, for spirits may pass through walls, may they not? And appear and vanish at will?"

"And make footsteps?" murmured Mr. Franklin, his eyes briefly fixed upon the room's drawn curtains. He regarded Cassandra Fairbrass. "The ghost had the face of your father, you say?"

She shuddered. "His very lineaments!"

"Yet it was dark in the corridor; the glow from Soho Square shone behind the spirit."

"'Twas Papa's face, I tell you!".

He nodded. "Are there mirrors in your house, Miss Fairbrass?"

19

"Some."

"In the second story corridor?"

"One."

He did not pursue this. "You wear a stone, I see."

Her long, thin fingers leapt to this stone, pinned upon her bodice, as they had done often in the telling of her story. It was small and blue-gray, no longer than an inch, and crudely cross-shaped, with white lines incised upon it; no gem but just a timeworn stone.

"I obtained it of a woman in Crook Alley."

"It is old, is't not?" asked Mr. Franklin.

"Of ancient Britain."

"And brings luck. Celtic, I believe. An amulet. Pray, who was this woman?"

"Mrs. Rook, who deals in such charms."

"Have you others?"

"Some. And books on such matters. I read much about the faeries one may come upon on lonely walks."

This too Mr. Franklin let be, with a smile that made no cavil. "When did you first note the sounds in the corridor, Miss Fairbrass?"

"Near a month ago."

"Came they ev'ry night?"

"Once they began, yes."

"And how long before your first venturing out?"

"A week, exact."

"After the first sight of the ghost you kept to your room, you say. For what time?"

"Five nights. On the sixth I ventured forth for the second time—and saw the terrible thing with my father's face."

"When in the night did these sounds begin?"

"Not before two."

"And ended?"

"I never heard 'em past four."

"In the darkest hours, then." Mr. Franklin pulled hard at his lip. "The sounds came from the corridor only? Never from above? Or below?"

Doubt pinched lines about Miss Fairbrass's eyes. "They may've come sometimes from elsewhere. I cannot be sure."

"Who sleeps above?"

"Emily and little Tim."

"No one else?"

"No."

"There are other rooms in this upper floor?"

"Two. The children play in one. In the other are odds and ends, in a jumble. It is locked."

"The servants of whom you spoke. Did they show evidence of having seen a ghost?"

"No."

"Does any person in the house sleepwalk, ma'am?"

"No one."

"You?"

Her voice was steady. "I am wakeful, but I do not walk."

"I see. This ghost—'dressed all in white,' you say? But why a ghost? May it not have been a person in white nightshirt or nightgown?"

"It moved as a ghost! It had dear Papa's face!"

"As you say. And what expression did it wear?"

"A staring look, eyes glitt'ring. The mouth was open."

"And made no other motion but to flee?"

"None. As I turned to hide my eyes from what I saw, Papa caught me in his arms. When I looked back, the spirit had gone."

"Down, you say. Might it not have gone *up?*"

"Why . . . I suppose it may."

"Or stepped through a wall, or vanished like smoke, if 'twas

21

a true spirit," mused Mr. Franklin. "You and your father did not search upstairs?"

"No."

"A pity." He shifted his feet. "This was a fortnight ago, by your accounting. Have you seen the thing since?"

"I have not had courage to peep out—but I no longer hear the sounds."

"Nor voices?"

"No."

"It seems gone, then, does it not? And how did your father behave after?"

"With great solicitude. He had heretofore been unwilling to listen to my fancies. Both he and Mama believe I am too much taken up with spirits and faeries—but I believe in 'em, I do! Yet now he said, 'A ghost, you say? May be,' with great concern, and told me to lock my door and gave me sleeping draughts for nights to come, but I did not drink these, though I did not tell him, for I must know if the spirit still walked. Yet I have not heard it to this day."

Miss Fairbrass's tale seemed concluded. She sat on the edge of the sofa clutching the small, cross-shaped stone pinned to her bodice as if all hope lay in it, whilst Mr. Franklin gazed for a moment into a chill corner of the room. Outside, London stirred, as if tossing in troubled sleep. From below came faint sounds of Mrs. Stevenson in her kitchen. Mr. Franklin asked, "Your father does not know you are come to me?"

"No one of my family knows."

"Yet the ghost has ceased its visits. How may I help you?"

She bent toward him. "O, Mr. Franklin, my house is damned! Dear Papa grows sadder by the day, and Mama is afflicted too. My brother James is not his cheerful self. Too, I have great fear. True, I have not heard or seen the ghost this fortnight past—but did it come to adjure me? Did I affright it betimes? Did it mean by its look to presage that Papa must die? Am I to do something to prevent this? I do not know." At this she began to sob, shoulders heaving, her kerchief clamped to her moaning mouth. Mr. Franklin gazed pityingly, and I too felt moved and fearful.

Mrs. Stevenson's case clock struck the half hour at the landing, at which the young woman started and leapt up. "I must be gone, Mr. Franklin, for I am to be home at seven. I bear such a burden in my heart! May you help?"

"I am no familiar of ghosts," said he, standing. "Yet I should be pleased to look into this." He patted her hands. "I shall do all I may to aid you and your family. Your father has invited me to the Christmas festivities at your house tomorrow, did you know? I shall begin my humble ministrations then, though I promise no result." He bowed his head humbly. "'Tis the best I may do."

"O, thank you, Mr. Franklin!"

Mrs. Stevenson fetched Cassandra Fairbrass's black cloak, and the young woman hurried out into the mud-tracked snow of Craven Street. Her two bearers lifted her chair. "Take heart!" called Mr. Franklin upon the stoop but returned quickly indoors. "Up at once, Nick!" commanded he, mounting the stairs with such alacrity, belying both fifty years age and painful gout, that I was hard pressed to keep at his heels. His chamber was as before, all dark. He hurried to its window. "See?" said he in some excitement, drawing me close and peering down. Miss Fairbrass's chair had reached the top of the street, its bearers moving rapidly, no doubt happy to gain warmth from their exertions. But this was not what Mr. Franklin's finger indicated. The small, closed carriage which had stood opposite was turning; it then went up Craven Street, at a pace which matched the chair's. Mr. Franklin

23

sniffed. "Coincidence that it departs as Miss Fairbrass does—or is she watched? Yet who may't be? The father keeping eye upon his daughter? Some other spy? Friend or enemy?" He tapped his brow. "A ghost, eh, Nick? Pah, 'twill prove a puppet, mark you, or I am not Benjamin Franklin. I begin to take interest in discovering who makes it walk—and why."

Mrs. Stevenson and Polly returned somewhat past eight from Christmas Eve services at St. Martin's, in the Strand. I had in the meantime thought much on Cassandra Fairbrass's strange tale without being able to draw any conclusions.

I saw by Mr. Franklin's ruminative silence that he thought on it too.

"And how liked you the sermon, dear lady?" inquired he as the women came in briskly from the cold.

"O, excellent, with much edification!" replied Mrs. Stevenson.

"Hum, I am a great lover of edification—yet I prefer the sermon of the ant; none preaches better than he who says nothing."

Our landlady wrinkled her nose, yet she could not remain long vexed with her lodger. She served supper in the room next the kitchen belowstairs, at the large round table. It was but cold meats, her grand Christmastide dinner to be brought forth tomorrow, yet there was much cheer. Candlelight warmed our faces and our hearts—as did good roast beef. I sat at Mr. Franklin's left side, his son William at his right. Then came Mrs. Stevenson and Polly. It being Christmas, two remaining places were set for Mr. Franklin's negro servants, Peter and King, who customarily ate in their attic room. Peter was tall and spoke excellent English. King was a small, crabbed fellow, of a glum disposition, who loved horses, spending much time in the stables with the mares, combing

24

and singing to them songs which he had learnt of his mother, now dead. I too had lost my mother; thus I met King's unhappiness with great sympathy, for I knew what it was to be cast adrift in the world. Peter was greatly content to serve Mr. Franklin, but King gave sullen service to William. "For poor King's sake I would send him back to Africa," Mr. Franklin had said, "yet that would serve little, for, being of a white father, he is of neither that land nor this. Indeed when I meet hostility amongst Englishmen, who regard me strangely because I plead Pennsylvania's cause, I too feel pinched. I have 'til now believed me to be an Englishman, yet I begin to see that, being of America, I am an hostile breed. Shall I one day be forced to choose between 'em? I heartily hope not."

After supper all went upstairs to the front parlor where the interview with Cassandra Fairbrass had been. "Bring in the yule log, Peter," commanded Mr. Franklin, and the servant soon returned with a piece of ash, whose stoutness all praised fulsomely, as if the tree itself, branches and all, had been delivered. "And now, Mrs. Stevenson—the faggot from last year's log."

"At once." She produced a blighted, blackened stick no bigger than a thumb, yet this was treated with such rev'rence as if t'were a bone of the Christ, Mr. Franklin proceeding solemnly to set it alight upon the grate. When it was burning, with other sticks of wood to help, he placed upon it the yule log, which soon caught fire, sending forth a flick'ring, merry glow and making shadows dance. He beamed. "Ah, 'tis the best of times—far more pleasing than this same day thirty-three years ago, when a callow youth first arrived on this shore, friendless, near penniless, with naught to make his way save some small skill at printing. I stayed eighteen months and learnt to love England. Thus, though my present purpose goes slow, I am happy to be returned. Such a time o' year!—it

25

may be Christmas has suffered; Puritans on both sides o' the sea have done much to starve him, and he comes not with his wonted gait (he is shrunk nine inches in the girth); but yet he is a lusty fellow. A toast to him, with lamb's wool, dear lady."

"The lamb's wool!" Mrs. Stevenson bustled out, returning but a moment later with a steaming pewter bowl of hot ale, smelling of cloves. In it floated peeled, roasted crabapples, whose whiteness gave the brew its name. Cups were handed round.

When all had theirs, Mr. Franklin sang lustily:

Come bring with a noise,
My merry, merry boys,
The Christmas log to the firing;
While my good dame, she,
Bids ye be free,
And drink to your heart's desiring!

All drank, and drank again: "Wassail!" There followed some business under the kissing bough, Polly and Mrs. Stevenson hugging me tight to their bosoms, which made my face go hot. Mr. Franklin bussed both Mrs. Stevenson's cheeks, at which she too turned red. Polly pecked Mr. Franklin's brow, but it was she who flushed as she did it. William Franklin made some awkward attempt to kiss Polly, but she turned her head, and he bumped his nose and cried out, at which she took pity and kissed him. At this he looked quite as if she had slapped him, stunned, and I vowed never to be smitten with any girl, not even one so pretty as she. We played Snapdragon, snatching raisins from flaming brandy. Mr. Franklin told riddles, which none but Polly could guess, proving her cleverness. Near eleven, mummers knocked and jingled in with their blackened faces and leering masks, and played pranks, led by their Lord of Misrule, who tweaked Mrs. Stevenson's nose, which only made her laugh and feed 'em cakes.

"Why is she not angered?" whispered I in wonder.

"'Tis topsy-turvy time," replied Mr. Franklin, "when servants may treat masters rudely, and masters may play servants, and all is set awry, an ancient custom."

Midnight drew on, Christmas day near. Mrs. Stevenson brought up a fat mince pie but would give us each but one small bite. "'Twill bring good luck to eat a little all the Twelve Days and on the twelfth to eat the last," said she.

Mr. Franklin glowered. "Avaunt superstition! I hold a man makes his own luck—though with less pleasure than by eating your mince pie." He swallowed his portion genially.

A cock crew somewhere in the night.

The gentleman turned his head to the curtained window:

> Some say that ever 'gainst that season comes,
> The bird of dawning singeth all night long. . . .

He laughed. "Let not this bird keep us wakeful."

"Shakespeare, father?" asked William by the fire.

"It is."

"But what play?" Polly plucked at William's arm. "May you say what play?"

"Why—" William frowned but found no answer.

"*Hamlet!*" Polly clapped her hands. "I know 'tis *Hamlet!*"

Mr. Franklin nodded from the great leather armchair which had been Mr. Stevenson's when he lived. "Marcellus says it—on a night when a father's ghost walks."

I did not like this reminder of Cassandra Fairbrass's tale.

"O, pray, do not speak of such things at this time!" exclaimed Mrs. Stevenson.

27

"Nay?" Firelight glinted from Mr. Franklin's eyeglasses as he bent forward, chair creaking. "You do not believe that on this night, when cattle kneel down in reverence, any soul who sees 'em perishes before dawn?" His finger suddenly pointed. "Look, look at the forms upon the wall!" Startled, we all turned, and indeed our shadows made a second company upon walls and ceiling, wavering giants. I shivered. "Do you not know what is told?" Mr. Franklin whispered, "—that any shadow which appears headless belongs to him who shall *die* within the year."

Mrs. Stevenson wrung her hands. "O, sir, you must not say such things!"

Softly chuckling, the gentleman rose. "Indeed I shall say no more of such superstitious folderol, for 'tis not true, dear lady, though many people hold to it. Most of such stuff is harmless, some causes peril, all is foolish. Yet I would not dispense with your mince pie, which is so pleasant a remedy." He stretched. "It has been a fine Christmas Eve, but 'tis time I retired. Pray, excuse me. Nick, shall you go too?"

At the top of the stairs Mr. Franklin bid me into his chamber, where he lit a lamp. He stood at his bow window a moment before turning. "Christmas—a curious mixture of the Christian and pagan, much deriving from the ancient Roman Saturnalia and Druid ceremonies, with sacrifices to deities of spring. I have read so in Gower's *Customs of Old England*." He squeezed my shoulder. "Well, I may disbelieve much, but I believe that God looks down." Yet he brooded a moment. "What made you of Cassandra Fairbrass's tale, lad?" asked he at last.

"It affrighted me, sir."

"Aye, the ghost. But did you think she spoke true?"

"She saw something in the night."

28

"But truly a ghost? The young woman is disposed to believe in 'em; how far, then, may we trust what she says?"

"She lies?"

"I do not say so. Truth and sincerity have a certain distinguishing native luster which cannot be perfectly counterfeited; they are like fire and flame, that cannot be painted. I believe Miss Fairbrass is sincere in much."

"In all?"

Sighing, he let go my shoulder. "All is a very great deal. Yet we may know more tomorrow, when we go to the party at the Fairbrass house. Will you accompany me, Nick? William is asked, but is off with friends to hear Handel at Covent Garden. Damn me, my son goes about a great deal too much for the good of his studies!"

Bidding Mr. Franklin good night, I crossed the hall to my own small room. In no very settled frame of mind I lit my stub end of candle and made some attempt at the fourth volume of *Tom Jones*, a gift from the gentleman, but the words would not settle into sense. Tomorrow I should visit a house where a spirit may've walked?

Gooseflesh sprang out on my arms, and blowing out my candle I pulled bedclothes tight over my head.

❧ 3 ❧

IN WHICH amidst the best of times the worst comes to be. . . .

Christmas dawned with new snow. Mr. Franklin's habit was to rise early; my former hard life had ingrained in me early rising too, so when light had barely broke I rose and dressed in bruising cold and knocked at Mr. Franklin's door. "Come," called he. I entered to find him in his cotton nightshirt by the bow window, casement flung wide, bending at the knee: up, down, which he did some two dozen times. This he called his air bath. Whilst I set a fire in the grate he dressed in the plain clothing he preferred: white muslin shirt and stockings, dark green waistcoat, brown worsted knee breeches and black buckled shoes. It was his habit to read an hour or two before going down to breakfast. Pulling *Hamlet* from the shelf, he settled in his leather chair by the stove; but, his eyes falling on the gold chain at my throat, which I always wore, a sad, ruminative look took him. I read his thoughts and drew from my shirt the small oval locket, opened it, and we gazed together at the silhouette within: my dear mother, Rose Handy. "Ah, Nick," sighed the gentleman. He had loved the woman. They had met in America, but she had been cruelly murdered four years after she came to England, leaving me in bad hands. Upon coming to England eight years later, Mr. Franklin had discovered her murderer and more: that he was my father, for I was indeed his natural child, offspring of his and Rose Handy's love. Though this fact remained a secret between us (he wishing not to discomfit his faithful wife, Deborah, who remained patiently with their daughter in Philadelphia, nor William, who studied at the Inner Temple), I felt no shame in my lineage. T'was a warm coal in my breast, making me proud: Benjamin Franklin, whom the King of France had thanked for his electrical discoveries, was my father!

I too sometimes read, these early hours. Yet I did chores for Mrs. Stevenson as well, and this morn she called me down to help in placing garlands of holly and yew about the house. This I did willingly, taking pleasure in the good woman's humming as she prepared the sucking pig, whilst Polly stuck oranges with cloves.

Near nine Mr. Franklin descended just as Mrs. Stevenson was directing me in hanging a wreath about the tall case clock.

"Very pretty," said the gentleman. "In Pennsylvania some German settlers carry a whole tree into their house and keep it there many days hung with sweetmeats."

The housewife's nose wrinkled. "A tree entire? 'Tis a custom the English are unlikely to take up."

"Yet custom may change, dear lady. Shall we breakfast, all?"

There was porridge and hot bread belowstairs, William Franklin joining us, but this meal was not to conclude pleasantly, for there came a loud snap from the kitchen, and a squealing, at which Mrs. Stevenson leapt up and scurried off and came back moaning and holding her temples as if she had the headache. "Another rat, Mr. Franklin. How I hate the creatures!"

31

We went into the kitchen. There on the floor by the brick oven was a brown rat, near a foot long, bloody, in the jaws of a trap. Yet the rat still lived and dragged the trap slowly as with a dreadful, high keening it struggled to escape. I flinched at its yellow-toothed grimace. There had been much trouble with the creatures of late. By vigilence and the stopping of cracks they might be kept from houses in summer, but the freezing cold had made 'em bold; finding ways into even tight-closed places, they plagued all London.

Mr. Franklin was no friend to rats. Crushing the suffering creature's head with his heel, he tossed it in the dustbin. "I am reminded, Mrs. Stevenson, that I may go some little way toward making the catching of these vermin both more sure and less vexing. Pray, excuse me."

I accompanied him upstairs, to the room behind his bedchamber, where I had played with the glass rod and filings. On his workbench lay a new thing: a cage of curved iron wires, with a little door. "I have had Mr. Crabbe, the blacksmith, construct this to my design. See you, Nick?" He raised the door, which was kept open with a tongue of metal held by a spring. "Lured by food, which we place here," (he indicated the back of the cage) "a rat enters. Yet the snatching of the food at once releases the spring, which drops the door. The rat is trapped with no blood and may be carried to the Thames to be drowned. A bucket of water will do as well. Many rats 'scape metal jaws, but none will free themselves of this. 'Twill be a gift of the season to our landlady."

Mr. Franklin was clearly much pleased. William walked in, and he showed his invention with the same eagerness with which he had shown it me, but the young man's thoughts seemed otherwhere: he made but cursory acknowledgment, and his brief gaze at me was haughty—no surprise, for he always addressed me coolly, though whether this was due to

Mr. Franklin's treatment of me, which William found un-wonted, I did not know. For my part I gave William all respect; I wished for his approval. He strode about in huffing agitation, whilst Mr. Franklin watched quietly over the tops of his spectacles.

At last William halted. "You lent Polly your *Shakespeare*, did you not, father?" asked he.

"I did. From which she learnt well."

"O, learning! Father, you fill her head with thoughts beyond her station."

Mr. Franklin did not respond at once. "'Twill make of her an amiable and desirable companion—for a man of proper sense," replied he evenly.

William started. He was handsome indeed, in very fine clothes, which he had learnt to wear as London fashion bid, taking proud pleasure in doing so; yet his present spiteful look twisted his face to ugliness. "I understand, father, that you like her too well! And she you!" He strode out, banging the door.

Mr. Franklin trembled. His calmness was rarely ruffled, yet I saw his jaw tighten, and he was plainly at some pains to keep from bursting out. "Foolish, spiteful boy!" muttered he between his teeth. Flushing, he looked at me. "Youth has warm blood, I must remember me." He picked up the trap. "Shall we take this down to Mrs. Stevenson?"

Stepping into the corridor we met her coming up. "Mr. Roderick Fairbrass waits below to see you, sir, announced she.

This gentleman stood in the front parlor, as had his daughter yesterday afternoon. The remains of last night's yule log lay cold upon the hearth, and the kissing bough hung above. "Benjamin!" said he, stepping forward and wringing Mr.

Franklin's hand. I looked close at this man whose house may've been visited by a ghost. Near fifty, he was tall and strongly built, in a dark blue greatcoat and black boots. He had the long, lean face of his daughter, with a similarity of expression: hers had been troubled; his too showed anxiety about the wide mouth and pinched eyes, yet he had kindly features, which struggled to express cheer. There was no evidence that he had been tippling.

Mr. Franklin gripped his hand warmly. "What brings you on Christmas day, Roddy?"

"Passing along the Strand and finding myself near, I bethought me to turn aside to make certain you meant to be amongst us this eve."

"I would not miss your party."

"There will be a play. *Saint George*. I myself shall play the saint."

"You? Come Roddy, might not your elder son James better suit the role of brave, young knight?"

"As for my son. . . ." Bitterness flickered in Fairbrass's eyes.

"Aye, sons," murmured Mr. Franklin, "—they do not always please. By the by, this is my young friend, Nicolas Handy. William cannot accompany me. May Nick take his place?"

"I should be happy." Mr. Fairbrass warmly squeezed my shoulder. "We shall welcome you, lad."

"Thank you, sir."

Wearing a close-fitting white wig, he began twisting his tricorn hat in his hands. "Your friend, Dr. Fothergill . . . he comes too?"

"I believe so," replied Mr. Franklin.

"I should especially wish to have him there."

"Especially? Why?"

34

"Why . . . because he is an amiable gentleman—no other reason." Fairbrass emitted a hoarse laugh. "I should wish my house filled with amiable gentlemen!"

"Fothergill is indeed amiable." I saw that Mr. Franklin observed his visitor closely. "Are you troubled, Roddy? Should you wish to tell me of your troubles?"

The parlor window was uncurtained, revealing snow softly falling. Wind buffetted the panes. Fairbrass puffed his cheeks. "Troubled? At Christmastide, Ben?" protested he.

"Troubles are no respectors of season."

"What cause have I for sorrow?"

"That is what I wish to know."

All pretense of cheer fell from Roderick Fairbrass's face, leaving it gray and old-looking. Yet he denied all: "Nay, Ben, I am well—*all* is well, and we shall have great joy this night." With another hoarse laugh, he clapped Mr. Franklin's shoulder. "You must think nothing on me. I shall see you at eight."

"As you say."

During this exchange I had noted Mr. Franklin's right hand moving about in his coat pocket. At the front door he shook Mr. Fairbrass's hand once more. The door closed, and with a thoughtful expression Mr. Franklin dropped some small flattened ovals of wax into the plain pewter snuffbox which he always kept in his waistcoat.

He saw me watching. "Aye, Nick, fingerprints—my whim. Roddy was most anxious that Fothergill and I be there this eve. Why? Well, we shall not disappoint him—and I shall be pleased to have your sharp young eyes with us, to be alert and see all." Returning to the parlor, he peered out. Beyond the panes the sky was sooty gray, and the snow fell more thickly. Yet the traffic of Craven Street was plainly visible, and I sensed the gentleman stiffen at my side. "See you!—that

35

small, closed carriage, which seems to pursue Roddy? The same that followed his daughter yestereve?" He adjusted his spectacles. "Yet it may not be; there are many such in London." Frowning, he gazed in the direction of the river. "Will the Thames freeze? I should like to try this new thing, called ice skating."

Savory smells filled the house all morning, Christmas dinner being served at two in the room looking upon the back yard, white with snow. Mrs. Stevenson carried in a plum pudding like a speckled cannonball. "Round!" exclaimed Mr. Franklin. "A kiss is round, the horizon is round, the earth is round, the moon is round, the sun and stars and all the host of heaven are round. So is your plum pudding." He himself carried in the sucking pig, crowned with rosemary, and an apple in its mouth:

> The pig in hand bear I,
> Bedecked with bays and rosemary;
> I pray you my masters be merry,
> *Quod estis in convivio.* . . .

All were present, including Peter and King. There was a prayer, which Mrs. Stevenson concluded by saying, "And let Mr. Franklin's work be done well and speedily."

"O, not speedily!" protested in Polly, "for that should take him from us."

We set to with forks and knives. "Eat not to dullness, drink not to elevation," adjured Mr. Franklin, yet he ate as much and as well as any, with much smacking of lips and praise of each morsel, which pleased Mrs. Stevenson into many smiles. The threepenny piece was discovered in my pudding. "Promising wealth, as you deserve, Nick," said Mr. Franklin. For his part, he found the thimble, which proclaimed he worked hard, all agreeing this suited him well.

There remained the ring, which Polly found but did not like and thrust upon William. "You, sir, are likely to marry long before I."

He lifted his chin. "Given your nature, I do not doubt it."

Polly only laughed.

Mr. Franklin's good friends, Dr. Fothergill and Peter Collinson, members of the Royal Society, and Mr. Strahan, the printer, looked in. Hearty greetings were followed by a warm concoction in the front parlor, served by Mrs. Stevenson. Talk of political and scientific matters ensued, to which I was privileged to listen from a stool by Mr. Franklin's side. He spoke of the Penns. "I have at their request drawn up some *Heads of Complaint*," grumbled he, "which their lawyer, Ferdinand John Paris, a haughty man, has placed in the hands of the attorney general. This languishes unanswered while I trudge about like some ha'penny errand boy seeking friends of my cause. I tell you, I have conceived for Thomas Penn a most cordial contempt! Yet though he balks me now 'twill in time be seen that the government and property of a province must not be in the same family: 'tis too much weight in one scale." Of scientific matters he told of his cloth-in-snow experiment. "Does this not teach that in the Indies, East or West, light colored clothing would suit best?"

"So it seems," agreed Dr. Fothergill. "I have a friend just returned from the Antilles. You must meet him and tell him so."

Mr. Franklin beamed. "How it pleases me to disseminate new aids to mankind, which the study of Nature reveals."

These gentlemen departed near six; then grew on the time to set out for Roderick Fairbrass's party. Mrs. Stevenson met Mr. Franklin and me as we came downstairs at seven-thirty.

"Have you caught a rat in your new trap yet, dear lady?" asked he.

"I have not set it."

"Let the experiment begin!"

It was black night, snow no longer falling, yet bitter chill outside when he and I, wrapped to the ears in coats and scarves, he in his round beaver hat, stepped from the stoop of Number 7, Craven Street, into the covered coach which Peter had brought round. Mr. Franklin had recently hired this conveyance after much complaint: "The hackney coaches at this end of town are the worst in the whole city, miserable, dirty, broken, shabby things, unfit to go into when dressed clean and such as one would be ashamed to get out of at any gentleman's door." We pulled the traveling rug snug across our laps. Mr. Franklin tapped the roof with his stick, Peter flicked the reins, and we rattled north toward the Strand.

I greatly looked forward to this party. Indeed I always liked to go about with Mr. Franklin. In my former, confined life in Moorfields, I had seen little of London. Now I peered eagerly. Streetlamps cut the darkness, and all manner of conveyances—cabriolets, jitneys, chairs— and people, from beggars to lords, passed in a ceaseless flow, so that the great, smoky city seemed a living thing lying restlessly athwart the Thames. From the busy Strand we turned right into St. Martin's Lane, then by Castle Street to Leicester Square and from thence up Greek Street to Soho Square. "'Tis not so fashionable as't once was," murmured Mr. Franklin. "The *ton* flee west, so I am told, but the new aristocracy of bankers and honest merchants and traders resides here; soon, who may tell the difference between 'em and men with coronets?"

Roderick Fairbrass's residence proved a large, three-story brick terrace house on the South side, with light spilling from many windows, and coaches drawing up. Ours joined this parade, and soon we were let out at the door. There were smiles on the ladies and gentlemen going up—yet all was not untrammeled jollity, for a wizened, white-haired old man stood to one side in a drift of snow blowing frosty breath and shaking his stick.

"Go home!" railed he in a screeching voice. "Be off! 'Tis blasphemy to sing and dance on this or any day. 'Tis devil's work, I say!" He waggled his stick under Mr. Franklin's nose. "Roderick Fairbrass is a wicked man; do not enter his house for fear o' the Lord!"

"O, I fear the Lord," replied the gentleman mildly "—that, having given me capacity for joy, He should be displeased if I waste it. Take heed before you accuse others of misusing time. Good eve."

A grimace of fury twisted the old man's face.

Six wide marble steps led up to the great front door, twice as large as Mrs. Stevenson's, with a fanlight surmounting. Both Mr. and Mrs. Fairbrass were just inside to greet us, he in a fine white wig and a handsome suit of clothes. "Ben, 'tis good to see you!" He squeezed Mr. Franklin's hand, his long face forming a look of warmth, though there was something too bright in his beaming eyes which affrighted me though I could not have said why. "Nicolas, is't not?" He shook my hand too, then presented his wife, Hannah, a handsome, pale woman, perhaps forty, near as tall as he, with reddish hair. She smiled as Mr. Franklin kissed her hand, but her features too seemed fixed with false cheer, like a mask barely fastened, which might slip or shatter at any moment. "Fothergill has arrived," informed Fairbrass. "You will find him in the drawing room." He waved us on. "Pray go in. Make merry!" New guests crowded behind.

Mr. Franklin's soft glance said, "Keep eyes peeled, lad."

A serving man took our coats, and we proceeded down a

39

long hall, at the end of which were wide stairs. I peered up them. Had Cassandra Fairbrass's ghost fled down these?

I could not repress a shiver.

Mr. Franklin wore a white wig and his best black suit. Mrs. Stevenson had fitted me out as a young gentleman, in a yellow waistcoat and blue jacket, my brown hair held back with a velvet tie.

It was with a mixture of pride in these clothes, finer than any I had worn, and some nervousness that I followed Mr. Franklin into the drawing room.

This was large and high-ceilinged, with flames licking in the huge mouth of the fireplace. All was music and a babble of talk: gentlemen, and ladies in pretty dress, and many children too. Mistletoe and holly hung from windows and walls. A trio of fiddlers played merry tunes in one corner, a manservant carried about cups of Christmas brew, and a long table groaned with all manner of food, from capons to cakes. Laughter bubbled merrily. This was no formal gathering but a celebration amongst friends.

A clown wearing motley pranced about giving gifts. To me he handed a prettily wrapped box, which contained a lead soldier.

"One good soldier makes an army, Nick," proclaimed Mr. Franklin. "What may you not now conquer?"

From out of the crowd came Dr. Fothergill in iron-gray wig to meet us with his wonted dignity. After greetings Mr. Franklin asked, "Do you know Roddy Fairbrass well?"

"Indeed, no," replied Fothergill, gazing about with his friend. "It quite surprised me to learn I was to be of this company. Not that I am not pleased. What little I have seen of Fairbrass on this and other occasions tells me he is a fine fellow."

"Is he ill?"

"Ill?"

"Some fever about him?"

"Why . . . no. I do not see it."

"What do you hear of his business?"

"That it prospers more each day."

"With no faltering?"

"The man has the touch of Midas."

"Which proved vexing to Midas."

"Eh?"

"Is there not some recklessness about the man? I hear that his career has been marked by risks."

"Which have rewarded him handsomely."

"As you say. Pray excuse us, we must pay our respects to Miss Fairbrass."

Cassandra Fairbrass stood at the edge of the room by the tall windows. She wore her auburn hair pulled up in curls pinned with a small lace cap. Her long dress was pale green. The cross-shaped Celtic stone, polished by centuries of hands, was pinned to her bosom. Her pale-blue eyes searched Mr. Franklin as he approached, as if in hopes he may've already vanquished her ghost.

"Miss Fairbrass," said he, kissing her hand and softly adding: "I am here, as I promised and shall see what may be seen." She acknowledged me with a brief, leaping flick of eyes, then she and the gentleman spoke some moments of the skill of the fiddlers and whether the Thames might freeze, she ever rubbing her hands or stroking her stone, with her frighted rabbit stare. For his part Mr. Franklin looked at perfect ease, peering about genially. He politely inquired after various persons present, about whom she obliged him as she could. Several gentlemen were merchants, like her father. Mr. Franklin pointed to a powerfully-built young blackamoor

41

who stood in livery by the door. I too had taken special note of this fellow, for he seemed to spy on us, though as to that his hooded ivory eyes, with great, dark pupils, slid everywhere in restless watchfulness. "Who may that servant be?" asked the gentleman.

"Cato Prince. He worked in Papa's brother's house in Jamaica but has come recently to us."

"Over so long a distance?"

"Uncle Lemuel knew we looked for a good man. He assured us we might discover no better than this."

"And does he serve you well?"

"He has never made cavil at anything and performs all with alacrity—yet there is something about him. . . ."

She said naught else, but I saw her misgivings. The man was not so black as Peter, and there was an arrogance about him; his gaze roved bluntly, whilst he held his head as if he were a monarch's son. He looked but a few years older than I. What were his thoughts of this assembly?

Mr. Franklin seemed already to have forgot him. "And that is your young sister and brother?" His gesture drew my eyes to two small children by the long table, plucking at sweets. The girl had her mother's reddish curls. The boy was darker haired, and very pale, with a strange, fey smile.

"Dear Emily and Tim!" burst out Miss Fairbrass. "I wish no harm to come to 'em!"

Mr. Franklin cocked a brow, "From ghosts, you mean?"

She clutched her runic stone. "From any quarter."

"I see. May I meet your brother James?"

She led us across the room, through the gaily chattering crowd, to a young gentleman at smiling ease by the fire. By this time all guests seemed to have arrived, for Mr. and Mrs. Fairbrass had left their post by the front door and roved amongst us with exhortations to cheer. "James, this is Mr.

42

Benjamin Franklin, Papa's friend," introduced Miss Fairbrass as the clown pranced by with jingling bells.

James Fairbrass was lean and bright of eye. He had the family's long face and broad mouth but none of their haunted look, appearing all open friendliness. "Mr. Franklin," exclaimed he heartily, wringing the gentleman's hand. "How pleasing to meet a friend of Papa's!"

"And how pleasing to meet his son. But your father has many friends, has he not?"

"O, he is much liked."

"And will you follow him in business?"

James Fairbrass laughed. "Perhaps. I have not much head for business."

"Fortunate, then, that your father does. But what then do you do? Study? Law? Medicine?"

"I have no bent for such things," pronounced he airily. "I go about. A young man must go about, must he not, to see many sights? That is what I do, making my catalogue of the world, so I may find my place in't."

"And what geography have you mapped?"

"Only London. I wish to go abroad, but Papa has thus far forbid it. He has a strong idea of removing to America, yet that is not what I look for. France and Italy are what a man must see. America is not civilized."

"You are rude, James," put in his sister. "Mr. Franklin is from America."

The young man's cheeks flushed pink. "Forgive me, sir."

Mr. Franklin waggled his head. "Beg no pardon. You are correct in believing there is much that is uncivilized in America—as there is in England. Your father thinks of settling in America, Miss Fairbrass?"

"He has said some such thing."

"He has fixed upon't, you know he has!" put in her brother

43

sharply. He gazed reproof at his sister. "Cassie does not always know of what she speaks." His smile broke out again. "But I am doubly rude, for I have not presented my friend, Caddy Bracegirdle." He turned to a man of perhaps twenty-five, dressed very fine in deep red, with much lace at wrists and throat, who had just come up. "Benjamin Franklin, this is Cadwallader Bracegirdle."

This new arrival's smile showed large white teeth, but this was his only fine feature, for he had a crudely formed face: thick lips, a flat knot of nose, and cheeks disfigured by the pox. He had deep-set eyes and black brows. One might have called him ugly yet he seemed not to think himself so but greeted us as if he were the prettiest gentleman to be met, and the most diverting. "Haw, Mr. Franklin!" he burst out fatuously as he squeezed Mr. Franklin's hand. "And Miss Fairbrass." He kissed her fingers, drawing her near as he did so, and I saw her shudder. "You are looking pretty, Miss," purred he into her face, then beamed at all of us as if he were the very deliverer of sunlight to darkness. "I heard you speak of America? Haw, I too would not wish to go to America. London is quite enough for me; it has pleasures for a lifetime."

"Pray, what pleasures?" inquired Mr. Franklin.

"Why . . . boxing, gaming, cockfighting, clubs—and beautiful women and fine gentlemen the like of Jimmy Fairbrass."

"You enjoy the cockfights?"

"Immeasurably."

"They are cruel," put in Cassandra Fairbrass.

"Haw, not to my purse! For I win much on 'em."

"Fortunate," said Mr. Franklin.

James Fairbrass beamed at his friend. "Caddy has shown me much of London."

"Has he? I too love the city. And of all you have thus far seen, Mr. Fairbrass," inquired Mr. Franklin, "what pleases you most?"

"Gaming! Jimmy loves gaming," crowed Caddy Bracegirdle.

The brother's smile faltered; his cheeks reddened again. "Why, I do not love it so very much."

"You do! You know you do."

"I protest—"

"Bracegirdle . . ." mused Mr. Franklin. "I have heard of Lord Bracegirdle. Are you his son?"

"No," said the pocked man quickly. "My people are of Devon; you cannot know 'em. Little wonder, for my father is as reclusive as a badger. He has a monstrous big house, which might be quite gay, and acres of land, but he does nothing with 'em but holes up with his company of flea-bit dogs and his stable of hunters and pursues the wily fox. I detest dogs!—give me music and beer! What say you, Jimmy, shall we quaff some of your father's fine ale?" He tugged the young man's sleeve. "Pleased to've met you Mr. Franklin. By'r leave, Miss Fairbrass. Haw!" And, making an elaborate bow, he led James Fairbrass away, his arm hard about his shoulders as if he owned him.

Cassandra Fairbrass's thin fingers clutched her stone. "Would my brother had never met that man!" cried she.

Spritely dancing had begun in one corner, jigs and reels, and a stout young fellow drew Miss Fairbrass to this, though she looked unwilling to go. Mr. Franklin stayed where he was, thoughtfully watching James Fairbrass and his friend lift cups of ale across the room. "Two young men out of the bounds of their fathers," murmured he. Did he think of his William? Shaking himself, as to recover from bad thoughts, he began to make his way amongst the crowd, I at his side. He

45

struck up acquaintance with great ease. He had a true interest in people. Too, there was a quietness about him, a ready smile, an inquiring look about his soft gray-brown eyes behind their small squarish spectacles. He asked questions and listened close to replies and took all in, and I began to believe that, though the Penns might presently thwart him, they must one day succumb to his persistence.

One man he spoke with was Captain Jack Sparkum, of Deptford, who sailed to and from the West Indies for Roderick Fairbrass. This was a glowering, taciturn, powerfully built tar, ruddy of skin, with a grim mouth that said it knew all the tricks of the sea and a piercing eye that said it saw how to skirt 'em. "Aye, I sail for Roddy Fairbrass," asserted he between his teeth. "A good man! None better 'pon this earth."

"What does he ship to England?"

"Some indigo. Cotton. Sugar, in the main."

"His brother works for him in the Indies?"

Captain Sparkum's slitted eyes settled upon Mr. Franklin as if upon an approaching squall. "He mans his watch, he does." He would say no more.

Mr. Franklin spoke also to Moses Trustwood, a red-faced, large-bellied gentleman who stood with his hands behind his back and rose and fell on his bright black heels as if this were his house and his party and His Majesty, George II, here to take his pleasure. Trustwood was in partnership with other merchants in Nash's Bank, one of many in Lombard Street. "A man makes money; he wishes his money to grow," confided he jovially to Mr. Franklin. "What better way than to lend it to others, who pay for the use of't, while the lender sits at home with his feet up by his fire?"

"How pleasant to earn money by the fire—especially in

46

weather such as this. Roddy Fairbrass makes money this way?"

"O, great deal."

"With Nash's Bank?"

"He keeps all his funds with us."

"Where they are lent at good rate?"

"Why . . . yes, until recent days. Is't not a fine assembly? Do not they dance well? Pray, excuse me, sir. My wife awaits, and I must try a jig."

Mr. Franklin observed Trustwood's departing back. "When a wife waits, a husband must jig—lest she jig with another," murmured he. Until recent days—what did the fellow mean? There came a small sound of laughter. I turned. A tall gentleman of middle age, wearing no wig, stood nearby, his thick, dark hair pulled straight back and tied behind, much as mine, accentuating strong, straight planes of face. He had a long, sensitive nose, his eyes large and warm, yet guarded. His laughter had been subdued and brief, and there was a reserved air about him, he standing as still as a statue, a man apart, though he replied readily when Mr. Franklin introduced himself.

"Pleased to meet you, Mr. Franklin. I am Joseph de Medina," said he in a deep voice whose accent told he was not English born.

"Of Portugal?" inquired Mr. Franklin.

"That is the land of my birth. I have settled in England."

"You are a Jew?"

Feeling stirred in the deep brown eyes. "How do you surmise this?"

"I see much money in this room. 'Tis not flaunted, but 'tis here. Some Portuguese Jews make money in England. Such a Jew would fit well in this company. Thus I draw conclusion."

"You are clever."

47

"I merely make one and one into two. Forgive me, but . . . what does a Jew at a Christian celebration?"

Joseph de Medina smiled. "I see little that is Christian here. People kiss under mistletoe. Did Christ prescribe that? They drink English beer. At Christ's bidding? They dance. To worship him? If so let them worship as they will. I keep my faith."

Mr. Franklin smiled back. "I admire a man who knows how to use the world—and who keeps his faith. Would that Englishmen kept the spirit of theirs. I count it a crime that despite the services of many Jews to the English Treasury the Jewish Naturalization Act has been repealed."

De Medina made an impatient flick of fingers. "London merchants engaged in the Spanish and Portuguese trade were against us."

"I have heard."

"You know much, it seems."

Mr. Franklin waved a modest hand. "My habit is to learn what I can. Their treatment of you is outrageous."

De Medina glowered. "To think that when the ancestors of the Right Honorable Gentlemen were brutal savages, mine were priests in the Temple of Solomon." He made himself smile once more. "Yet I must not say so, I must bite my tongue. You too are a merchant?"

"Of a kind. I trade in right, striving to persuade Parliament and the King they must trade in't too, though the scales presently tip against me." He explained his mission. "What is your business?"

"Gold. Gems. Easily transported goods. The value of a diamond depends little on the whims of a nation, nor may it be tarnished by the breath of persecution."

Mr. Franklin nodded. "You too have discovered that in the great world one must learn to ride a tide or drown."

48

He spoke to some other gentleman, and some ladies too, one of whom persuaded him he must dance, which he did with great energy and a round, laughing face. Standing quietly aside, I saw in this Christmas assembly no lords and ladies in high, white wigs but sturdy gentlemen of commerce and their wives and children, dressed well enough but (except for some few, like Caddy Bracegirdle) naked of airs. I saw that there was money here, as Mr. Franklin had observed—not money resting in land, where it did little save breed indolence, but money which pumped like life's blood, driving ships across seas, building roads and squares, delivering goods to market, buying and selling sugar and coffee and silks and making the world change.

The music ceased. There blew an anticipatory stir as if a door had been opened—and of a sudden a fat, white-robed fellow carrying a wassail bowl and crowned with holly appeared amongst us, his crinkled face wreathed in smiles:

> In comes I, Father Christmas,
> Welcome or welcome not.
> I hope old Father Christmas
> Will never be forgot!

With a wink he lifted his bowl and toasted us all, and children laughed and clapped their hands. The jolly fellow then made up a game of Oranges and Lemons, with even the servants of the house, at Roderick Fairbrass's urging, stepping in. We sang a song of English Church Bells, concluding:

> Here comes a candle to light your bed,
> Here comes a chopper to chop off your head,

at which arms fell and captured a person for the Orange side or Lemon side. I was taken prisoner just after the servant,

Cato Prince, and stood behind him in the tug o' war. He pulled with great ferocity, as if winning were all in his life. Caddy Bracegirdle stood behind me and uttered his loud, barking "Haw" as we toppled the Lemons, amongst whom Mr. Franklin ended in chortling merriment on the floor amidst a tumble of skirts and breeches. Though Cato Prince had pulled well, Bracegirdle treated him with contempt, turning up his nose as their eyes met. Yet the young blackamoor did not look away, but faced down Bracegirdle, who strode off with loud huffing. Standing nearby, I found Prince's blazing eyes turned suddenly on me. My mouth went dry; I was held as strong as if he gripped my arms. What anguish, what pride, what hope burned in those liquid orbs. Being grateful for any good fellow on my side, whatever his station, I spoke out: "You pulled bravely, sir." But he only stared the harder, hostilely, as if he despised a boy's opinion, and walked away.

Shaken by this encounter, I rejoined Mr. Franklin. Roderick Fairbrass stood near him. "How I deplore the loss of the old games of Christmas, open to one and all," proclaimed he, whilst his little daughter clung to one leg and his little son to the other, gazing up as to ask: What surprises next, father, dear? The man was pale; perspiration wet his brow. He knelt tenderly. "Dear children, you must let your Papa go for a time, for as I told you I am to be St. George in our mummer's play."

"Mummers?" inquired Mr. Franklin.

"I have hired a band of players."

"Who do not provide a St. George?"

"They are short a man. I like to play a part." Yet his look belied his words, for he seemed shaken, his smile weak and faltering. Bending and clasping his children tight once more, he vanished out the door.

Mr. Franklin watched him go. "Damn me, what torments so good a man?"

There was no time to ponder this. Mrs. Fairbrass proceeded to draw the company to one side of the room, where we formed a crescent about the center. At one end of this stood James Fairbrass and Caddy Bracegirdle, Joseph de Medina near them in quiet talk with Moses Trustwood—two men of money sharing views. Mr. Franklin and I were at the middle, with Dr. Fothergill. Cassandra Fairbrass stood to our right, rubbing her stone, her mother beside her. Some three or four servants, Cato Prince amongst 'em, gathered at the other point of the crescent, with some dozen or so children, including Emily and Tim Fairbrass, clustered in front, so they might see best. Candles flickered. Sparks flew up from the huge log on the grate.

I looked forward to this mummer's play, a new thing— yet I felt pricks of ill ease. Mr. Fairbrass's gloom had seeped into me. Too his daughter's thin hands, ever chaffing her magic stone, were in my sight, her handsome mother looking tense as a cat beside her. Glancing up at Mr. Franklin, I read a watchful look in his eyes, which for all their mildness saw as sharp as an owl's. The fingers of one hand opened and closed at his side, whilst with the other he gripped my shoulder hard.

It began.

There was but one entrance to the room, the door from the hall, the lintel hung with holly. There came a murmur and bustle from this, which quieted us; then a hobby horse bedecked with fantastical ribbons burst in prancing and neighing. The children clapped their hands as the creature pawed the polished wood.

> St. George's gallant steed am I,
> Bravest steed under the sky.
> Pray, give us leave to play our play!
> England's King will clear the way.

Then came the second player, boldly, a grand, fat, waddling fellow in a glittering crown, as beribboned as the horse, and masked too so one saw only his mouth behind a straggling beard of straw. "I am the King of England!" boomed he, with much striding about and slapping of his wooden sword. He hated the infidel, he averred. This infidel must be beaten— and his son, George, was the champion for't.

Then followed St. George, beribboned too, and masked, with a plumed helmet and broadsword, though his sword was metal, not wood, and caught the firelight. His visor covered his eyes and nose, but Roderick Fairbrass's broad mouth was clearly visible beneath.

> I am Prince George, a worthy night.
> I'll spill my blood for England's right!

Loud huzzahs greeted this speech. St. George took his turn at noisy striding about, yet falteringly, I thought, for one who was meant to be so brave a knight.

Mr. Franklin bent near. "'Tis a play from the time of the crusades, oft performed at Christmastide. Many an old custom rides upon the holiday."

Then came another knight, visored to the chin and fluorishing his metal sword.

> I am the bravest Turkish man,
> From the far-off Eastern land.
> Your George's life be full of sorrow;
> No sun shall rise on his tomorrow.

Hisses greeted this, which only made the Turkish Knight more bold in his swaggering. Then the two warriors began to circle one another, whilst ohs and ahs flew up from all watchers. The battle followed, in which there was much thrusting and parrying, metal clanging on metal. "Oh, dear, oh dear!" wailed Tim Fairbrass's small, high voice. The boy gazed with open mouth and wide, fearful eyes at the men whose joining must seem as real to him as the floor on which he stood. His thin face was strained and white beneath his dark curls, his hands twisting pitifully. Did he recognize his father? Mr. Fairbrass made a poor show. His steps were unsure; he lurched against the long table, upsetting a clattering plate of meats. The Turkish Knight pursued him near the fire, and the two men's long shadow's circled above us.

And then Mr. Fairbrass seemed to recover. He made a great slashing show with his blade, forcing the Turkish Knight back, near the left-hand point of our crescent, where Joseph de Medina and Moses Trustwood and James Fairbrass and Caddy Bracegirdle watched. He was about to stab the infidel—voices cried for him to do't—and he did strike, but awkwardly, and missed, and the Turkish Knight thrust his sword. This nicked St. George's hand. I saw the spot of blood. 'Twas but a small cut, one I might have ignored, yet St. George made a great show of being mortally wounded:

O, woe to me and England's land!
Death has played his hand.

With great drama he fell heavily upon the floor, though his heaving chest said he but feigned death.

The Turkish Knight strode about in triumph, swinging his blade, whilst the King of England, who had observed all, wrung his hands. "Is there no one who may undo this evil deed?" Bending, he inquired of the children, the youngest of whom, with large eyes, said, no, they knew not what to do;

but some, who were older and had seen the play, shrilly chanted: "The Doctor, fetch the Doctor!"

"And so I shall!" crowed the King. "Doctor! Doctor!"

At this in strode the most fantastically garbed man of all, so masked and bedizened one could see no inch of his face. He carried a motley bag.

> I can cure whatever you please:
> Diseases of the nose and knees.
> I cure the itch, the stitch,
> The palsy, quinsy, and the gout,
> And if the devil's in a man,
> I can fetch him out.

The King begged his fee, which was a guinea. "Done!" The Doctor proceeded to rummage in his bag with great noisy show, pulling forth all manner of odds-and-ends: a broken salt pot, rusted nails, a horseshoe, a capon's chewed leg, until with a cry of triumph he drew out a small glass vial of bluish liquid, which he held up for all to view.

> Opliss-Popliss drops, you see,
> From death our Knight to free.

Much cheer greeted this. St. George lay at Joseph de Medina's feet. All eyes turned that way as the Doctor knelt beside the slain hero and held the vial to his lips. There was a breathless moment whilst St. George drank. His hand lifted; it grasped the vial, and I thought I heard words—the Doctor speaking? St. George? The Doctor held St. George's head. The brave knight ceased drinking and trembled all over, and there came a *Hurrah* for this shaking must signal the moment when he cast off death and leapt up and vanquished England's foe. The Doctor rose and stepped slowly back from St. George. Beaming, the King cried:

> My son, arise,
> And make a show of valor for men's eyes!

But St. George did not arise. There came an uneasy stir amongst the watchers. The King again repeated his incantation, this time in some alarm, yet St. George lay still, unmoving. "Come, sir . . . come, Roddy," sounded voices, urgent and full of sudden dread, for they too must see, as did I with a horrible sinking in my breast, that Roderick Fairbrass's chest no longer heaved. "Dear God," I heard Mr. Franklin murmur. "Fothergill, quickly!" These two rushed as one to the prone man's side. Fothergill knelt over his chest, listening, whilst Mr. Franklin held a small round glass to the man's lips. Only the spitting of fire marked this moment. The men stirred and exchanged glances and slowly stood, looking about grimly and shaking their heads. "He is gone, poor man," said Mr. Franklin, at which with a pitiful cry Mrs. Fairbrass fainted upon the floor.

I was struck cold to the marrow. All eyes fixed upon husband or wife—save mine. Only I, it seemed, glimpsed the movement by the door, marking the masked Doctor's stealthy exit.

And where was Cato Prince?

*IN WHICH Mr. Franklin shakes many
hands and feeds a rat some pie. . . .*

S ee to Mrs. Fairbrass, John," urged Mr. Franklin to Dr.
Fothergill. He gazed grimly down at the pitiful, still
form that had been Roderick Fairbrass. "Nothing may
be done for this poor fellow now." Yet I had the sense he said
this as much to have freedom to act unfettered as to aid the
stricken wife, for immediately Dr. Fothergill was removed
Mr. Franklin knelt and furtively plucked at the dead man's
chest.

I went to him.

Standing, he drew me aside and showed a sprig of green.
"*Rosemary, that's for remembrance,*" said he in deep, frowning
puzzlement. His eyes met mine. "How came such a sprig
upon the dead man's chest? 'Twas not there before. See you
rosemary about the room, Nick?"

"Why . . . no, sir. I see holly, mistletoe, yew—but no
rosemary."

He started. "Where is the mumming Doctor?"

"Vanished, sir. I saw him creep out."

"Damn his slyness! Observed you more, Nick?"

"Cato Prince gone too, sometime as the play was being

56

played. It may make little matter, but I heard the Doctor say some word or words to St. George as he gave the Opliss-Popliss drops. Yet it may've been St. George spoke to him, I am not sure." I felt a sudden wrenching. "O, Mr. Franklin, has the ghost's promise come true?"

"Bethink yourself, Nick—'twas no ghost! Further, it promised nothing. Yet why did the thing have the face of Cassandra Fairbrass's father?" Gravely slipping the rosemary into his coat, he knelt once more and opened the fingers of the dead man's right hand, from which he plucked the small, glass vial of Opliss-Popliss drops, some half inch of bluish liquid yet in't. The cork lay upon the floor nearby. This too he took, and stoppered the vial. "Keep this, Nick," whispered he, glancing about. "See nothing spills." Yet it seemed some may've spilled, for there was a wet spot amongst the dead man's ribbons, just below his neck. Mr. Franklin gazed at this as I secreted the vial in my coat. "And this wetness . . . ?" said he touching fingers to it. "How came it here?" He waggled his head. "There is much amiss. . . ."

All this took but a moment. Mr. Franklin's business went largely unheeded, for the company of guests, stunned and rooted, seemed not to wish to look at the body, as if they might deny death. Instead they fixed their stricken gazes upon the circle of friends who attempted to rouse Mrs. Fairbrass. Now came a stir all round: a murmuring and shifting of feet and small cries. At last Mrs. Fairbrass came to her senses amongst many helping arms and sat up in gasping sobs. Her elder daughter was white as flour and clutching her stone, as if she too might faint. "Where is Papa? Where is Papa?" cried Tim Fairbrass in a small, lost voice, his frighted sister Emily clasping his hand and staring too and opening and closing her mouth though no sound came. "Poor dears," cooed a woman, whilst two gentlemen proceeded to herd the dozen or so small children toward the door.

James Fairbrass had come to his father. He knelt trembling, then turned his long face up to Mr. Franklin. "'Tis true, then? He is dead?"

"At peace," amended Mr. Franklin, "free of a troubling world."

Just behind stood Moses Trustwood and Joseph de Medina, fixed with twin looks of dismay. As for Caddy Bracegirdle he stared, mouth open, his pitted face whiter even than Cassandra Fairbrass's, muttering over and over: "It cannot be . . . cannot!" whilst he slapped his fist against his thigh, though whether in sorrow or fury I could not tell.

Joseph de Medina stepped forward. Swiveling his solemn brown eyes about the room, he spoke with dour authority: "A sad event has marked this eve, which was to be given over to joy. 'Tis best to leave our friends to their grieving." He lifted his arms. "Come, let us to our homes. We may deliver condolences at more settled time." Firmly he gathered the nearest of the assembly and began to urge them toward the door. "Come . . . come." This was all that had been needed. Relief was palpable though sighs burst out as most obeyed. Everyone glanced back at the stricken relations and called regrets as they shuffled to their coats and the wide world beyond: "So sorry, dear Cassie . . . take heart, James . . . such a good husband, Hannah."

Caddy Bracegirdle went too, though in apparent reluctance, with a seething, black look. "Truly dead, is he?" demanded he as he passed Dr. Fothergill. "Truly?"

The doctor coolly nodded.

Mr. Franklin leapt to the pocked young man at the door. "So sad." He wrung his hand. "Would it were not so, eh?"

Bracegirdle pulled free and stalked out.

Yet Mr. Franklin stayed by the door squeezing Joseph de Medina's hand before that gentleman left. Moses Trustwood's too. Others.

After each pressing of hands I saw him discreetly drop small, oyster-colored bits of wax into the waistcoat pocket with the snuffbox.

Thus most of the guests departed. The fiddlers went as well, their instruments which had played so lively silent by their sides. Father Christmas trudged out, ashen, as did the hobby horse, the King, the Turkish Knight. Mr. Franklin looked as if he would wish to stop 'em all and put close questions, yet he merely resumed his quiet stance near the body. One might have thought he mourned, as helpless as any soul, yet I saw by the stitching of his brows and the grim set of his mouth and his quietly darting eyes that his mind worked behind the small, squarish lenses of his spectacles.

And what then? We were left in a dismal air, the gay decorations seeming to droop, flames dying in the hearth, fat congealing about the meats on the long trestle table. Three servants huddled in a corner, though Cato Prince was not returned. Mrs. Fairbrass had been got to a chair, a close friend, Mrs. Busk, bending to comfort her. Her son James went to her; so did her elder daughter, though not before halting before Mr. Franklin with a shattered look. "You see?" Her neck cords strained as she thrust her tear-stained face in his. "If I had heeded might I not have prevented this? Might I not?"

Mr. Franklin tutted. "Blame yourself for nothing, Miss Fairbrass," urged he.

"Yet I do, I do." Clutching her stone she turned and with her brother and mother formed a composition of sorrow.

Reminded of my mother's death, I forced down the lump in my throat.

In the first rushing to the body Dr. Fothergill had loosed the costume at the neck. Now he knelt and gently pulled the helmet from the head. How changed Roderick Fairbrass appeared in death! His face had a slackness and grayness and looked altogether thinner than before, as if shrunk by the dire event. Gazing upon this pitiful visage, I hated death. But the ghost—surely Mr. Franklin was right: it had not predicted this; there would be found reason behind it.

Whilst the doctor made more thorough examination, Mr. Franklin quietly gathered up St. George's sword, holding it gingerly by the blade. In startlement the Turkish Knight had dropt his sword, and this too Mr. Franklin plucked from the floor and set both by the door.

He came to Dr. Fothergill.

"His heart, Ben," said Fothergill, standing and rubbing his hands with a white kerchief. "Such spasm as we observed is oft seen when a man dies thus. You asked if he was ill. Do you know that he was? How he sweated in the tug o' war! In any case, the exertions of the evening—the dancing, the game of Oranges and Lemons, the swordfight—were sufficient to bring on death. Too, I have heard the fellow was given to drink; that may predispose a man to such an end." He peered into his friend's face. "Such a look, Ben. Do you doubt?"

Mr. Franklin met his gaze. "Doubt the poor man's heart has stopped? I am no such fool."

There came a sudden gruff bark. All the while Captain Jack Sparkum had stood at the edge of the room watching out of his squinting eyes and rubbing his knuckles. Now he strode angrily forward. "A man must be treated decent, dead or alive! Have you not done your mutterin' o'er the poor soul?" He gazed down. "A good man, a good'un. None better." Pulling off his coat, he spread it over the slack, gray face, then turned. "I shall stay with the family, to see things are dealt

60

with proper. You gentleman are nor needed nor wanted; go with the rest."

I thought this rude, but Mr. Franklin made no cavil. "Mrs. Fairbrass must be grateful to leave matters to so able a man," said he with a small, deferring nod. "Come, Nick. Come, Fothergill. We have done all we may." Going to the mother, seated between son and daughter he bowed. "My deepest condolences. If I may be of any aid, please call at Craven Street."

Mrs. Fairbrass lifted her handsome face, framed by reddish hair. Tears swam in eyes which seemed neither to see nor know who spoke. "Yes . . . yes. . . ." murmured she.

The gentleman nodded solemnly to James and Cassandra Fairbrass, then led us to the door, where he scooped up the swords he had laid there as if they belonged to him. Dr. Fothergill made eyes at this but no comment. Outside, Soho Square was quiet, most houses dark, no moon or stars to be seen in the frosty sky. Snow softly fell, and eleven o'clock bells rang out. How cruelly indifferent seemed the world to the torment of the family we had left behind!

But not all was peace.

The wizened old curmudgeon stood where we had seen him two hours ago. Keeping stubborn vigil all that time? "Dead, is he? God's punishment, I say," brayed he. Mr. Franklin paid him no mind but brushed past. Dr. Fothergill climbed into his coach, we into ours, and Peter set off, our wheels crunching on the blanketed cobbles, the swords softly clinking together on the floor.

I felt disheartened, lost, bewildered—but glad to have Mr. Franklin by my side. Yet he too seemed confounded. "Why did not Mrs. Fairbrass go to Roddy?" muttered he as we moved through a London of few coaches in frigid, darkened

61

streets. "True, she fainted, but when she woke why did not the loving wife rush to her dear husband's side?"

I awoke next morning with a start, having spent the night tossing amidst dreams of Father Christmases who masked evil intents behind sly smiles, hobby horses that neighed of death, and visored knights who hacked and slashed with gore-daubed swords. Wanting company, I rushed into my clothes in dim dawn light and crossed the landing to Mr. Franklin's door, where I softly knocked. There sounded no reply. Firmer knocking brought a like disconcerting silence. Might the gentleman be in his workshop just behind? I looked into this room, but it proved chill and untenanted.

There came a soft cry of triumph from belowstairs.

Descending two flights to the kitchen, I found Mr. Franklin barefoot in his dressing gown on the frigid flags, holding aloft the trap which he had designed for Mrs. Stevenson, in it a huge rat writhing and hissing, baring wicked yellow teeth. "See you, Nick," crowed he. "Is't not a success? And just in time, for we have business with this fellow. Come."

We passed Mrs. Stevenson on the stairs, descending to light fires. She gave a shriek at sight of the rat. "O, kill it, sir, kill it!" cried she.

"After my fashion," replied the gentleman, hurrying by. "Must we not have some half dozen of these traps made up, for to cleanse us of such vermin?"

He led me to his workshop. Though 'twas freezing cold, he was so intent on his purpose that he showed no chill. I had seen him often thus, capable when presented with a problem of so bending himself to't that all else became air which went unheeded save to breathe. Setting the trap on his workbench, the rat lashing against its strong wires, he pulled from his

62

dressing gown the vial of bluish Opliss-Popliss drops. From another pocket he drew forth a bit of meat pie, wrapped in parchment. He placed finger to lips. "Never reveal to Mrs. Stevenson how I employ her good food. Now—" Setting the small square of pie upon a dish, he unstoppered the vial and peering intently through his eyeglasses dropped three drops upon the pie, which left some quarter inch of liquid in the glass. This he restoppered. The meshes of the cage were large enough to force the pie through an opening. Having done so, Mr. Franklin drew me back some paces. "Observe," hissed he, very still and watching. It was so cold our breaths showed in little clouds. Faint sounds of Mrs. Stevenson came from below, and I heard a stirring above, of Peter and King rousing themselves in their slope-ceilinged attic room. The rat had turned to the pie, yet I had the sense it watched us, whiskers twitching, wanting to eat yet mistrustful.

Suddenly it grasped the bit of pie and downed it in a gulp. The creature twitched, shuddered, stretched, lay still.

"Quod erat demonstrandum." Mr. Franklin poked the rat triumphantly with one of his glass rods. No mistake: its limpness and glazed, staring eyes proclaimed that it was dead.

"Poison," pronounced he grimly.

I stared at him. "Murder, then?" breathed I.

"Murder, indeed," mused the gentleman as we came down-stairs to breakfast some half an hour later. "Miss Fairbrass asked me to aid her. Sad that 'tis too late to save her poor father, yet I must prevent more harm occurring. This vile murderer must be made known. My heart is moved, Nick. No time must be lost."

In the kitchen Mrs. Stevenson was just uncovering eight fat meat pies, which had sat overnight under cloth.

63

"Such plenty, dear lady!" exclaimed Mr. Franklin. "Surely we cannot consume it all."

She tapped her mole. "O, sir, and will not be asked to. They are for the poor. 'Tis Boxing Day."

"Boxing Day?" asked I.

"Aye, when charity is the rule."

"'Tis named for the alms boxes which used to be placed in churches," Mr. Franklin explained.

"What's this?" Mrs. Stevenson squinted hard at one of her pies. "Some small piece of this has been took. And such a neatly-sawed square." Her eyes narrowed at Mr. Franklin. "Done with a knife, was it? Cut by our fastidious rat to eat before he was caught?"

The gentleman faced her unblinking as a saint. "Ate it, dear lady, and was punished for so daring."

"Punished 'aright. All such pie thieves should be hung in stocks!"

Peter and King again joined us at table against custom, for there were gifts to be given, small earthenware boxes, one to each, which they were charged to break before we ate. Upon doing so they discovered money within. "Because our servants please us so well," proclaimed Mr. Franklin. Peter accepted his graciously, though King fingered his so glumly that the soft chink of the coins had a sad, lamenting ring.

To my surprise Mr. Franklin presented me too with a box. "Break it, Nick," urged he. This I did, upon the edge of the table, and found some shillings and pence. "With which you may purchase what you will," proclaimed the gentleman, smiling and touching my hair, and I flushed with pleasure at his kindness and thanked him heartily, though William's disapproving glance dulled my joy.

"Was't a gay party at the Fairbrasses'?" asked Polly when we had bowls of steaming porridge before us. "How I should like to have been there."

"You should have been sorry, had you been." Mr. Franklin said what had occurred.

Mrs. Stevenson paled. "What? Mr. Roderick Fairbrass, who was here just yesterday? Dead? Poor man. Yet his daughter came too, with news of a ghost." Her eyes lit. "Was't this spirit which brought death?"

Mr. Franklin scowled. "No more than the lark's song brings the morn, dear lady," replied he curtly.

The company inquired after every detail, which Mr. Franklin gave, though he said nothing of removing the Opliss-Popliss drops or the swords, which he had secreted in his workshop. Nor did he say how the rat had died. "Poor Fairbrass's heart was weak, it seems"—his way of putting an end to questions.

Yet he had questions of his own and had his coach brought round an hour later. "I am fixed upon looking into this matter," said he to me in his chamber, pacing. "Accompany me, Nick. I wish you by my side."

"Yes, sir." Life had a keener edge by Mr. Franklin's side.

We stepped out the front door at ten, the sky clear but gray, with a biting chill in the air. Chunks of ice still bobbed in the Thames. Yet we did not depart at once, for a sprightly singsong turned our eyes to some half dozen ragged boys marching along Craven Street as we descended the stoop:

The wren, the wren, the king of birds,
St. Stephen's Day was killed in the furze.
Though he is little his honor is great,
And so, good people, pray give us a treat.

They carried amongst 'em a sort of litter on rude wooden poles, on which lay a dead wren spitted on a stick, on a bed of evergreen.

65

Mr. Franklin looked sad. "This too is a custom of the season, poor bird." He dropped twopence into the little wooden box of the head boy, who tipped his greasy cap, and the troop marched merrily on. He watched them. "Strange, is't not, how death is a theme of the happy time? St. George too was killed, though he was meant to revive. He is the spirit of the year, who dies in winter yet revives in spring—so says Mr. Gower in his book on ancient customs. There is much of strange old times still living. Yet our St. George defied custom. Why?" Cursing gout, he climbed into his coach. "That is what I mean to discover."

❧ 5 ❧

IN WHICH the investigation begins. . . .

M r. Franklin wore an intent, pleased look, a softly smiling glow, a bright glint of eye, as our coach swayed and jounced in its progress toward Charing Cross. He was a man who grew glum when no purpose lay to hand; clearly the search for Roderick Fairbrass's murderer was a fresh breeze in the doldrums where he paced the deck whilst his business with the Penns sat becalmed.

"Where do we go, sir?" asked I.

"To seek a watchman. After breakfast I sent Peter to discover from the Superintendent of the Watch the name of the man who walked Soho Square last night. It is he whom we seek—and shall find off Castle Street, if we are informed aright."

"Yes, sir," said I.

The Strand bustled with all manner of toing and froing in spite of the chill: costers and merchants aselling and house-wives abuying. Everywhere chimney pots spewed their haze of sifting gray. Peter turned into the Royal Mews, and shortly we were in Orange Street, a narrow lane of overhanging houses banked with dirty snow, in which small children tumbled with shrill abandon. Mr. Franklin knocked at an oaken door.

It opened at once.

"Is this the home of Watchman Tree?" inquired he of a kerchiefed old dame.

"Aye," said she readily, and, aye, he might speak to her husband, who was just up having his pipe. She led us to a crowded parlor, which showed the pride of hardworking souls: nothing fine but all clean, in place, and loved. A lean old gentleman with bushy white brows was just lighting up with a coal. He unfolded himself in a cloud of smoke. Aye, he was Mr. Rupert Tree, said he, wringing Mr. Franklin's hand, and, aye, he was Watchman for Soho Square. "Down Greek Street I walks, and up Thrift Street, and I keeps an eye out and calls the hour, from seven to two exact."

"Perchance were in the Square at half past ten?"

"Aye, thereabouts."

"And saw what?"

"Why . . . naught save a canting fellow, Josiah Skint, who I had earlier warned must keep his peace. He spits at my feet—my very feet!—when I silences him, yet he shuts his mouth, for he knows wot's good for him. Yet he does not move off but stands stiff as a weathercock by the Fairbrass house and wrinkles his nose at its lights and music."

"You saw no one else?"

"No one."

"No one in fantastical garb, beribboned and masked?"

"Nay."

"Nor any other soul?"

"None at the hour you name, though some short time later comes a procession from the Fairbrass house, calling for their coaches, very sad for the season—women weeping, the men as grave as deacons. T'were early for the revels to end."

"A man died within."

"Tut, at such a time. Pray, who?"

"Roderick Fairbrass."

Rupert Tree shook his head. "A good man." Blackened teeth clamped hard on his pipe. "I am sorry to hear it." He peered shrewdly. "You were amongst that company?"

"I was."

"And are come to say 'tis a matter for the constable?"

"I shall tell you if I discover so. May you say more of Josiah Skint?"

"I know no more, save that his is the house next the Fairbrasses'. Last night be not the first the old fool ranted 'gainst honest pleasures."

"I thank you, sir."

"The watchman did not see the mumming Doctor flee the house," grumbled Mr. Franklin when we were once more in Castle Street, climbing into our coach. "Where then did he go? Yet a sly fellow may escape a vigilant eye—perhaps even so vigilant an eye as Rupert Tree's." He winced as he settled in his seat. "Damn Mrs. Gout!—my capering last night has inflamed her temper; the harridan reproves me." Snatching the rug across his lap, he thumped the roof with his bamboo stick. "Soho Square, Peter! At once."

In daylight the Fairbrasses's three-story brick house looked little changed from last night, its rows of white-trimmed casements giving no clue it was a place of sorrow. Yet a second-story window of the house to the left was not so mute, seeming to wink as a curtain was let fall. Josiah Skint, keeping watch?

"Aye, Nick," murmured Mr. Franklin, who had spied too.

We mounted the marble steps, a maidservant (one of the three who had huddled together after the death last night)

69

admitting us. "I have business of some urgency with Mrs. Fairbrass, if she is able," pronounced the gentleman, at which the maid scurried off. He lifted his round, bespectacled face as if sniffing the air. "Ah, what secrets are hid within these walls . . . ?"

The maid returned some moments later. "The mistress will see you, sir," said she and led us to a small sitting room to the right, curtains drawn. There Hannah Fairbrass sat in dim light, dressed all in black, as still as wax, her reddish hair veiled, her eyes bleak, yet her jaw set, as if she would face what had come bravely—as if, indeed, this were not her first tragedy. The room lay blanketed in sorrow, save for one bright note: four scarlet nightingales in a cage.

Mr. Franklin approached. The woman tremblingly looked up. Her voice was a beleaguered whisper: "Sir. You were friends with my husband."

Mr. Franklin tilted his head. "In a small way. We met sometimes at the White Lion; we had pleasant conversation. I am sorrowed at his passing."

"Many are so sorrowed."

"You recall my young friend, Nicolas Handy?"

Mrs. Fairbrass made wan acknowledgement.

"Very sorry, ma'am," said I.

"Forgive my intruding so soon after your bereavement," said Mr. Franklin, "but a matter of some gravity has arisen."

The woman's eyes struggled to take him in, "Yes?"

"May I ask some questions? It was your husband hired the mummers who played the play last night?"

"'Twas."

"Pray, where may they be found?"

"Why . . . in the Lambeth Road. The Queen's Rest, I believe."

70

"Yet, forgive me, your husband himself enacted St. George. Why?"

"Two days ago the chief player came hat in hand to say they had lost a man to some distemper. My husband was never one to stand on dignity." The woman's voice broke. "It gave him pleasure to take the part."

"So he told me. Forgive me once more, but . . . had he enemies?"

Mrs. Fairbrass's damp lashes blinked.

"Enemies, ma'am," pressed Mr. Franklin softly, ". . . who might wish to poison him?"

The woman stared, her mouth working, and some inner strength, a determination, drew her shoulders back. Her voice rose out of its whisper. "Do you wish to demean him, sir? And me?"

"Nothing like it. I take no pleasure in inquiring thus, yet you must hear a tale." Briefly he told of the Opliss-Popliss drops and the rat.

She watched his face intently as he spoke. "You are mistaken," said she firmly when he was done. "Some other cause killed your rat. Have I not troubles aplenty without talk of poison?"

"Surely, ma'am, having heard the result of my experiment you cannot insist t'was only the exertions of the evening did in your husband?"

"I do insist! Only?" Tears flooded her eyes. "Were those exertions not enough?"

Her sobs clearly discomfitted Mr. Franklin. His hands fidgeted, and he hemmed and hawed. "As you say," murmured he at last. "May I then inquire: had he been in ill health?"

She swallowed her sorrow. "He had palpitations of the heart."

71

"And seen a doctor for 'em?"

"He did not trust doctors."

This surprised me. Mr. Fairbrass had shown no mistrust of Dr. Fothergill, especially asking him to be at the Christmas party.

The poor, dead man might better have mistrusted mummers, thought I, though I kept my counsel.

Mr. Franklin too made no comment. "Was't these palpitations which made your husband so downcast of late?" inquired he.

She stared. "Downcast?"

"Some misfortune in business, perhaps?"

"Why . . . no such thing."

"Family troubles, then?" This was put in the kindest manner. Mrs. Fairbrass looked pained but shook her head. Standing near the nightingales, which softly stirred and preened, I had the sense that though she was much shaken by her husband's death she was not sent awry; there was steel in the woman.

Mr. Franklin was silent a moment. "Dear Mrs. Fairbrass, I do not wish to press you at this trying time, yet what if I am not mistook about the poison? You do not like news of't; indeed, I myself do not like rain when it wets my collar. Yet it discomforts me nonetheless, and I must shelter or suffer. Poison does no mild injury; poison kills. I do not insist that I am right, yet I beg, would you not consent to answer some few questions more, which, if acted upon, might shelter your family should there prove to be danger?"

At this the woman looked like yielding, and I was moved. Her expression seemed to plead: *I cannot take all upon myself.* Yet a kind of desperation effaced this brief look, as if she dared not give in, even to so well-meaning a man as Mr. Benjamin Franklin, and she grew hard again, knotting the

72

black kerchief in her hands as if't held her very soul, which must be stifled. Her lips pressed tight, to deny the gentleman; yet peering into his face she relented, though stiffly; "Very well, be seated and put your questions."

Mr. Franklin took a chair. "Who will see to your husband's business now he is gone?"

"Captain Sparkum has offered to help sort things through. Afterward I suppose I must do't myself."

"Not your son?"

"O, my son . . . !" Her face twisted bitterly.

Mr. Franklin made no comment. "Your daughter spoke last night of an uncle. Why not he?"

"He is far away, in Kingston, and needed there."

"He is your husband's brother?"

"Younger brother. Lemuel is his name."

"May you say more of him?"

"What more?"

"His character."

"'Tis of the best. He had some dissipation in his youth—but he is reformed."

"Did the brothers get on well?"

"What? You have heard that they did not? All rumor. As betwixt many brothers there was some jealousy, some rivalry as they grew up—but that was long ago. They are devoted. Lemuel would do anything for my husband."

"It will be a great blow, then, when he hears of this."

"I shall not like writing of it."

"Does any inheritance pass to this brother?"

"He has some small interest in my husband's business, but very little."

"There are no other relations?"

"Some cousins in Norfolk, whom I have not seen in years."

"And will you remove to America?"

73

There came another start. "Whyever do you ask?"

"Last night your son said his father had made some such plans."

"James speaks out of turn. It is true my husband entertained the thought. He had quite given it o'er, but yet. . . ."

"Yet—?"

Bleakly she shook her head. "How death changes all!"

"True. But son and father got on well?"

Mrs. Fairbrass colored. "They had the disagreements of a father and a son of twenty who is blind to the traps life sets."

"Life indeed sets traps. Yet your son's new friend, Cadwallader Bracegirdle, takes him in hand."

"The worse for James."

"Your daughter too does not care for this Bracegirdle?"

"Rightly despises him!"

The nightingales fluttered and hopped. "Speaking of Cassandra, how has she received this terrible blow?"

"By taking to her room. She wishes to blame herself for her father's death."

"Pray, why?"

"She believes. . . ." Mrs. Fairbrass bit her lip. "But yet I do not know."

The nightingales settled. The brownish, curtained gloom of the room wrapt us round. Mr. Franklin rubbed his brow. "I shall take little more of your time. Your daughter said last night that her uncle Lemuel sent you recently a new man, Cato Prince. A remarkable servant, by his report. Why did he not keep him for himself?"

"As I told you, he would do much for Roderick. He knew we looked for a man; he said we must have this one."

"Must? And how long has he been here?"

"A month and some days."

"And serves well?"

74

"With great loyalty."

"Sailed with Captain Sparkum?"

"From Kingston, in November."

"One last matter: you said your husband had no enemies—yet your neighbor, Josiah Skint, hates him."

Mrs. Fairbrass laughed without humor. "Pay no mind to Mr. Skint. He is a crabbed, pathetic man who complains of one and all. He would find sinning in a saint."

"It must be a trial to have him near."

"We are tolerant, as he is not."

"Wise to be so." Mr. Franklin arose. "I shall trouble you no more today, ma'am. I pray my fears prove groundless."

She stood too, in some anxiety. "Wait. What do you mean to do with your knowledge?"

"Why . . ."

She stepped forward. "Do not go to the magistrate!—you may not, you have no certainty."

He bowed his head. "As you wish." His gaze fixed upon her. "Yet I would desire to make more inquiries, in your interest."

Her mouth made its thin line, whilst her eyes glittered urgently in the gloom. "I consent—but do not bestir already troubled waters, I beg you. I have suffered greatly. I wish only peace, for me and my children, to heal our loss."

"I wish you well mended." Moving to the door, Mr. Franklin touched the bars of the nightingales' cage. "Pretty birds. From Jamaica?"

"Another gift of Lemuel."

"Arrived with Cato Prince? In November?"

The woman nodded gloomily as she sank into her chair.

"Come, Nick." Mr. Franklin led me from the sad, shadowed room. When we were in the hall he murmured, "Damn me, does she truly believe her husband cannot have been

75

poisoned? And is't mere coincidence that Cassandra Fairbrass began to hear night sounds at the same time this young blackamoor, Cato Prince, was delivered as so sacrificing a gift?"

The maid made to show us out, but Mr. Franklin stopped her by the front door. She was a short, plump, moon-faced girl with very black brows, wearing an apron and little cap. Her eyes were swollen, as if like Mrs. Fairbrass she too had been crying. Mr. Franklin smiled kindly. "Your name, my girl?"

"Mary, sir."

He asked about the servants in the house.

She sniffled as she spoke. "Why . . . yes, sir—there are four besides myself: cook, Mrs. Peters; Mr. Marker, the coachman; the manservant, Cato Prince; last is Miss Box, the governess." She herself tended to Mrs. Fairbrass and her elder daughter, she said. Roderick Fairbrass and his son, James, were seen to by Cato Prince. As soon as she uttered Mr. Fairbrass's name great tears began to roll down her cheeks. "Poor master, dead."

"There," soothed Mr. Franklin. "You were fond of the man?"

"He was so good to us all."

"Everyone tells of his goodness. The coachman, Mr. Marker, where may I find him?"

"He has took Mr. James to the undertakers, to see to the burial."

"Then I should wish to speak to Cato Prince."

"He too is out."

"O?"

"On some errand with Captain Sparkum, who stays with us some days."

"Captain Sparkum takes things well in hand? The blacka-

76

moor has served the household but short time. Does he get on well?"

Mary dabbed her eyes with her apron. "If you mean, does he do his duty, he does." Yet there was a hint of pique.

Mr. Franklin peered close. "You have some dispute with the fellow?"

Mary's black brows knitted. "He puts on airs, he does! And sneaks everywhere! I do not like him."

"Yet he does his duty."

Sullenly: "I give him that."

"Was your master in ill health before he died?"

"Ill? Nothing to show that, sir, but—"

"Say what you will."

"—but poor Mr. Fairbrass seemed so *sad* of late. And—O, sir, is't right to tell?—he fought with his son."

"About what?"

"I do not know. Mr. Fairbrass closed the door when the fights began."

"Many fights?"

"But two or three."

"Father and son were, then, not in habit of disputing? Do you sleep well, Mary?"

"Why . . . well enough."

"In what part of the house?"

"Below."

"Have you seen or heard a ghost?"

Goosebumps sprang out on her forearms. "You speak of what Miss Cassandra saw," breathed she.

"You know of it?"

"O, yes, sir, for Mr. Fairbrass woke us, me and cook, coming down with her one night, and they poked about everywhere whilst she kept saying she had seen a spirit. They found nothing."

"Yet have you yourself seen or heard a ghost?"

Mary gazed about, large-eyed, as if the walls might listen. "Not to speak on. Yet the house makes sounds at night, as ev'ry house makes sounds, and who may say some are not spirits up from their graves?"

This made me shiver, but Mr. Franklin merely wrinkled his nose. "Superstition, pah!" exclaimed he when we were out upon the snow in Soho Square. "It blinds men—and women—to reason and truth." Thoughtfully he tapped his jaw. "Hum . . . as Mr. Marker and Cato Prince are not to be met, shall we next door, to Josiah Skint?" Chuckling, he patted my shoulder. "Gird yourself for the encounter, Nick. And keep your wits."

The house to the left was narrower than the Fairbrass house, tell and crabbed, little more than two windows wide, which seemed to suit Josiah Skint's pinched nature. The sharply squinting old man himself answered Mr. Franklin's knock, flinging open the door as if he had observed our approach and waited to spring the latch.

"Well, what is't?" demanded he, thrusting out his wrinkled face.

Mr. Franklin met this abruptness stoutly: "Roderick Fairbrass died last night," replied he. "So pleased did you appear at this news that I have wondered if you yourself poisoned him."

Skint's skull-like head darted back, and his gray eyes in their nests of lines shot wide. "Poisoned? I be no poisoner, though I had little use for Roderick Fairbrass." Cunning crept into his expression. "Poisoned, was he? Ye say he was *poisoned?*"

"May be. If so, 'tis a matter for law, and all his enemies will be suspect."

"Ha, you are no magistrate's man."

"Yet I am His Majesty's loyal subject, who hates murder as much any citizen, and I shall do all in my power to bring justice. Why did you hate Roderick Fairbrass?"

"Hate? Despise, more like! The sinner dared offer music and dancing and playacting on a holy day. Plays are sucked out of the devil's teats. As for poison, music serves up a cup of it, brimful, to the world. Wickedness, I say! Such festivities are no glory but an affront to the holy season, a scandal to religion, a sin against our Lord."

Mr. Franklin gazed serenely into this ranting. Meanwhile a bedraggled-looking maidservant, hair afly, had crept up behind her master clutching some garment in her arms. She looked terrified of speaking.

"That is all that set you against Roderick Fairbrass?" asked Mr. Franklin.

"There were comings and goings at night."

"Of what sort?"

"Persons sneaking in and about. Who knows who they might be?" Glimpsing his servant, he flung up his hand as if to strike her. "What is't, ye cowering fool?"

She flinched. "Begging your pardon, sir . . . 'tis just that I plucked this from the dustbin and wondered if 'twas meant to be there." She held out in her arms, for all to see, the beribboned costume of the mumming Doctor.

❧ 6 ❧

*IN WHICH mumming mischief comes to
Craven Street, and Mr. Franklin prints
with wax. . . .*

An Oliver Grumble, is he not," said Mr. Franklin of
Josiah Skint when we were rattling back to Craven
Street. "Yet as the same man cannot be both friend
and flatterer, may not the curmudgeon prove useful? We may
oft learn more truth from an enemy than a friend. These
comings and goings at night, for example—are they not
suggestive?"

"The ghost entering and leaving, sir?"

"The intruder, Nick. Yet what might an intruder seek night
after night? I must speak again to Mrs. Fairbrass. To young
James and Cassandra as well." He fingered the mumming
Doctor's costume, which lay in his lap. It had been hid
beneath parings, so said Josiah Skint's trembling servant, only
some small glimpse of a yellow ribbon drawing her eye to't;
otherwide t'would have been carried off in the dustman's cart
next dawn. Josiah Skint had screeched in outrage that one of
Roderick Fairbrass's mummers had dared deposit it on his
property. "Why the man placed it there is of more interest, is't
not?" Mr. Franklin had inquired, yet Skint was so sunk in fury
he seemed not to hear. A feigned anger? A narrow alley ran

80

behind the houses on that side of Soho Square; here was where Skint's dustbin—indeed all dustbins—were kept. Was't, then, by this hidden way that the mumming Doctor had escaped unseen by Rupert Tree?

Mr. Franklin held up the Doctor's mask, which also had been found. "I am no friend to license, Nick," said he, gazing solemnly into its slitted eyeholes, "yet I am an enemy to excess, of whatever sort. Thank God the likes of Skint have lost their power. An hundred years ago the Puritans prohibited plays, carols, the keeping of Christmas itself, both here and in America. Such fear o' human nature is sad stuff; it pinches the spirit, it stifles the mind. I pity Josiah Skint."

"Yet may he have poisoned Mr. Fairbrass, sir?"

"How? Watchman Tree saw him out o' doors at the time the deed took place."

"May he have hired someone to do't?"

"He may, spite urging him on. Yet would not Skint's righteous professions forbid the sin of murder? Still, you may be right, for wickedness oft dresses itself in good."

"Did he himself thrust the costume in his dustbin?"

"Again, he may. Pah, how I dislike this proliferation of 'mays'—they breed like flies."

"If t'was put there by another, was't done to point the finger at Mr. Skint?"

"I do not think so. The servant said it had been thrust to the bottom; t'was not meant to be found. Yet you inquire, Nick, weighing all matters. Perhaps you outrun me? May you tell who murdered the man? Come, lad, say who did it."

Our mare's hooves clopped. "I cannot," confessed I, all bewilderment. I pictured avuncular, kind-faced Roderick Fairbrass bending to clasp his two young children; it was the last I had seen him alive. "He seemed so good!" said I.

Mr. Franklin plucked thoughtfully at his lip. "Aye, they say

81

so, one and all: a good man. Do you know the story of Job? Once home, we shall peruse it, for your edification, for it too asks why a good man should suffer." Yet this solemn question was replaced by a smile. "Damn me if we shall be whipped into gloom! I am pleased at the season. Twelve days have we of't; let us make what joy we can." And he burst into song, to the swaying of our coach:

All you that to feasting and mirth are inclined,
Come, here is good news for to pleasure your mind:
Old Christmas is come for to keep open house;
He scorns to be guilty of starving a mouse.
Then come, boys, and welcome for to diet the chief:
Plum pudding, goose, capon, minced pies and roast beef.

Mr. Benjamin Franklin's laughter mingled with the bustle of the Strand.

Yet there was no joy when, near two, we returned to Mrs. Stevenson's house, for Craven Street had been broke in upon, and our landlady was all adither.

"O, Mr. Franklin, I could not stop 'em, for 'tis the custom o' the season, and I dared not stand athwart it. Yet I did not know they would be so rude nor go on such a rampage. I am sorry, very sorry. Pray, forgive me, good sir."

We stood in the hall, just come in. "Calm yourself, dear lady," urged Mr. Franklin. "Rampage? What do you mean?"

Her white cap flapped as she spoke. "Why, the mummers, sir! And their Lord of Misrule." She tapped the mole by the side of her nose. "I ought to've known by his red hair they could be up to no good. Yet they were all smiles behind their masks when they burst in, and I knew that such were about, for I had seen many bands of 'em in the streets and heard no bad report. So they made a capering—no harm in that—and held out their hats, into which I put some small coin, thinking t'would satisfy 'em; but it did not, for they would have their mischief and ran over the house, from kitchen to attic, and tumbled things about. In your rooms 'specially, sir: your bedchamber and workroom, which are thrown much awry."

"How many men?"

"Three."

"Masked, you say?"

"Aye, with hands and necks rubbed with black, as mummers do, and visors on, and bells."

"This Lord of Misrule—he had red hair, you say?"

"Quite red."

"A wig?"

"Why . . . I do not know, for he had a fool's cap on as well."

"Did he speak?"

"There was some jabber, all nonsense. Yet I thought he spoke your name once, to one of his two men—though how that could be I do not know, for how should he know you lodged here? I did not like his laugh—t'was low and mean; it gave me chill! But there was no one to be called, for your good son, William, was at the Temple, and Peter gone with you, and King to the butcher with Polly. Indeed t'was just after she left that they knocked."

"As if they watched and waited for you to be alone?" The gentleman patted her hand. "You are not to blame, Mrs. Stevenson. Come, Nick. We shall see what damage has been done."

We mounted rapidly to a distressing disarray. In his chamber all was flung about, as Mrs. Stevenson had described: bedclothes atangle, drawers pulled and emptied, books scattered. In the workshop some glassware had been broke and

papers tossed to the floor. The dead rat still lay in its cage, yet
the cage had been moved on the bench. Mr. Franklin knelt
and looked under the bench, where he had strapped the two
swords. "They did not discover 'em," said he and looked too
in back of a cupboard, at a secret place where he sometimes
hid things. "Nor did they find what remains of the Opliss-
Popliss drops." He turned, lips compressed.

"Not truly mummers, sir?" asked I.

He was grim. "This had no mere mumming purpose."

"They have, then, to do with Mr. Fairbrass's murder?"

"What else? I do not think the Penns, even in their
arrogance, would pay such nice attentions." Windowlight
glinted from his spectacles as his fingers opened and closed at
his sides. "I hate this red hair for affrighting Mrs. Stevenson.
If I had any thoughts of letting the Fairbrass matter lie, as it
seems the widow heartily wishes I would, this has stifled 'em.
Yet we must learn caution."

Our landlady appeared in the door. "Please you, sir, I shall
set to straightening your bedchamber." Mr. Franklin thanked
her, and he and I began to set things aright in the workshop.
On the floor lay bits of stone which he collected, some with
animals long dead impressed in 'em, and charts on which he
kept record of winds and temperatures. A thermometer had
been broke. The glass tube, with which I had experimented
with the metal shavings but two days ago, also was shattered.
I glanced at Mr. Franklin's Philadelphia Machine. Would that
the intruders had meddled with its discharging point, whose
electrical spark would've knocked 'em to the floor. Yet it
seemed untouched, as if they knew to avoid it.

"What is a Lord of Misrule, Mr. Franklin?" asked I as I
gathered scattered papers.

"A custom of the season, Nick, with origins long lost. 'Tis
the time of turning things upside down: masters play servants,

84

servants masters, men dress as women and women as men. The overseer of such revels is the Lord of Misrule, who devises pranks that would not be countenanced at other times o' the year. He is customarily a masked fellow—you will have observed such a one leading bands of mummers about the London streets, though the custom is much abated and is more observed in the country, so I am told. When they knock on your door you are expected to let 'em in and suffer their outrages and give food or money."

"Why did Mrs. Stevenson say she should've been warned by the man's red hair?"

"Because Judas is reputed to've had red hair. A Lord of Misrule with red hair is said to bring ill luck."

I shivered. "And was't the same mummers broke in here as played St. George at Mr. Fairbrass's house?"

Mr. Franklin picked amongst shards of glass. "I ask myself the same. Damned if I shall not ask the mummers to their faces."

We were near an hour putting back that which had been tossed and jumbled. Afterward Mr. Franklin repaired to his desk to write some necessary letters, whilst I went down to help Mrs. Stevenson at chores. After peeling potatoes, I carried the bucket to the pump at the top of the street to fetch water, my hands and nose stinging in the cold. Upon my return it was left for me to inform Polly, just come in with her joint of beef, of the adventure at Craven Street. She made much wide-eyed exclamation— "O, tell all, Nick!"—and seemed so truly sorry to've missed the event that Mrs. Stevenson chid her for a foolish girl. Around four I went up to find Mr. Franklin still at his desk. He read a long letter to his wife, Deborah, telling of all he sent her and their daughter, Sally: "'. . . carpeting for the best room, a damask table

85

cover, gowns for you both, a pair of silk blankets just taken in a French prize ship such as were never seen in England before.'" He sent, too, a beer jug to stand in the cooler: "'I fell in love with it at first sight, for I thought it looked like a fat, jolly Dame, clean and tidy, with a neat blue and white calico gown on, good natured and lovely—and't put me in mind of . . . somebody.' What think you, Nick?"

"I think they shall be well pleased, sir," said I.

"Pleased. . . ." said he, gazing off. When he had told me of my mother, and how his affair with her had come to be, he had spoke too of his Deborah—or Goodwife Joan as he oft called her. Deborah Franklin was no match for his mind—he could not speak to her of ideas (as he had been able with my mother)—yet she was a steadfast, loyal wife, a true helpmeet. He was fond of her and indeed might have brought her with him to England if she had not feared sea voyaging.

I too fell into private thoughts. Should I ever meet Deborah Franklin? His daughter? Should I ever see America?

The gentleman shook himself from his revery. "Time," said he, drawing the small pewter snuffbox from his waistcoat pocket, "for some printing, lad."

I followed him to his workshop, where he shut the door and lit a lamp 'gainst the darkening day. From a cabinet drawer he drew out a miniature brayer, no more than two inches round, and placed it upon his workbench; likewise a large sheet of fine white paper, and a quill pen and bottle of ink. We sat together before this. "Now. . . ." He opened the snuff box to reveal inside the several thin, flattened disks of oyster-colored wax which I had observed him slyly place there after shaking each of several hands. His trick was this: to warm the wax secretly in his pocket and then to press a small ball of it against thumb or fingers of the person whose hand he took, producing an impression of tiny lines. So clever was he at doing this that the person never noticed. He now took the brayer and carefully inked the first circle of wax, then pressed this lightly against the upper left corner of the paper, thus fixing the pattern of lines upon the paper.

Beneath it he wrote: *Thumb, Cadwallader Bracegirdle.*

He proceded to do the same with each of several more bits of wax, which he had in order in the box, so he knew which belonged to whom—the thumbprints or forefingerprints of Joseph de Medina, Moses Trustwood, Jack Sparkum, Hannah Fairbrass, James Fairbrass, Cassandra Fairbrass, the servant Mary, Joisah Skint. There were a few last bits of wax, which he had done when Mr. Fairbrass visited us on Christmas morn. *Three fingers, Roderick Fairbrass*, wrote he beneath the print of this in his neat, clear hand. "Done, Nick." He leant back whilst I too gazed upon the rows of marks in the lamplight. He had told me how, when a young man laboring in his brother's shop in Boston, he had first observed the phenomenon, which he called fingerprints. The printers always had ink on their hands; they left marks everywhere. Being keen-sighted, "and of a mind to learn even from trivial observations," he had noted how the patterns of each man's fingers were unique to each. "Thus they may identify a man—or a woman."

"Well, well," grumbled he, "they are not perfect. T'would be best to ink each hand direct, all ten fingers, and press 'em on paper—but as I cannot do that (I should be thought mad) this must suffice." He removed the swords from under the table, with handles black as ebon. These he dusted with a white powder which I knew, from having seen him do a similar thing before, to be snuff. We looked close. "Suggestions of prints on 'em, Nick," observed he, "but naught conclusive, damn the luck." He brought forth the small vial of bluish Opliss-Popliss drops, which he had heretofore handled with great care, touching only the cork stopper and rounded bottom of the glass. Onto this he blew very fine coal dust and peered close. "Pah!" He turned to me. "May your young eyes help?"

I squinted but could make out only smudges. "I am sorry, sir, no."

"I hoped for too much." He held up the vial, frowning. "What poison is this, so quick acting? And how obtained?"

"And why given to Mr. Fairbrass? And by whom?"

"You ask aright."

"But why did you take the swords, sir?"

"Because of the cut which Roddy Fairbrass suffered. Might the tip of one sword have been poisoned? An odd thought, yet I take it from Shakespeare. I have been perusing his *Hamlet*, a play which you must read, as well as *Job*, for excellent wisdom (as well some fol-de-rol) abounds there; in it such a double assurance of death is planned. Was't so in this case?" He shook his head. "If so, what desperation to wish poor Fairbrass so surely dead! Leave that. Shall we to supper?" He winked. "Thank God we need fear no poison in Mrs. Stevenson's hearty fare."

After supper William Franklin hurried off to *George Barnwell* in Drury Lane. Polly curled on the back parlor sofa with another book which she had borrowed of Mr. Franklin, though Mrs. Stevenson clearly would much rather have seen her at her needle. "I do not read books, and I am a happy woman!" cried the landlady, yet I saw more than reproach in her eyes. I saw some hurt, that Polly reproved her by such study, as if her daughter said by't that to be as her mother did not suffice. Polly's eyes flashed pique at such treatment, as if she would like to retort that her mother's ignorance and superstition could not be for her; yet Polly bit her lip and held her peace

88

and buried her nose in her book, for which I was glad, for I loved Mrs. Stevenson and would not wish her hurt. Yet I loved Polly too and knew not on which side to stand.

In thorough confusion I went upstairs.

Mr. Franklin, who had observed some of this dispute, beckoned me to his room. "You see how 'tis between 'em, Nick, and is ever thus between parents and children, son or daughter not following the clear line which the parent has surveyed." He settled in his chair by the fire, whilst I sat on the edge of his bed. "So it seems in the Fairbrass family, the daughter skittish and mired in her belief in faeries and spirits, the son too at some odds with his father, sufficient to cause fights if their servant is to be believed. Yet there is more. The cheerful husband falls into gloom—I myself saw it, as did the maid, Mary—yet his wife denies it was so. What put Roddy Fairbrass down? Why does Hannah Fairbrass deny he was unhappy? Why is she so set against the belief he was poisoned? Is't only the wish to avoid more pain for herself and her children?" He thumped his chair. "I cannot believe it. Would you not wish the murderer of a loved one discovered? Surely Hannah Fairbrass hides something. What and why? I must go careful with her, Nick. Her brother-in-law, Lemuel, would do anything for her husband, said she, yet she did not assert that her husband would do likewise. Was the husband then not devoted to his brother? And Cadwallader Bracegirdle, what shall we make of him? O, the foppish fool!—he that falls in love with himself shall have no rivals. Yet he was remarkably took back to see Fairbrass die—or seemed so. Cato Prince, too, a mystery. He arrives from the Indies, a gift of Lemuel Fairbrass, and six weeks later Roderick Fairbrass is dead. Does this signify? I wish to learn more of the Fairbrass brother."

"Did Mr. Fairbrass truly mean to remove to America?"

"There is dispute about that."

"And the ghost, sir."

He nodded. "Ever the ghost. Assuming 'twas not a creature of Miss Fairbrass's imagining (and I believe 'twas not), what was't? Did it search for something? And then there is this." From the small round table beside his chair, which customarily held his *London Chronicle*, he plucked the sprig of rosemary which he had taken from the dead man's chest. He twirled it in his fingers. "Has it some meaning? Who might've dropped it? The mumming Doctor? The son, James, also stood near, as did Caddy Bracegirdle. For that matter, so did the Portuguese Jew and the banker, Moses Trustwood. 'For remembrace. . . .'" He gazed long at the sprig before his eye rose to meet mine. "Such a *public* death, Nick, for all to see. And for Fothergill to affirm. . . ."

He seemed to suggest something by this, though I knew not what. "And the wetness upon Mr. Fairbrass's collar."

"Indeed. Might't have been . . . ? Yet why . . . ?" But he said no more on this, sinking into a torpid rumination, to which I left him, crossing the hall to my little room, that night dreaming on a red-haired, masked Lord of Misrule who turned all upside down at Craven Street.

My awakening cry in inky dark seemed feeble defense 'gainst such capricious invasion.

✤ 7 ✤

IN WHICH we seek truth of a talking cat, a dead man's daughter, and an empty room. . . .

T
he sleeping fox catches no hen. Up, Nick!" called Mr. Franklin at my door before seven next morn. "We have much to see and hear and discover." We were by half past eight climbing into the gentleman's coach at the stoop of Number 7, Craven Street, a feeble sun shedding light on snowy cobbles and rooftops. Mr. Franklin had said we must take as much joy as we could in the Twelve Days of Christmas. 'Twas now the second day. I found it hard to summon joy, yet a species of't glimmered in the gentleman's bright gaze. The mystery of Mr. Fairbrass's murder was to him as the mysteries of Nature, which must be probed 'til they gave up their secrets, and I sensed a bloodhound's eagerness about him as he commanded Peter to drive to Westminster Bridge. Round beaver hat pulled snugly to his ears, he sniffed the air as if to catch scent. His eyes crinkled, and he sank back with a great sigh of satisfaction as we set out.

"Where do we go, sir?" asked I.

"Why, to the mummers, Nick, where else? To enquire of murder."

"I, too, should like to hear what they tell."

The iron rims of our wheels clattered as we moved under shop signs in the Strand: hosiers, confectioners, apothecaries. We passed Mr. Porberry, the toymaker. Though shoppers were yet few, birds of the season, turkeys and geese, swung for sale in icy gusts.

An idea stirred my brain. "I have bethought me, sir—may there be some great mistake? Perhaps 'twas not Mr. Fairbrass who was meant to be poisoned, but the player who customarily did St. George?"

"St. George was masked, so the murderer knew not the difference, eh?"

"That was my thought."

"Clever lad! I too have wondered the same. The wrong person killed . . . *Hamlet* is suggestive in this, as in other regards, for the like occurs at Elsinore, to the dismay of a canting old fool named Polonius (with, yet, some wisdom in him) and a weak-willed queen." Mr. Franklin pulled thoughtfully at his lip. "There is a ghost in *Hamlet* too, full of dire news. And players. However, London is not Denmark—though there is much rotten in both. We shall soon meet our players. Let us greet 'em as befits: we must not saw the air nor act the town crier; we shall speak trippingly," he nudged my ribs, "—but subtly, Nick, mark you, with great craft."

I nodded and took to watching the city pass by our windows. Our journey carried us south, along Whitehall and Parliament Street. Mr. Franklin scowled as we passed these seats of government. "I come to know this part o' the city too well," muttered he, "—its antechambers, where I cool my heels awaiting some officious fool to say me nay, yet I am the beetle who burrows in the oak; the oak must fall." We turned onto Westminster Bridge, thirteen arches of white Portland stone under which the Thames, broad and bleak, flowed sluggishly, with more ice than I had seen, great bobbing chunks. "London's second bridge," told Mr. Franklin, "completed but seven years ago so people in the west need not travel back to London Bridge to cross to Kent and Surrey." I looked down. Already watermen steered their wherries to and fro, and barges plied, with footstuffs and timber. Gazing to north and east where the Thames bent, I was almost able to spy Craven Street. The city shouldered the river, and I had a sudden vision of wood, stone, brick, hovels and spires, broad streets and bent, twisted ways crawling out of the Thames as if it spawned 'em. The city's size, its noise, its maggot seething thrilled me. "Aye, Nick," said Mr. Franklin as if he read my mind, "the largest city of Europe, half a million souls, the center of trade. What glory!—what corruption. I care little for Cadwallader Bracegirdle, yet I concur with him in this: a man might spend a lifetime quizzing London."

Yet ten minutes effected great change, for by the time we reached the crossing of the New Road with Lambeth Road south of the river the city had vanished. Black, leafless trees and frost-rimed grass inhabited here, all the restless sound of close-packed souls vanished, with St. George's Fields as still as death nearby. An inn stood at the crossroads, the Queen's Rest, its half-timbered galleries rising above us on three sides as Peter drove our conveyance through its gate. Passenger coaches from the south coast stood in a spacious yard; too: a post chaise, a gig, three or four carrier's carts, and a wagon groaning under a load of potatoes. As it was near ten, the stagecoaches prepared to take travelers on. Ostlers loaded baggage. Men stomped their boots and blew on their fingers to warm 'em. A horse whinnied as the lash of a whip drove it and its fellows out upon the frozen turf.

I followed Mr. Franklin into a large, low ceiling room where a smoky fire fought the chill. "May you be the landlord?" inquired he of a red-nosed fellow directing the removal of mounds of baggage.

"I am, and welcome. You and the boy seek rooms?"

"Not at this time o' day. You lodge some players, do you not? Mummers?"

"I do. You shall find 'em there." the man ordered a sniffing, sullen boy to take us to a large back room of the inn, where we came upon some half dozen men in motley dress. Four leant back in chairs and watched whilst two enacted a scene in which one strove to play a boy named Dick and the other a cat. The seated four scowled and cried *Nay* and niggled—"Do it this way, Walter! That's never a cat, Ned."— and made bawdy suggestions, at which the two players gave redoubled effort, the cat player licking his hands as if they were paws and cleaning himself as many a cat, meowing and slinking about. I thought him excellent; his antics made me laugh—yet I felt my cheeks burn red when he pounced near with arched black brows over a squinting stare. "Oho!" cried he, brushing imaginary whiskers and creeping three times round me, flicking a ragged bit of fur tucked at his backside. He was stout yet agile, with bristles of hair sprouting from a round, thick skull. "You like it, boy? You laugh?" He drew himself up proudly before his fellows. "See you, I play Pussy well—though I curse the season which calls upon me to do't; I was born for greater roles."

"You play other parts, do you?" asked Mr. Franklin in his quiet way.

The stout man's glittering eyes fixed upon the gentleman. "You seek players, sir?" He made a flourishing bow. "We can enact whatever you will."

"Comical?"

"Or tragical."

"Tragical-comical?"

94

The man's eyes shone even brighter. "Pastoral-comical, historical-pastoral, tragical-historical, tragical-comical-historical-pastoral, scene individable, or poem unlimited. *Hamlet*, is't? Should you like *Hamlet*?" He rubbed his palms. "We serve up a rousing *Hamlet*."

"I fear me, no, I have had a deal too much of *Hamlet*. I am Benjamin Franklin."

The player wrung his hand. "Ned Ivy, at your service."

"Do you do *St. George*?"

"We do." Yet he appeared disappointed that no grander effort was required.

"And have men to play all parts?"

"You shall need a Father Christmas, a hobby horse, a King, an Infidel, St. George himself, and a Doctor. Six, and we are six."

"Pray, who should play the Doctor?"

"Why, Walter Brownjohn." Urging forth the young fellow who had enacted Dick, Ned Ivy winked. "An excellent physician for your pox or scurvy."

Mr. Franklin peered mildly over the tops of his spectacles. "All which he cures with his Opliss-Popliss drops?"

"And cures well, too. Settled, is't? Where and when shall we hold forth—providing, that is, that other engagements do not prevent."

"Yet I believed your St. George was ill."

"Ill? Never!" Ivy drew a tall man from his chair. "Can you not see our Jim Bones' hearty nature?" He thumped the man's chest. "How should he be ill?"

"Roderick Fairbrass told me that he was."

There was a sudden silence, in which the three seated players scraped up from their chairs. "What's this about Roderick Fairbrass?" muttered Ned Ivy. "The poor man is dead. How could he speak such a thing?"

"Indeed you were present at his death," said Mr. Franklin. "You played the King of England. He told me the day before he died that your St. George was ill; that is why he himself must play the part."

"Why . . . then he lied—or you do. He *asked* to play the part, for he loved to act, he said. T'would give family and friends much amusement to see him do't, he said."

"T'was his idea?"

"Do I not say so?"

"His, only?"

"Never mine." Ivy gestured round. "Never ours."

The six players watched as still as stone as Mr. Franklin drew from under his coat the Doctor's beribboned costume and unfurled it before 'em. "How came this in the dustbin of the house next Fairbrass's in Soho Square?"

"My costume!" exclaimed Walter Brownjohn.

Ned Ivy peered sharply. "Here, now, why are you truly here?"

"To discover truth, which you shall deliver, if you have nothing to fear. Come, I ask, how came this to be tossed where it was?"

Ivy glanced at his confederates, who moved round us in a threatening circle. Mr. Franklin seemed to pay little heed, yet I saw that with his right hand he gripped his bamboo hard. I had seen him lay about with this sturdy stick, and knew that, though he was past fifty and would rather reason than butt heads, he was no man to be trifled with. Indeed he himself had taught me just where to strike a man, to take his wind, and I prepared, small as I was, to do my best if trouble brewed.

Yet there were six against two, and one of the two a boy.

Ned Ivy muttered, stomped, cursed. At last he turned to

96

Walter Brownjohn. "Tell all, Walter," grumbled he. "We have naught to hide."

Brownjohn faced Mr. Franklin squarely. "'Tis just as Ned here says: Fairbrass himself asked to play St. George. And then, the night o' the play, as we are dressing, comes a *hsst* at my ear, and an arm beckons me to a side room, some antechamber, small and dark. The arm belongs to a man, and the man is wearing a mask, though I pays little heed, as masks are common at revels. 'Here, now, I wish to play the Doctor,' says he. It cannot be, says I. 'O, may this not ease the way?' says he, twisting a guinea—a guinea, I say!—back and forth beneath my nose. Yet I mistrusted. Who are you? asks I. 'A great friend o' Roderick Fairbrass,' says he. 'Roddy loves a good joke, and I shall play one on him tonight.' All the while he keeps atwistin' the coin, like a fly for a fish. 'Come, sir, no harm, and a guinea to ease the way?' Might I refuse so harmless-seeming a request? So I gives up my costume, which he puts on. But do you know the part? asks I. He does not answer. 'I know all I must do,' says he in a sort of shiv'ring sigh that makes me misgive—but by this time the hobby horse is neighing 'midst the assembly, and shortly the stranger goes to play his part. The rest you know, as much as I or any man."

"Not as much as any man," murmured Mr. Franklin. "You gave him the Opliss-Popliss drops as well?"

"Aye."

"Who mixed 'em?"

"I did, as always—though there is little enough to't, for they are but cochineal in water."

Mr. Franklin drew himself up. "You, then, poisoned Roderick Fairbrass."

Brownjohn blanched. "Poisoned? Why, I never . . . ! *I? Poison?*"

97

"And you," Mr. Franklin rounded on Ned Ivy. "Were in confederation with Walter Brownjohn."

Ivy snorted. "Madness! Poisoned Opliss-Popliss drops? The drops never killed before. Fairbrass just died." Yet there was some faltering in his voice.

Mr. Franklin shook his head. "The drops not poisoned? You cannot believe so. Let us suppose Walter Brownjohn tells true; you must nonetheless have noted that the man who bribed your confederate slipped out in the first confusion, the only man to do so. When all departed and you rejoined your fellow players outside, you discovered that 'twas not your man who played the Doctor but some stranger who paid for the privilege. Did that not rouse suspicion? Too, this stranger was thoroughly masked; clearly he did not wish to be known. If you are as innocent as you assert, you must have had doubts. Why, then, have you not spoke to some constable or magistrate?"

The six men's eyes darted. "We do not seek trouble," growled Ned Ivy.

"Yet it finds you. Or do you cause it?"

"I tell you, 'twas as I said!" exclaimed Walter Brownjohn, trembling.

Mr. Franklin was silent a moment, with a closed look behind his small squarish spectacles, as if he shut up his mind in a chamber. "May be," said he. "And if you have naught to hide you will speak more truth. This stranger—you saw nothing of his face?"

"Not a whisker."

"Nor the color of his skin?"

"The room had little light, I say."

"His hair . . . red?"

"I do not know."

"His figure?"

"Tallish, as mine."

"So he might be mistook for you with ease. You practiced the play with Mr. Fairbrass?"

"We did," replied Ned Ivy.

"Where?"

"At his house."

"How oft?"

"Twice."

"Who else was present?"

"Some servants, who looked on awhile. The wife and son and daughter watched sometime too. And the small children. No one viewed our rehearsals entire; they came and went. You must trust our answers, sir."

"I shall trust no one 'til the murderer of Roderick Fairbrass awaits trial in Fleet Prison. Was one of these servants a young blackamoor?"

"There was such a fellow present, yes."

"And did you connive your way into my lodgings yesterday, and frighten my landlady and fling my things about?"

A chorus of *Nos!* greeted this query, the guard's horn and muffled clatter of yet another departing coach echoing after. Mr. Franklin looked down, up. "And what of . . . *Quimp*," asked he, very soft yet with a peculiar distinction, so that the last word came like a small discharge of powder—yet there was little result amongst the six players.

"Quimp? A person? Place?" inquired Ned Ivy in what seemed genuine bewilderment.

Mr. Franklin gave no sign that his shot had misfired. "A person," replied he grimly, "—and yet a thing too, of uncertain shape yet much peril." I was surprised at this mention of Quimp—and not surprised, for Quimp was such a creature to bedevil. I thought of the huge, circling shadows of Knight and Turk on the walls of Roderick Fairbrass's house

99

two nights ago. I peered at Mr. Franklin, who took a turn about the room, all eyes upon him as if he were the very engine of justice.

Halting before Walter Brownjohn, he thrust the Doctor's costume in his hands. "See that no one buys the use of this again. You stood not far from the men who played that final scene," said he to Ned Ivy. "Did one of 'em speak?"

"The Doctor . . . yet there are no lines as he leans over St. George."

"Which ought further to have fed your suspicions. What said he?"

"I could not hear."

"Surely—?"

A firm shake of head. "I could make out nothing, I say."

"One last question: there was some dampness on Roderick Fairbrass's costume, about the neck. Did you see how that came to be?"

"I did not. Spilt Opliss-Popliss drops?"

"There was too much of wetness for that. Now, sirs—" drawing himself up, Mr. Franklin fixed each player with such a stern stare that I was amazed at how the gentleman, customarily so self-effacing (reminding me of no animal so much as a soft, brown mole, content to be left to its ways), could assume such commanding aspect, "I hope you do not lie. It bodes ill for you if you do. If any new thoughts come—or if anyone else inquires as I have done—seek me out at once, at Number 7, Craven Street, the Strand. Come, Nick."

Following him out, I glanced over my shoulder, the players seeming caught in a net of discomfitted stares, one to another. Guilt trapped there? A struggling secret?

Ned Ivy flicked his ragged cat's tail.

In the inn yard the usual sly-eyed watchers of every such

100

waystation hung about: thieves or lookouts for thieves, eager to cheat unwary gentlemen of their coin or baggage, women of their virtue. The Queen's Rest felt an unsafe place, evil, and I was glad when we were once more a mile away, upon Westminster Bridge.

Mr. Franklin sat silent for many moments. "Quimp, sir?" ventured I tentatively, above the sweep of icy water.

He stirred. "It may not be . . . no certain evidence . . . I merely conjecture. And yet we well know Quimp's penchant for disguise and tricks." He drummed his fingers. "Strange, a play within a play: those two men, Roddy Fairbrass and his unknown assassin, acting out a ritual of death. The Doctor's rapid fleeing shows he well knew he had murdered. Damn me, who may he be?" He cocked a brow. "Did you believe the mummers' tale?"

"They seemed to speak true."

"If they did, Roderick Fairbrass lied. Why?" He sighed. "Well, I too am inclined to credit them—though we must remember that they are dissemblers by trade, and there is much dissembling in this." He thumped the roof. "Soho Square, Peter," called he. "To winnow lies from truth."

"Shall you speak to Mrs. Fairbrass again, Mr. Franklin?" asked I three-quarters of an hour later, as Peter turned into Soho Square beneath a soiled-looking sun.

"I wish first to pay my respects to poor Roddy," replied the gentleman as he stepped from the coach. He had instructed me to wear black coat and breeches; he too wore black, and the wide fanlight door of Fairbrasses' house greeted us dressed in the same funereal shade. The maid of yesterday admitted us. Removing his beaver hat (I too removed my cap), Mr. Franklin added his card to those upon the salver in the entrance hall, thumbing quickly through other cards as he

101

did so. "The Jew has been here, I see, and the banker, Moses Trustwood. . . ." From thence we proceeded to the large assembly room, so ripe with cheer two days ago, before death struck its blow. All traces of that night's festivities were gone, the room too hung with black, curtains shut, candles flickering in sconces. A coffin sat upon a trestle in the center, but one other person present, a man, who bent strangely close over the bier. I could not see his features, yet his scrutiny appeared unseemly: he stared into the dead man's face. Mr. Franklin's hand halted me. The man was clearly unaware of us, and snorted and muttered and bent yet nearer, as if the corpse might whisper secrets in his ear.

He straightened.

"Dead! Damned dead!" came his exclamation.

He turned, and we saw the pocked, ugly face of Cadwallader Bracegirdle.

He started, yet, before his features had time to alter, their expression was strangely mixed: pleased or angry to assure himself once more that death had done its work? I could not say.

At sight of us his look slid to hypocritical gloom. He strode forward. "Mr. Franklin, I see." He gave the gentleman's hand a single sepulchral squeeze. "What a blow to poor James to lose his father. A blow to the family. A blow to the world. I shall leave you to pay your respects." Dour mask in place, he slunk out.

Mr. Franklin glanced askance. "Did I not say there was much dissembling in this?" pronounced he.

We stepped to the coffin.

Mr. Franklin stood long, gazing at the dead man, thinking his thoughts. I did not like to look; I had several times set eyes upon death, the first my mother's, the second when I discovered my dear, kind printing master, Ebenezer Inch, stretched upon the frost-rimed grass in the yard of Inch, Printer, Fish Lane, Moorfields. Forcing myself to examine Roderick Fairbrass's rigid, waxen lineaments, I was flooded with sadness and horror. How death diminished a man! He appeared not like one struck down in his prime but as if wasted by terrible disease, his flesh already sunk into his bones.

"Could he but speak. . . ." murmured Mr. Franklin, shaking his head.

As we exited the room we passed other visitors, come to pay their respects: merchants and their wives, faces familiar from the revels, all hangdog, somber, and ashen. As she had yesterday, Mrs. Fairbrass sat in the small side parlor off the entrance hall. We glimpsed her like a creature of darkness in her dim room, receiving friends, a soft litany of condolences and the sniffling of noses making their music of regret.

Mr. Franklin crept quickly past this door to seek out the maid. "Tell Miss Fairbrass that Mr. Franklin is come and wishes to speak to her."

"O, sir, she has shut herself away. I do not think—"

"Deliver my name," said he.

Five minutes later Cassandra Fairbrass descended the stairs. She was pinched and drawn, all pale in her long black gown, clutching a book to her breast. As ever she wore the rude, cross-shaped stone with its pattern of white, incised lines. Her deep-set eyes were glazed with despair as she plucked at Mr. Franklin's arm. "I should have heeded the ghost, should I not, sir?" queried she hoarsely. "I should have took better care of my father?"

He patted her hand. "Tut, child, you did all you might." He glanced round. "May we speak apart?"

In some hesitancy, looking so frail she might faint, she led

103

us to a room beside the assembly room, small, with some two or three chairs, and closed the door.

Mr. Franklin examined this room. "Was't here the mummers changed into their costumes?" asked he.

"I believe so."

He glanced into an alcove. "And here the stranger accosted Walter Brownjohn."

"Stranger?" Miss Fairbrass hugged her book.

Helping her to a chair, Mr. Franklin sat opposite. "I must tell you sorry news. Gird yourself, child." He took deep breath. "I believe your father may've been murdered."

I stood at Mr. Franklin's back. Miss Fairbrass's book fell into her lap so that I could see its title: *Signs and Other Wards against Evil*. "Murdered?" echoed she in a voice little more than a whisper.

"I fear so." Mr. Franklin told of the Opliss-Popliss drops and our morning encounter with the mummers.

For a long moment the young woman's lips seemed incapable of speech. "But who should wish to do such a thing?" wailed she pitifully at last.

"That is what I wish to discover. May you answer some questions? Did anyone bear your father a grudge?"

"No one could."

"Was he a danger to any man?"

"Danger?"

"Did he know aught that might ruin someone, I mean."

Miss Fairbrass drew herself up, and for a moment I saw her mother's spirit in her. "I do not know. But I know this: if he had such knowledge Papa would never use it. He was too good; he would not harm another."

Mr. Franklin did not reply for a moment. "Yet many men would willfully harm others, for the wicked pleasure t'would

104

give 'em. But forgive me; your father was not such a man. No revisitation of your ghost these few nights past?"

She shuddered. "Not since the time two weeks ago, of which I told you."

"Pray, did your father have some mistrust of doctors?"

"Why . . . no."

"But he had palpitations of the heart?"

"Palpitations? Not to my knowledge. Why do you believe that he did?"

"Your mother spoke of such a thing. It may've been that which so fretted him. Indeed it may be that alone which killed him—it is what she holds."

The daughter's eyes grew large. "But the poison in the drops? And the ghost?"

The gentleman nodded. "As you say: the poison, the ghost. Your uncle, Lemuel—your mother told of some dissipation when he was young. What might that have been?"

"Gaming, I believe. But that was long ago; he has conquered the weakness—so I understand. Why do you speak of my uncle? He is far away."

"Merely to know your family the better. Are you fond of your uncle?"

"I have never met him."

"Never?"

"—that is, met him to remember him. He left for the Indies—for Jamiaca—when James and I were young (I was less than four), and has not been back since."

"I see. Much needed there, your mother said."

"A great aid in Papa's business."

"His diligence, then, matched your father's goodness. Did you father keep a diary?"

"Yes, of a sort. He was in the habit of jotting the day's events in a leather-bound book. I picture him now in the parlor, doing so." She pressed knuckles to her mouth. "Dear Papa! Why do you inquire?"

"To trace the spoor of his murderer. Perhaps some clue—"

"Surely you would not read his private thoughts!"

"Yet where is this book?"

"In his strongbox, I believe."

"Where did he keep this strongbox?"

"In his bedchamber."

"Has the box been opened since his demise?"

"I do not know."

"Miss Fairbrass, this diary may reveal who should wish to murder him—but 'tis, as you say, private," added Mr. Franklin quickly. "We must then not depend upon't. Yet if all else proves fruitless. . . ." He let this suggestion hang.

Miss Fairbrass bent forward. "Mr. Franklin, you *will* discover who murdered dear Papa?"

"I shall try. A grave injustice has been done. The balance must be righted." He rose, as did she with his hand on her elbow to support her. "I am told that Captain Jack Sparkum sees to your family."

For the first time color came into the young woman's cheeks. "Kind Captain Sparkum! Mama depends upon him. The provisioning of his ship has drawn him back to Deptford, but he assures us we may call upon him for any need."

"He sails soon?"

"I believe so." Miss Fairbrass trembled, as if the interview had exhausted her. "I should like to return to my room, now, if I may."

"Do not imprison yourself there. You are to blame for nothing that has occured."

The young woman bowed her head.

"By the bye," said Mr. Franklin at the door, "you said that in the time of seeing the ghost your father gave you a sleeping draught, which you did not drink. Have you this liquor still?"

"In a little stoppered bottle."

"Will you give it me?"

She blinked. "I will, but—"

"By way of trust, so I may know all. Pray, where did your father obtain this draught?"

"Surely of some apothecary?"

"No doubt. Shall I go up, to receive it?"

"If you will."

The gentleman smiled thinly. "Accompany us, Nick."

We mounted the wide stairs, which led to a long corridor. This, as Miss Fairbrass had told Mr. Franklin on her visit to Craven Street, traversed the house, from front to rear. Her chamber proved halfway along. At her door I peered back in the direction of Soho Square, where a narrow window opened out. I shivered. She had stood where I stood now, seeing in dark night, silhouetted by the lamplight from the square, her ghost glide along the hall, turn, descend. Horrible! Truly a spirit? Mr. Franklin would chide me for asking, yet I could not suppress doubts—might not dead souls make themselves visible, to frighten, revenge, warn?

The pale young woman stepped into her chamber. We remained outside, yet I could see all within: a plain room containing little more than a high, four-posted bed spread with a white counterpane, a dressing table, a chair, with little of warmth or comfort in any corner. A dozen or so books sat upon a little shelf; I could read some titles, all of the superstitious sort which she had carried down.

She brought the sleeping draught from a drawer beside her bed. Mr. Franklin tucked it in a waistcoat pocket. "Your parents' bedchamber lies opposite?" inquired he.

"It does."

"And your elder brother's room?"

"Just next it, at the back of the house."

"May I view the top floor?"

The maid, Mary, had come upstairs. "Show Mr. Franklin the top floor," commanded Miss Fairbrass. Her trembling hand brushed her brow. "Forgive me, Mr. Franklin, for I must lie down."

"Rest, child. You have suffered much."

Cassandra Fairbrass shut her door.

The maid led us to the stairs we had ascended, from which more stairs arose, and we mounted to a corridor very like the one we left below, with its own window overlooking the square. A door was open some twenty paces along, from which issued a happy din. Coming to it, we discovered the two younger Fairbrass children, Emily and Tim, at play amongst toys. Emily served biscuits to a large doll, more than half her size, with great green buttons upon its dress and staring glass eyes and a pink, painted smile, whilst Tim set out on a baize cloth field some dozen lead soldiers, cannon, and cunningly fashioned horses, which he moved about intently in a great, noisy battle.

"Children, children!" came a stern voice. A thin, high-colored woman stood suddenly beside us with folded arms. "How unseemly, your father just dead! Play quietly, Tim," adjured she. "Emily, you must restrain yourself." At this the children's faces blanched—yet they looked bewildered too, to be told that joy was forbidden at this time. Though I was little older than they, I felt sadly wiser, moved to anguish by their white, upturned faces. What could they, seven and five, know of death? In their minds their father lived still and would rise from his bier in a day or so, when his strange, still sleep was done, to cuddle 'em as before and tell over his dreams. I knew

108

this, for I had believed the same of my own dear mother; it would take time for this thing called death to show its true, stony visage, as a creature to steal forever what we loved.

"This is Miss Box, the governess, sir," said Mary. "Mr. Benjamin Franklin."

The gentleman made a small bow, to which the thin woman nodded, her gray eyes measuring, asking why he should be here though her tongue did not voice the question. Within the room Emily murmured softly to her doll, and Tim now obediently moved his chargers as if timidness might win battles. The boy glanced at us, and I saw again his fey look, as if he, like his elder sister, communed with spirits. Miss Box stepped into the room to touch Tim's hair, and I saw that she limped. "Poor little ones," clucked she, "to be bereaved so young."

"A terrible thing," concurred Mr. Franklin. "May I see their sleeping chambers?"

The governess looked unsure why he asked but showed them readily, two rooms opposite, one Emily's, one Tim's.

The gentleman peered in but displayed little interest. "There is another door," said he. "What chamber is that?"

The governess glanced at this door, some way along the corridor at the rear of the house. "One little used," replied she, "containing odds and ends of the family."

"Locked?"

"Customarily."

"I see." Yet when Mr. Franklin went to it and tried the latch it turned.

"Why . . . open," murmured Miss Box in some surprise.

Mr. Franklin entered. We all followed, the governess and Mary with curious looks, as if they were never admitted here. Yet to my judgment there was little to be seen—a large space, chill, with a slope of rafters at one end and a musty smell, as

109

of candlewax and dust and old tobacco. There were some tables stacked and mismatched chairs and a cupboard and sofa and a dozen paintings leaning in a corner amongst other oddments. Mary brought a lamp at Mr. Franklin's request, and with it he poked here and there, making small hums to himself, whilst the maid and Miss Box exchanged glances.

Coming to us, the gentleman held up the lamp, smiling. "And have you seen a ghost in this house, ma'am?" asked he of Miss Box.

"I do not believe in ghosts," replied she curtly.

He pulled at his lip. "You are then of my mind—though they sometime disregard what we believe to show themselves nonetheless." He turned to Mary. "I wish to speak to Mr. James Fairbrass."

The black-browed maid curtsied. "I shall tell him you are come."

8

*IN WHICH a son is subject to scrutiny,
we are followed to Craven Street, and
Mr. Franklin plays cards. . . .*

As we descended past the second floor landing, Mr. Franklin paused to hold up a hand, appearing to test the air. His eyes flicked to mine. *See you, Nick?* their gray-brown depths seemed to inquire, though I could not surmise what he might mean. Nodding, as if he had proved some theory, he continued down, I at his heels.

Mourners still shuffled in to pay respects to Mrs. Fairbrass, with the huddled, straitened air of people gathering round a death. Shortly James Fairbrass met us in the small room where Mr. Franklin had spoke to his sister. He entered with a soft step and searching eyes, and his resemblance to his father—long nose and jaw, and wide mouth—momentarily took me aback, as if by some miracle the dead man had come alive as he was at twenty.

The young man too was dressed in black and peered with a kind of helpless blankness at Mr. Franklin. "Why . . . thank you, sir, for your thought in coming," murmured he, wringing the gentleman's hand.

"Do not mistake me," said Mr. Franklin. "Though I am come to offer condolences (I am heartily sorry at your father's

111

passing), I wish to have words for other reasons. I should be glad to give over 'til some better time, yet they must be talked on now. Shall we sit?" They did so, I standing near Mr. Franklin's side. As he had twice before, gently, yet leaving out no detail, he told of the poisoned Opliss-Popliss drops.

James Fairbrass blinked and stared, his blue eyes struggling to comprehend. When Mr. Franklin was through there was a silence, broken only by a whisper of sobs from beyond the closed door. The son's Adam's apple bobbed. "B-but . . . what may it mean?" stammered he.

"That your father was murdered," said Mr. Franklin.

The son's mouth worked. "Murdered? But . . . no." He clutched his breast. Though his mother had shown fortitude—his sister too, in her courage in facing a ghost—James Fairbrass looked weak as water, as if the news might prostrate him.

"Steel yourself, young sir," said Mr. Franklin firmly. "I am sorry to trouble you with this, but you must see that quick inquiry must be made. I have told your mother and sister that I shall do what I may. Will you answer my questions?"

James Fairbrass gave a stunned nod.

"Do you know of any enemies of your father?"

The young man's eyes seemed to seek escape. "N-no."

"Can you conceive any reason he might be poisoned?"

"None." Uneasily he twisted his hands.

"Your father was downcast of late, was he not?"

The son clearly did not like these questions. "I cannot say," muttered he.

"Come," urged Mr. Franklin. "I myself marked the change in him. What fretted his mind?"

James Fairbrass remained grudging: "I do not know."

"What, then, of your father's mistrust of doctors?"

112

The young man looked up sharply. "He had no such mistrust."

"But what of his weak heart?"

"Weak? Father's heart was as strong as any man's."

"He did not complain of palpitations?"

"Never."

Mr. Franklin tapped his fingers on his chair. "Your mother does not wish to believe your father was poisoned. As to your sister—" He related Cassandra Fairbrass's tale of the ghost. "In short, she believes this spirit plays a part in your father's death."

Contempt twisted her brother's mouth. "You cannot believe her tale. She is a foolish, superstitious girl. This is some dream or fancy."

"You do not believe in spirits?"

"I do not."

"And you neither saw nor heard anything during the nights she names?"

"I sleep deeply. I am not troubled by ghosts."

"And are troubled now by nothing more than your father's death?"

James Fairbrass swallowed hard and writhed upon his chair as if he longed to bolt and flee.

Mr. Franklin leant forward. "Should you not wish to unburden yourself?" urged he gently.

"Of what?" Hot eyes flashed. "Of what, I say?"

"Only you may answer." Mr. Franklin sat back. "But let be. Someone must now assume your father's business. Shall it be you?"

A bitter laugh. "I? I should not know what to do."

"Yet you might try. Necessity is a great teacher, and—"

The young man flared: "I have tried, I tell you! I have failed! Father told me so, and it was true. I cannot do't.

113

Mother may. And Captain Sparkum says he will guide matters for a time, but—"

"Yet you, as the son—?"

"The son! Am I a good son? Dutiful? I have caused my father much disappointment. I cannot follow in his steps."

Mr. Franklin pulled at his lip. "Perhaps your uncle may return from Kingston. He may help, may he not? He went there when you were young?"

"When I was but five."

"Do you recollect him?"

"Little."

"The servingman he sent you, Cato Prince—a good man?"

"Excellent."

"Was he—is he—a slave?"

"We keep no slaves, here or in the Indies. Father would not have it."

"You asserted that your father was determined on removing to America, yet your mother denies the fact."

"Why, then, mother does not remember aright."

"Why should your father contemplate such a change?"

James Fairbrass continued to grind his hands together, as if by doing so he milled truth to dust between 'em. "I do not know," replied he sullenly.

"When did he first speak of it?"

"June, I believe. Midyear."

"Six months ago, then. And did you love your father, Mr. Fairbrass?"

The young man started. "How can you ask! I loved him as . . . I loved him more than. . . ." Burying his face in his hands, he sobbed.

My hands squeezed to fists. I was surprised at Mr. Franklin's question. Truly wonted? It seemed cruel. Did the gentleman suspect James Fairbrass of want of feeling?

He observed the son's heaving shoulders with apparent sympathy. "Forgive my unseemliness in asking," said he when these sobs began to die. "I am sorry. And forgive me for this as well: in what way did your father feel disappointed in you?"

James Fairbrass lifted his wet face. "I have told you: I showed no skill at business."

"He was not also disappointed in your friends? Caddy Bracegirdle, for one?"

At this the young man grew even paler than grief had made him. "He complained of Caddy, yes."

"Why?"

The voice was near inaudible: "Gaming."

"You learnt to game?"

"Some."

"Which Bracegirdle led you to?"

"He introduced me to a house, yes."

"Which?"

"The Hazard."

"Hazard?"

"A gentleman's club. Near Pall Mall."

"You diced?"

"I did."

"And played at cards?"

"To my regret."

"But did not win?"

James Fairbrass looked sunk in misery.

"Tut, you are not the first to learn that Fortune lures men to cards only to trap 'em. Caddy Bracegirdle played too?"

"Much."

"And fared well?"

"At times."

"Yet also lost?"

"Fortune deserted him too."

"Often?"

"I have seen him go down an hundred pounds at the turn of a card." Young Fairbrass seemed almost to plead: "But he is a cheerful fellow! He laughed at such losses!"

"O, prodigious," murmured Mr. Franklin, "—a man who can laugh at such a loss. His father must be rich indeed, and care little how his son squanders his money. Your father knew of your gaming?"

The reply was delivered with a defeated air: "He did."

"And paid for your losses?"

A great sigh.

Mr. Franklin rose. "The way to wealth is not amongst paper kings and queens—or knaves. I do not wish to trouble you further." He pressed the young man's shoulder. "Out of sorrow may come strength. You shall be surprised what you find you may bear. Good day."

We left James Fairbrass in his chair.

In the entry hall Mr. Franklin asked the maid if he might speak to Cato Prince, but the young blackamoor was again out on some errand.

"Another time," said the gentleman airily, as if it made no matter, and led me to our coach, Peter at once turning south into Greek Street. I drew our travelling rug close about my knees. The sun was vanished under cloud, and the biting three P.M. chill said the cold spell which gripped London had not loosed its frigid hold.

Mr. Franklin leant to peer behind us. "Does a small, closed carriage pursue us, Nick?" said he after a moment, sinking back. "Look as we turn into West Street."

Heart leaping, I did so—and indeed such a conveyance seemed to keep pace behind, though 'twas difficult to be

116

certain due to the traffic crowding the way. Its driver was muffled to the eyes. "It appears as you say," replied I in some alarm. "The same which followed Cassandra Fairbrass's chair the night she came to Craven Street?"

The gentleman pursed his lips. "It seems so, does't not? What may it signify? That we are watched? Mistrusted? Found displeasing? O, I am happy to displease!—it says we make progress, it proclaims that we veer near to truth." He tapped his brow. "But we must keep watch and take care. Eyes open, lad, for coaches, for red-haired mummers, yes, even for ghosts." Winking, he smiled, sank back and began to hum a merry air.

"Ah, Nick," sighed Mr. Franklin when we were once more in his second floor chamber in Craven Street, coals glowing in his grate, "I do not willingly intrude upon sorrow." He sank into his chair. "It pains me to press Mrs. Fairbrass and her children at this time. Yet how else discover who murdered Roderick Fairbrass? And why?"

I was happy to be back in these safe invirons. Kneeling I helped tug off the gentleman's damp boots, which he replaced with the fleece slippers his wife had sent as gift of the season. "Indeed, how, sir?" agreed I.

His mouth twisted. "There is concealment in that house, Nick!"

"There seems so," agreed I, "—though Cassandra Fairbrass appeared to conceal nothing."

"True. Yet her mother does not wish me to pursue the matter. And the son showed great reluctance to answer my questions. Damn me, what does he hide?"

Rising, I glanced out the bow window, to see if the mysterious coach which had followed us lingered on the icy cobbles—but to my great relief I spied nothing save the familiar bustle of the street.

I turned. "You do not believe the family has aught to do with the murder?"

Another sigh. "'Twould not be new in the world, for blood has raised its hand 'gainst blood since Cain slew Abel. But I form no judgment. Too little is known. He who theorizes on insufficient knowledge is like the cat who pounces betimes; he loses his mouse. Did you see me hold up my hand upon the landing? 'Twas to seek for wind in the upper hallway, and indeed air moves there, of no little force. Many a house lets in such draughts; perhaps one day I may turn my mind to some method to prevent 'em—yet that must be at more settled time. Might this wind in the Fairbrass house cause a loose-fitting garment to billow in ghostly fashion?"

"And thus resemble a spirit? I see your thought. And the mirror, sir?" added I.

"Aye, Nick. It stood very near her door, 'gainst the wall opposite. Yet I cannot see how it plays a part. I believed that in her agitated state, Miss Fairbrass may've glimpsed her father in the glass and mistaken him for her ghost. Yet the ghost, as she tells it, fled towards the *front* of the house. Her father emerged from his chamber behind her. Only when the spirit had vanished did she turn to fall into her father's arms. What make you of't, lad?"

"I do not know what to say of the mirror, nor do I know if the ghost has any relation to Mr. Fairbrass's murder. But I have wondered: though the ghost fled, is't possible Miss Fairbrass was *meant* to glimpse it? Her susceptibility to the supernatural was well known."

Mr. Franklin lifted a brow. "Indeed a like idea has stirred my thinking. Yet why might someone wish her to see a ghost?"

118

"To prevent her seeing—or hearing—something else?"

The gentleman beamed. "Excellent! But let us not yet give this theory too much credence, lest it lose us our mouse. We must consider more: Roderick Fairbrass's character, universally praised as the best of men; yet though Cassandra Fairbrass protested that he would never use damning knowledge against a man, did she know all of him? Principle is ever compromised by necessity. If he knew of wrongdoing, might he not give over the criminal to the law? Too, might he not sacrifice someone if't meant sparing his family?"

"Mr. Fairbrass may then have been a peril to some man, providing sufficient motive for murder?"

"Or to a woman, Nick. Or to a woman."

I took this in. "And yet—" said I.

"Speak."

"I only wonder . . . why strike the poor man down in such a fashion, with all gazing on?"

The gentleman rose to stare broodingly out his window, where day sank toward dusk, London turning to somber silhouette. "Why, indeed?" muttered he. "So *visible* a death . . . so elaborately planned, very like a play, with its audience gathered to witness the show. . . ." He turned, yet seemed far away, his voice murmuring. "Witnesses . . . is that what we were? As much puppets as the players we watched . . . ?" Pacing, he thumped a fist into a palm. "Yet, still: why. And again, why? And why and why and why?" His gaze met mine. "Reason, Nick—that is the key to all. Ever is. I am determined to resolve this *discordia concors*." Going to his desk he dipped pen in ink and scribbled a note, which he blotted, folded, handed me. "Tell King to deliver this to Mr. William Strahan, at once. I was to sup with Straney tonight—ah, how I hate to give my old friend o'er—yet I must hie me elsewhere: to the Hazard, the club which James Fairbrass

119

frequented. A gentleman's club?—ha! 'Twill prove a gentleman's club if you conceive a very imperfect idea of a gentleman. Yet I shall go there tonight. I shall play me some cards. I shall learn of this house where the Fairbrass son lost sufficient money to turn his father gray with grief. You, Nick, remain here. Write today's events in your journal. Perhaps in doing so you may make more sense of 'em than I have been able. Practice style. Speak clearly and write only truth."

Mr. Franklin's fellow agent, Robert Charles, called upon him, they putting heads together for half an hour as to how to further Pennsylvania's cause. Mr. Franklin then writ some two or three letters at his desk whilst by the fire I practiced the lesson in ciphering which he had set me. As ever I took comfort in Number 7, Craven Street, the familiar creaking of its boards, Polly's hum in the corridor, the smells of good huswifery: Mrs. Stevenson baking in her kitchen. Near six William Franklin came in from his studies. He and his father discussed law for some time, at which Mr. Franklin proved proficient on many points. "The boy does sums, does he?" said William with a cool eye as he prepared to depart. "You are fortunate, boy, to have so excellent a master."

And then, near eight, eschewing supper yet submitting to Mrs. Stevenson's admonitions that he must bundle warmly if he would go out on such a night, Mr. Franklin took coach. From the bow window I watched Peter drive him to the top of the street before vanishing in chill night. I very much wished I might accompany the gentleman, and I was little pleased to be left alone with thoughts of red-haired mummers, ghosts, and poison, yet I set myself to my task: writing all which had occurred that day.

I am grateful to've done so, for my journal has been my guide in telling all that befell Mr. Franklin.

A hand gently waked me to the tolling of eleven bells. Lifting my head from the desktop, I found Mr. Franklin gazing kindly down. "O, sir. . . ." said I, scrambling up and rubbing sleep from my eyes. My candle had burnt down, but he had lit another.

"Nay, sit you, Nick." Shaking snow from his coat, the gentleman briskly rubbed his hands. "I shall warm my feet by the fire." He groaned into his chair. "Pah!—will Mrs. Gout never let be?" His eyes found me. "You have not forgot the shorthand, which I taught you?"

"No, sir."

"And are sufficiently waked to hear my tale?"

"O, yes sir."

He placed his stockinged feet upon a stool near the grate. "Then set down the chronicle of Ben Franklin, gamester."

This is what he told:

. . . 'Twas bitter cold, Nick. How age diminishes a man's heartiness! Yet the lure of truth warmed me for the journey. The Hazard is in Bury Street, off St. James's Square, in that devil's acre east of Hyde Park, where the vices of the gentry hold sway. Many clubs are tucked in those lanes and ways, some of a truly vile nature—though many respectable too, such as White's, where only the finest gentlemen may be met. Yet gaming is the soul of 'em all, a magnet for recklessness, where five thousand pounds may depend upon a single card at faro, fortunes are lost in a night, and men are found hanged in their garters at dawn. A sad state, a waste, a loss. Yet the gentlemen will do't. Ladies too, I am told, at card tables in their homes, where polite smiles mask heartless play. Such is human nature.

The Hazard is a fine stone house, once a residence but now given o'er entirely to gaming. I had little difficulty of admittance, once I showed I was a gentleman of means with some desire for play. Inside were many rooms, handsomely fitted out, from which came the rattle of the dice box and the crack of the billiard stick. There was much light everywhere, from many lamps, yet it could not dispel the air of desperation, cries of hope sinking to dismay. A fever coursed there, Nick, a hard need; I felt it, and it made me fear that in wagering I too might catch the disease and perish of't.

I was for an hour but an observer, of which there were many; and, such is the hope of winning, that even these men standing aside would sometimes bet amongst themselves, in sharp whispers and with twitching fingers, at what numbers might be rolled upon the table or which cards might fall. 'Tis a paradox that losing often teaches no lesson but to try again. Yet it is so. Cards are the great favorite, and there were tables of ombre and loo, vingt-une, quinze, faro, roly-poly, more. Gin and other spirits flow freely. Too, odd superstitions are observed, some men believing that turning their coats inside out will bring luck. Some wear leather to protect their lace ruffles, and some wear masks to hide looks which they fear might reveal the nature of their cards. How strange a sight, to see four such masked fellows at table, white-knuckled, muttering, one crying out at his win, the others silent but betting ever more, sneering at the winner and cursing luck.

And there is cheating, Nick. I saw it, for, as you have heard, I know something of card trickery, having practiced the sly manipulations in my youth for the pleasure of discovering their secrets. I watched a wretched young man lose near a thousand pounds in half an hour and stagger from the table as white as flour. And he was cheated of't, Nick, ev'ry farthing! Yet he did not see it, nor did the men standing round like vultures seem to see but only took pleasure in his loss, as if it damned him into their company, like dead, venal souls

122

welcoming a fresh sinner. The man who did the cheating was a jolly fellow who smiled broadly as he fleeced his lamb—yet he was not skilled at his tricks; I saw ev'ry one and was filled with such fury (though I kept it hid), that immediately the young man was gone I sat me down in his place and like a bumpkin allowed this sharper to win some few hands before I turned the tables. Up comes a red queen—a great surprise!—at which the jolly fellow's smile stiffened, and I swept the table of as much as the young man had lost, and more, and excused myself as fatigued, at which my sharper grit his teeth. Had I not done well? But, no. I sought out the young man and pressed his loss into his hand and bid him learn from the night's play where better to spend his time. Yet he did not learn. I saw from his eager look that he was already lost and some time later found him gaming again as hotly as before.

I saw Bertie Hexham there—aye, Nick, the foppish son of the woman who murdered your mother. He has survived his family's ruin and looks to be in the employ of the Hazard, to lure fools to gaming. I saw Caddy Bracegirdle too, at piquet, his pocked face smiling as he lost, just as James Fairbrass said he did. How is he so free with his coin?

Yet as I went about I felt watched. There are eyes everywhere, some choosing men to inveigle into play—fresh grist for the mill—and some cutpurses too, noting who has won, to rob 'em in the street. O, one must take care! Yet there are other eyes, a black pair belonging to a great, burly fellow named Mr. Bumpp, whose task is to see that no gentleman strikes or stabs or shoots another should the play go heavily against him. Indeed tempers frequently flare; anger simmers near the boil. At one point a man accused my sharper of cheating. Bumpp was there in an instant, and before the accuser could make a scene had near strangled him before flinging him into the street, where I should not be surprised he picked himself up with broken bones. Was there any protest? None, the remaining players yawping at this great joke.

This sharper surely plays for the house.

And who owns the place? A particular set of eyes followed me, belonging to a tiny, ferretlike man hardly taller than you, long of face and tooth, in an elegant gray coat and breeches, with little built-up heels on his black buckled shoes, and carrying a lace handkerchief with which he ever dabbed his lips. He seemed to be everywhere, insinuating, watching— yet after my win he took particular note of me.

He minced to me on those black-heeled shoes. "You are new here, sir," said he in a voice so soft and strange it gave me chill. He dabbed his lips, which are rouged, his face powdered white, with a patch upon his chin.

"I am," said I.

"Gideon Kite." He shook my hand in a soft, quick grip. "You are in my house."

"And pleased to be so. I am Benjamin Franklin."

"You do not play a great deal, I see."

"I know little of gaming."

His smile would've curdled mother's milk. "Yet in your only sally you won against Mr. Wilkes."

"O, fortune sat at my side."

The tiny man's eyes looked made of agate. "Indeed, I hope 'twas only Fortune." The handkerchief touched his lips. "But as you will, Mr. Franklin, play as you like, and welcome to do so. I wish you well." The fellow minced off, but as he did so I saw him catch Bumpp's eye and bob his head my way, as to say: watch this man.

And thus was my evening, Nicolas. For show I played me some few more hands of cards, and rattled the dice box, and

124

departed with no more nor less in my pocket than when I arrived. I ask myself: was James Fairbrass's fate the same as that of the young man whom I attempted to save? If so, what were the results? I tell you, I am determined on learning more of this Gideon Kite. Of Caddy Bracegirdle too. But now to bed, for I am fatigued by my gadding. Some more nights of it, and tongues shall begin to wag! You have writ all? Sleep well, then; have pleasant dreams. . . .

❦ 9 ❦

IN WHICH Mr. Franklin learns from the blind, and we follow a dead man to his grave. . . .

M r. Franklin was out much of the morning and early afternoon of the following day, the third of the Twelve Days of Christmas. Left behind, I helped Mrs. Stevenson as I could, for there were ever chores to be done, and such was my gratitude at being taken into the house that I was eager to do my part. So I scoured blackened pots and swept the kitchen hearth. I had studies too: "If ten angels blowing on ten golden trumpets are needed for each of the five continents to wake on Judgment Day, how many trumpets must the Lord dispatch?"—such like. "Angels? Trumpets? Pah, ignore the matter of these questions," Mr. Franklin had said, "—but seek answer, for he who does not master numbers is at a great loss in the world." So I multiplied trumpets to five hundred—though I preferred to imagine they were pirates' muskets. Too, I read six pages of John Locke's *Treatises on Civil Government*, as I had been bid, though this could not be resolved into muskets nor into much else in my mind. Yet I saw this idea: that in the long run the mass of men, rather than kings, knew what was best for them.

126

This, I knew, Mr. Franklin fervently believed.

The negro, King, set out on some errand for William Franklin near noon. Sunlight glistened on snow, yet icicles clung tightly from rooftops, and frosty breath blew from ev'ry mouth in Craven Street as the black man trudged from the door. As ever he looked glum. I pitied him. Mr. Franklin had saved me from my dismal captivity at Inch, Printer, yet there were many others in the world, I saw, for whom there could be no such liberation, and though King might walk free at any time (Mr. Franklin had said as much, often), where should he go?

These reflections made me think of another blackamoor: Cato Prince. He was lighter of skin than either Peter or King. I pictured his proud lift of head the night of the Fairbrasses' party. Such fierce, intelligent eyes! Coincidence solely that Cassandra Fairbrass's spirit began to walk at the same time this fellow arrived in London? Unable to say, I fretted at my labors. A ghost, mummers, poisoned drink, gaming; further, a coach which pursued us through the London streets—what to make of 'em all?

Mr. Franklin returned near two, humming. He loved to go about, to dinners, inns, clubs, coffee houses, where conversation was the rule. He had been this morning in friendly dispute with the Honest Whigs, he informed. "Yet I did me some business as well," whispered he slyly as I accompanied him up to his chamber. "No, no," called he to Mrs. Stevenson at the top of the stairs. "I desire no luncheon. Nick has ate? I am pleased to hear so, for we shall shortly go out."

Behind his closed door he glowed with an air of triumph. "Do you know what I have discovered? That Cadwallader Bracegirdle is a liar." Eyes bright, he strode briskly as he spoke, from window to hearth. "O, I knew the fellow could

127

not be straight. I have made me some friends amongst the gentry, enough to learn of the Bracegirdles of Suffolk. Should it surprise you to find that they have been ruined near forty years? 'Tis true, in the bursting of the South Sea bubble. They clung to some land, but that too was forfeit a dozen years ago, and both father and mother are long dead. Where then does young Bracegirdle obtain money to gamble so frivolously that he can laugh at the loss of an hundred pounds which might keep a family well for a year? I smell me some plan, Nick, a stinking thing, to bring ruination. What may't be? I will nose it out. We shall sniff round the door of the Blind Beak, to see what he may tell. Come, lad, your coat and scarf, for Peter waits at the reins."

"I am very grateful, sir, to be let to go about with you," said I to the gentleman when our coach swayed and clattered west ten minutes later.

"Tut, Nick, you are my son, and though I do not openly acknowledge you—indeed though there is no certain proof of the relation save circumstance and your lineaments—I nonetheless owe you an upbringing. And so your books. And so life too. Have you not heard of Jack, so learned that he could name a horse in nine languages, so ignorant that he bought a cow to ride on? I am determined you shall know a horse from a cow."

"I hope I have learnt that, sir," said I.

"Learn, too, to tell false from true. That is wisdom."

Such fatherly affection warmed me to my soul, but I could not revel in't as I should like. The hairs at the back of my neck prickled as I peered back ever and again to see if we were once more followed, yet so thick was the midday bustle that I could say neither aye nor nay as to whether a small black coach crept behind. A quarter hour's journey delivered us to

Bow Street, a row of two-story brick and slate. Peter pulled up before a green-shuttered house on the west side, Number 4, which I well knew: the home of Mr. Fielding's People. We pushed through drifts of snow to be admitted to the entrance hall by Mr. Joshua Brogden, who greeted us in far warmer fashion than he had three months ago, when we had first applied to him in the investigation of the murder of Ebenezer Inch.

"Mr. Franklin!" cried the wizened man, giving a delighted little hop. His bulging eyes danced. "You have come at excellent time, for there are no sessions today. Murder again, is't?" He rubbed his hands. "O, I pray 'tis murder, for the last which you discovered proved most intriguing. Come, sir, this way."

In less than a moment we were past the Justice Room, where a dour portrait of King George frowned down, and in the inner sanctum of Mr. John Fielding, Principal Magistrate of Westminster.

This was a small, plain room. Mr. Fielding sat behind a broad desk, a great, doughy man of formidable presence, with three chins resting upon his ill-tied cravat. I was sure I should shiver in my boots if I were ever brought before his court. His huge, white-bewigged head, squashed near neckless upon his shoulders, quavered as we entered, and before Mr. Brogdan could announce us, his ears, like great curled shells, seemed to stretch with alertness. "Mr. Franklin, or I'm damned!" his rumbling voice pronounced. "And the boy with you, too? Nicolas Handy?"

Remarkable, for Mr. Justice Fielding was stone blind.

His chair creaked as he bent unerringly toward me, his sightless eyes squinting slits. His breath blew hotly in my face. "Are you a good boy? Do you do your duty? Do you obey the law?"

129

"Y—yes, sir," quavered I.

His chins trembled. "'Tis well, for the Tyburn hangman awaits if you do not." The froglike man swiveled to Mr. Franklin. "Welcome, sir. Sit you down, sit you down."

Mr. Franklin did so, I taking the wooden chair beside him. It was a wonder that in his state Mr. Fielding had become the chief crime fighter of London, yet he had. His remarkable hearing, keen as a dog's, was some of the reason. Too, his uncanny memory, deep intelligence, and driving will made him a man to be reckoned with. Further, he was no trading justice, to be bribed. Mr. Franklin had told how he had taken over the position after his half brother Henry (who had writ *Tom Jones*) had died in office. Henry Fielding began reforms which John forcibly continued, and such was the reputation of the Bow Street court that the constables under him, handpicked men, were known as Mr. Fielding's People.

A beak was a person of authority. The mere whisper of the name Blind Beak made criminal London start and peer as if doomsday lurched at its shoulder.

Mr. Franklin and Mr. Fielding spoke some time of the wretched state of the city's streets, where disorder, riot, and robbery were common, and where a wise man carried a cudgel to protect his purse. They lamented too of the sad state of justice, where the watchman took money and the constable took money and the magistrate himself took money, so the criminal might bribe himself free to rob or bludgeon once more. Mr. Fielding tightened his fingers across his belly. "Yet I believe I begin to make some change," said he. "I have discharged three men from office who showed such contempt for the law that they did their business in taverns. I have admitted men of the newspapers to my court, that they might report truly of what passes. And I have begun to exchange

130

information with county justices, that an interlocking system of records may be established."

"I am glad to hear it," said Mr. Franklin. "And what of gaming houses? What do you, to hold them in check?"

"Little, I fear," grumbled the Justice, "for their victims willingly step in their doors. Fools! They are like rabbits longing for the poacher's snare. Too, these dens are well-organized, with a director, who supervises the rooms; an operator, who deals cards at cheating games; some crowpees, who watch close and gather money; puffs, who are given coin to decoy fools into play; a clerk to keep close eye on the puffs (no one is trusted); a squib, who deals cards; a flasher, to swear how oft he has won; a dunner, to make certain men pay out what they have lost; a waiter to see the gamesters' glasses are well-filled; and a captain, who fights any man peevish at losing. All which makes strong meshes. These tricksters are not to be found in the best clubs, where gentlemen play honorably, though no less recklessly, amongst themselves; yet they are found frequently enough."

"In houses such as the Hazard?"

"In just such places." Justice Fielding pounced upon the hint. "You take particular interest in the Hazard? In Gideon Kite as well?"

"What do you know of him?"

"A ferreting little devil! There is no more than four feet of him, yet every inch a danger. But last month a man—a good man too, save for his weakness for dicing—shot himself after two hours of Gideon Kite's hospitality, and the widow and her babe must now seek for home in the streets."

"May one prove cheating against him?"

"How, when he has swearers aplenty who will perjure themselves in his behalf?"

131

"The buying and selling of truth is a great crime. Do you know of a fellow named Cadwallader Bracegirdle?"

"I have heard the name, a seeming foppish fellow, yet sly. Why do you ask of him?"

Mr. Franklin told all he knew of the murder of Roderick Fairbrass.

The blind magistrate listened, his breath softly wheezing. "But, given your strong evidence, how can the widow refuse to believe her husband was poisoned?"

"She *says* she does not believe it. What she *thinks* is a different matter. Something makes her fear to have the business looked into."

Fielding cocked a brow. "She herself had a hand in it?"

"I know not. I should not say so, though it may prove to be."

"And why do you take such an interest?"

"A promise to the daughter that I would help."

Mr. Fielding's raw laugh shook all three chins. "O, promises—cheap enough these days, with only one man in ten honorable enough to keep 'em. Yet you are one such. Indeed, Franklin, I wish you might be amongst Mr. Fielding's People. Better still, a magistrate, to dispense honest justice."

"That should steer me from my promise to Pennsylvania, to make the Crown yield to reason."

"Reason—as scarce a commodity as honor. Well, I am sorry to tell you we are hard-pressed in Bow Street and can spare no man presently to look into so uncertain a thing as this Fairbrass matter."

"I look into it myself. I wished merely to alert you to't. And to inquire of the Hazard. The gaming houses are well-organized, you say. You spoke at another time of a criminal enterprise which casts its net over robbery, bawdry, even murder, the head of it a man named Quimp."

"Whose true face is unknown."

"Fond of disguise, you said. Might he have a hand in the business of gaming in London?"

Mr. Fielding's chins sank gloomily upon his chest. "I have long suspected that he does, indeed that he, rather than the dwarf, Kite, is the force behind the Hazard—and other hellholes too. He seeks power and envies any man his success. Gaming is an excellent way to bring the mighty low. Take care, Franklin. Quimp likes a clever adversary—likes him to crush him. And you, boy," growled he to me as we rose to depart, "see you walk the narrow path of right."

We returned to Craven Street amidst a keening wind, the city appearing more and more gray, mired and slowed, as if at last the long cold spell went to her very veins and congealed her blood, so that the throngs in the streets seemed to sleepwalk, wrapped to the eyes as they groped their way over dirty snow. The sky was an oppressive pall of cloud and smoke. Were we followed? So biting was the wind that I dared not poke out my head to see.

Mr. Franklin sat in pondering silence.

Back in the warmth of his chamber, he stood by his window watching snow lift from rooftops to whirl madly in air. "Roderick Fairbrass's funeral is this eve—inclement weather for't, yet the man must be put underground. I shall pay my respects. Will you accompany me?"

I did not relish once more freezing my fingers and toes but said that I should like to go.

"Good." The gentleman tapped the rims of his spectacles. "Two pair of eyes shall then keep watch."

133

Thus, near six, when night had wrapped the city for an hour, we plunged again into winter's harsh chill and chaffed our hands to keep 'em warm 'til we arrived in Soho Square. There the procession was already forming before the Fairbrass house, the mourners presented with black scarves and weepers. We had torches too, whose spitting light cast strange shadows in the icy night. Mr. Franklin and I found a place in the forming line, though only after he had gazed about in his sharp fashion to see who might be present. He spied Joseph de Medina, to whom he nodded, and Moses Trustwood and Cadwallader Bracegirdle wearing a hypocritical look of woe on his pocked, ugly face. There were the family too, the youngest, Emily and Tim, like little, black-wrapped dolls. With them stood Captain Jack Sparkum, his weathered face uplifted as if 'twere a ship's prow in a storm. The servants made the tail of the procession, Cato Prince standing at its very end; yet (we passed close to him as we sought our place) the man's chin trembled, and I believed I saw tears in his eyes. This, from so stoic-seeming a fellow? I was much startled—moved too—but there was no time to draw Mr. Franklin's attention, for black plumes were just then raised before the coffin, the bearers lifted their burden, and we trudged off at sober pace.

I thanked God that city parishes were small, for this made our walk short, and in ten minutes we entered Saint John's churchyard to the shuffling whisper of our steps. A fresh grave gaped amongst the stones—how trying a task must it have been to break that frozen ground! As the preacher droned the service I could see anguish writ large on Mrs. Fairbrass's handsome face as wind fluttered her black veil. On either side of her stood Emily and Tim, to whom she clung as if at any moment they too might be snatched away. Nearby was

134

Cassandra Fairbrass, one hand clutching her runic stone, and next her, her brother James, ashen and stiff.

Mr. Franklin's fingers pressed firmly into my shoulder. I glanced up to find his mouth pursed, his small squarish spectacles glinting as he took in all.

And then the thing was done, earth flung with its terrible, hollow thud upon the coffin in the grave. Wind lashed and flapped our garments. Mrs. Fairbrass sobbed, joined by an echoing chorus. We struck out our torches on the ground and made our way back to the Fairbrass house, where, as customarily, friends would take supper with punch and wine.

What a contrast was this to the gay scene of the Christmas party three days past! Then, before the play (and save for Mr. and Mrs. Fairbrass's odd, strained manner) had been music, dancing, gaiety. Now all was grim-set lips, furrowed brows, downcast eyes, tear-smirched cheeks and the sepulchral muttering of regrets. Mr. Franklin too spoke his condolences, and tutted, and agreed how sad an occasion was this. Yet he kept watch too. "Damn me, where has Cato Prince gone?" murmured he when guests began to excuse themselves. The black man had helped to serve supper; he had stood for some time by the door with his proud gaze (no trace of tears), but was now nowhere to be seen. Mr. Franklin stepped into the entrance hall, amongst departing mourners. As I went with him both our gazes were drawn by a flash of livery in a servant's doorway to the right.

"Follow, Nick!" The gentleman hurried to this door.

A narrow flight of stairs led down. Just before descending, I glanced back to find Mrs. Fairbrass's large brown eyes fixed upon me, in amazement or fury I could not say, and I near bumped into Mr. Franklin at the foot of the stairs, in a narrow, dark way. "He has come here," breathed he determinedly. "I

135

saw him." He made his way along, and shortly we came to the kitchen, a large room with still-warm oven, where two women in aprons—one the maid, Mary—tidied after the collation which had been served abovestairs.

Hearing a faint sound, I turned to discover Cato Prince not three feet away, gazing down.

My heart thumped as I gazed back. So powerful was the man's frame that it seemed it might burst the seams of his livery. His huge hands opened and closed at his sides, and he fixed upon Mr. Franklin a look of mistrust and ire.

"Cato Prince," said the gentleman in as easy a manner as if he met an acquaintance at a club.

"That is my name, sir." The servant's voice was deep, his tone guarded.

"I wish to put some questions," said Mr. Franklin.

The black man said nothing.

"You came to London little more than a month ago?"

"I did."

"Pray, why?"

"My master sent me from Jamaica."

"Lemuel Fairbrass. Yet, still: why?"

"To serve his brother."

"Your master was dissatisfied with you?"

"He was not."

"Pleased with you?"

Proudly: "I was a good servant to him."

"Then why part with you? Could not Roderick Fairbrass find his own man?"

"I know naught of that. Mr. Lemuel Fairbrass wished me to come to London, and so I did."

"Are you a slave?"

Cato Prince's eyes flashed. "I am not!"

"Yet you submitted to your former master's request."

"It was he who freed me. He said I need not leave him, yet he wished me to do so, to help his brother. I wished to please Mr. Lemuel Fairbrass. That is why I came to this house."

"And were you to help Roderick Fairbrass in any particular way?"

"As his personal manservant."

"Did you find him a good master?"

"He was kind and fair."

"As was Lemuel Fairbrass before him?"

With trembling voice: "Just like."

"Tell me—was Roderick Fairbrass happy?"

Cato Prince's yellowish eyes narrowed. "'Twas not for me to judge what he thought or felt."

"Come," adjured Mr. Franklin.

"I have answered as best I may."

"How old are you?"

"Eighteen years."

"So young! Born in the Indies?"

"Born there, yes."

"How came you into Lemuel Fairbrass's household?"

"My mother was a slave, whom he bought of another man."

"And freed?"

"With great generosity."

"Your mother worked for Lemuel?"

"Hard and well."

"Thus you were raised in his household?"

"I was."

"You speak English excellently. Do you believe in ghosts?"

The black man's mouth worked. "There may be such things."

"And have you seen 'em here, in this house?"

Firmly: "I have not."

"Yet you have heard that one may've walked?"

"Servants talk. They say Miss Fairbrass saw a spirit."

"Do you believe she did?"

"I do not think on't."

"O, you think more than you say. Do you sorrow that Roderick Fairbrass is dead?"

At this the servant's lips twisted; he bit 'em, and for a moment I thought tears might spill forth again. Yet he mastered himself, with a terrible show of will, though he remained rigid and shaken.

How like James Fairbrass's reaction!

Mr. Franklin was silent a moment, with bowed head. "Your feeling does you credit," said he softly. "I have discovered that Mr. Fairbrass may've been poisoned. Do you know aught of this?"

"Nothing."

"Yet the eve of the tragedy you left the assembly room before the play began. Did you not meet the man who acted the Doctor? Did you not see his face?"

"I went directly below," murmured Cato Prince. "I saw no mummers."

"But—"

Mr. Franklin's words were cut short by a rustle of garments. "You shall answer no more this evening," came Mrs. Fairbrass's strained voice. We turned. The widow stood in the corridor, a bar of kitchen light illuminating her taut, pale face. "Go upstairs at once," said she to Cato Prince. "See the house is shut—but do not lock the front door. Mr. Franklin will depart soon." The blackamoor bobbed his head and passed her silently, and the woman fixed her gaze upon the gentleman. *Friend or foe?* her desperately searching eyes inquired. "You pry everywhere, I see," said she. "Well, I gave you

138

permission—yet I did not give you freedom of my house. Hereafter you shall apply to me before nosing about as you have done." She wrung her hands, her voice a piteous wail: "Ah, sir, you know not what you do!"

With this wretched exclamation the poor woman turned and fled.

❧ 10 ❧

IN WHICH Mr. Franklin pursues a coachman, a banker, and a Jew. . . .

D o you know, Nick," said Mr. Franklin near eleven next morning, the twenty-ninth of December, "not only gentlemen have their clubs, but servants too, where they gather to imbibe and converse as their masters do, though their talk be not the same, for 'tis of the masters themselves. I know some such haunts: The Two Chairmen in Haymarket, The Running Footman near Golden Square. The Coach and Four resides in Brook Street. It is where coachmen go on free days, to let loose the reins of their horses and drink some pints of beer. Peter, clever fellow, has discovered this, and more: that the Fairbrass's own man, Mr. Harley, repairs there, to put up his boots." Mr. Franklin shrugged into his greatcoat. "Indeed Peter has just come from keeping watch on the Fairbrass house to say that now is one such time. I mean to engage the man, for what he may tell; for he, more than any other, will know of comings and goings in Soho Square." He regarded me, where I sat with my copybook. "Leave studies, Nick. Your coat and cap. Brisk air awaits, as does Peter in his box."

I was very glad to go out. Below we climbed into our coach

amidst more lashing wind. One reason Mr. Franklin had settled upon Craven Street, amongst many other lodgings he might have took, was Mr. Tisdale's printing shop next door. "So I might be within smell of printer's ink, and stop in now and again to set me some lines of type." Indeed I too loved printing, from my days at Inch, Printer, where I had learnt the craft. Mr. Franklin and I waved to Mr. Tisdale on his stoop as Peter took us by. Then we were once more in the Strand, heading west into Charing Cross.

"Sir," said I as we swayed along, our breaths frosty plumes, "did you see Cato Prince's tears as he stood in the funeral line?"

"Shed tears, did he? Many?"

"They near made icicles upon his chin."

"Sharp-eyed!" The gentleman pulled at his lip. "The young blackamoor near wept, too, when I asked about his new master's death. Do you recall the spot of damp on Roderick Fairbrass's shirtfront when he died? Fallen tears? Dropt from the eyes of the mumming Doctor? Yet why should a poisoner weep as he murders his victim—what sense in that?"

Having no answer, I huddled close to Mr. Franklin. Twenty minutes delivered us to Brook Street, where a creaking wooden sign painted with a coach pulled by prancing dappled grays showed we had found our destination: the Coach and Four. Entering, we discovered a tidy public house, fire merrily chirping, whilst some dozen or so men in livery of varying colors, all neat and trim, sat at ease on benches with pewter mugs and gossiped of the lords and ladies they served, or of men of money from the City.

A quiet inquiry of the landlord soon discovered Mr. Franklin his man, sitting amongst his cronies.

We drew near.

Mr. Harley seemed in some dispute with his fellow coach-men as to the grandness of their respective establishments. "Trouble in your house, Bill?" I heard one of the tribe chide. "Where's the money, eh?" Mocking laughter broke out, but the coachman only sniffed, as if this made no matter. Mr. Franklin bent and whispered in his ear, and he scraped back and went to sit at a small corner table with us. He was a small, lean fellow, with a bald, burnished knob of head, strong, knotty fingers and long wisps of eyebrow that drooped over peering, gray eyes. He proved friendly and willing to answer any questions—once he was assured that no whisper of his complicity should fly to Soho Square.

Mr. Franklin asked much that he had asked others before: of ghosts and the state of Roderick Fairbrass's mind.

"I know naught of ghosts, thank the Lord!" exclaimed Bill Harley. He nodded with deep solemnity. "Aye, the master seemed downcast of late." He wished to buy Mr. Franklin a hot flip, "Rum, molasses and beer—just the thing for a dev'lish cold day," but Mr. Franklin declined, though he allowed a mild sillabub for me, delivered with a plate of jellied eels. It was the family's goings about in which he was most interested. In low tones he inquired closely as to where Mr. Harley had driven Mr. Fairbrass and Mrs. Fairbrass and Cassandra and James Fairbrass over the past many weeks, but especially in the days just before Christmas. Bill Harley told this willingly. Miss Cassandra Fairbrass went out but little. Her brother, James, was frequently in the company of Cad-wallader Bracegirdle, whom Mr. Harley condemned as bad business. As to the Hazard, the coachman well knew the way, due to Mr. James's spending many hours there. "But that was some time ago; he's not gamed in months. Yet I took his father there now and again."

Mr. Franklin stirred. "His father? Many times?"

"P'rhaps some four or six in all, the first time near half a year ago."

"Recent visits, too?"

"One, a fortnight ago. When the gentleman come out he were not pleased, amutterin' and agrindin' his teeth."

"He had lost at gaming?"

"'Twas not for me to ask." Bill Harley also described recent visits to Moses Trustwood and Joseph de Medina.

"Was Mr. Fairbrass in the habit of calling upon these men?"

"More likely met 'em at some club—yet 'twas not there nor at their houses that he saw 'em that week afore he died, but in their offices in the City."

"Long visits?"

"Half a hour each."

"And where else did he go?"

The coachman's long eyebrows drew together. "The day afore Christmas he stops by Porberry's, to buy a doll for Emily and some soldiers for Tim—poor littl'uns. And Christmas day he visits a man in Craven Street, though I do not know his name."

"I am that man. And what do you make of the new servant, Cato Prince?"

Bill Harley sniffed. "He cannot be faulted for shirkin'." He bent across the table. "But the servants has their ways, Mr. Franklin. They sticks together. I don't mean against the masters, never that. But there is, well—*ways*. This Prince fellow is not one o' us; he does not act aright, too high and mighty, and always akeepin' to himself. When he comes in a room he seems to be sneakin' and aspyin'."

"The color of his skin has nothing to do with your dislike?"

Bill Harley's gray eyes swelled. "And what if't may? A blackamoor? To be given the priv'lege o' servin' Mr. Fairbrass?"

143

"I see. Finish your sillabub, Nick. I thank you, Mr. Harley, for speaking so roundly. I assure you my questions are for good purpose. One last." Mr. Franklin gestured across the room. "What did your friend mean just now when he asked about money?"

The coachman's eyes glittered. "No word to Mrs. Fairbrass that I spoke? 'Tis because rumor gets about that there is trouble with money in the house, now the master is dead. A maid heard the mistress speak of it to young James; 'tis not much that servants do not know about their masters. 'Twas my mistake to carry the story here, for I have been rid hard about it."

"Rumor whips even the bearer. What trouble with money, pray?"

Bill Harley snorted. "Why . . . not enough." He grinned broadly. "Is that not ever the trouble with money?"

"Roderick Fairbrass paid visits to the banker, Moses Trustwood, and the financier, Joseph de Medina, shortly before Christmas day, did he?" mused Mr. Franklin under his round beaver hat as we climbed into our coach. He sank back. "I remember me, the eve of the party, some hesitation in Trustwood's manner when I inquired after Fairbrass's investments at Nash's Bank." He thumped the roof of the coach. "To Lombard Street, Peter. Let us see, Nick, what Mr. Trustwood has to say of this."

Yet other thoughts were on my mind. "Is't not of more interest, sir, that Mr. Fairbrass was more than once at the Hazard?"

"O, 'tis of very great interest. You have rubbed the glass rod in my workshop to see how the electrically charged object draws metal. In this matter money is much like a charged thing, to draw the facts of our case: money, won or lost, at the

Hazard; money lacking in the Fairbrass household; money invested at Nash's Bank."

"But what does this money draw?"

"A ghost. Murder, surely—though but one, I pray. I do not say this makes all clear, yet light begins to gleam." The gentleman leant out as we turned into New Bond Street. "Oho!" There was a peculiar, tremulous satisfaction in his voice as he settled against his cushion once more.

My heart thudded. "What is't, sir?"

"Our small, black coach, which sticks to us as a fly to a mare. What close attention!—does that not suggest we pursue a right path? Yet who should keep such strict watch?"

I wondered the same, but the passing London scene drove this from my mind. We moved east: Covent Garden, Drury Lane, the Inns of Court. Throngs swarmed by like blackbeetles in wainscoting. South, over rooftops, sprang up a forest of ships' masts, while ahead I glimpsed now and again against the chill, pewter-gray sky the dome of St. Paul's. The Strand dissolved to Fleet Street. "London is many cities," said Mr. Franklin. "We have long left her most fashionable precincts. Here, by the river, from the Temple to Fleet Ditch is that part known as Alsatia, where footpads lurk, and bludgeoners, and whores. A man's purse may be worth his life in these streets; I should not like to set foot in 'em." Thus I was greatly relieved when we passed into the ancient City, marked out long ago by the old Roman wall, of which Mr. Franklin had told me. "Parliament may sit in Westminster," observed he, "and the King may sup at St. James's, yet there is power at this end of town, that of hardworking men who cultivate their business to great prospering. Then they may rise to challenge men of ancient right." His mouth became a hard, flat line, and I knew he thought of his fight with the Penns. "Such

145

diligence was the way of Ben Franklin, a penniless boy from Boston," said he.

I took all in. Passing through the maze of lanes about St. Paul's, we turned into Cornhill Street, the towers of St. Michael's ahead, and from thence to the portico of the Royal Exchange. "Here is where men of money come to do business," said Mr. Franklin, directing Peter next to turn into Threadneedle Street, so I might see the Bank of England next the Church of St. Christopher-le-Stocks. "And here is where the Government itself begs in satin breeches with its fine leather hat in hand." He winked. "Did I not say there was power in the City?"

Yet there were private banks as well, several in Lombard Street nearby, to which we now repaired, pulling up before Nash's, a small, elegant building of gray stone which bespoke respectability and trust. As we stepped down I looked about for a particular small black coach, and believed I glimpsed one such amongst many others on the snowy cobbles but could not be sure, for its hooded driver drove it quickly, like a scuttling thing, into Gracechurch Street.

We entered Nash's Bank.

Here was a marble solemnity, with clerks scribbling at high desks, their quill pens seeming to whisper of accumulating wealth. Moses Trustwood remembered Mr. Franklin, to whom he had spoke both at the party and the funeral. Red-faced as ever, and as paunchy in his tidy, tight-fitting suit of clothes, he tutted over Mr. Fairbrass's death as he led us through the large outer chamber into his sanctum, a snug little room whose damasked walls were hung with paintings of racehorses. Bidding us be seated, he settled genially behind his broad oaken desk, folded his small white hands, and smiled. "And what brings you, Mr. Franklin? Should you wish

146

to place some funds with Nash's Bank? 'Twould be most wise."

"No," replied Mr. Franklin in his soft voice, "I am come to seek after Roderick Fairbrass's business here. Did he not withdraw a great deal of money in recent days?"

"Why . . . I cannot speak of this, Mr. Franklin, you must know. 'Tis private business, which may be known only by Mr. Fairbrass and Nash's Bank."

"But Mr. Fairbrass is dead."

"That makes no difference."

"Murdered."

Moses Trustwood looked to right, left, up, down. "Murdered?" breathed he as his little eyes settled on Mr. Franklin once more.

"Poisoned."

Fingers fidgeted on desktop. "Whyever do you say so?"

The gentleman told all, from Opliss-Popliss drops to the small, closed coach which might at this moment lurk nearby.

The banker fanned his brow. "Murder? Truly?" The redness had drained from his face.

"Some doubt it. I do not. I further believe that Mr. Fairbrass's fortune, such as it may've been, is the reason for't. I mean to learn more of that reason, and to uncover the murderer's vile hand. I have spoke to you frankly. Pray, do the same with me."

Moses Trustwood opened his mouth, closed it, gazed here, there, shifted papers about, shut them in a drawer. At last he lifted his hands only to let them fall. "How did you know that poor Roddy had recently withdrawn funds?"

"A surmise. He did so, then?"

"On the twenty-first of December. All he had placed with us."

"All?"

147

"To the last farthing."

"A great deal?"

"Many thousands of pounds. Profits from his business over a dozen years, which he carried away in notes. Foolish, foolish. We were friends, Mr. Franklin. I asked why. I asked if 'twas wise. But he was firm, he would not say. 'It must be done,' averred he in a most strange mood, as't had been these past months, full of sorrow and anger. He was determined, sir; he had some plan."

"Plan?"

"Would that I knew it. I should tell you if I did, to help you in your seeking. But there is more." Lowering his voice, as if some authority secretly listened to chide him for speaking, Trustwood said, "He sold his business too, all goods and holdings, here and in Jamaica."

"To you?"

"To Nash's Bank."

"Why did he this?"

"Plain stubborn will. Madness? I cannot say. I advised 'gainst such rash action—yet I must stand for the bank too, and in the end bought all from him, for he was willing to sell at very fair price. Indeed I felt I robbed him, but he would have it so. He was all in a fever, a rush, as if time ran out in some clock."

"But what of his brother?"

"The man in Jamaica?"

"You know of him, then. Had he no interest in the business?"

"None. The papers were clear; Roddy owned all. Yet you must know more: another has inquired after his transactions."

"What man?"

"A woman, old and bent, yet dressed well, as a lady. She claimed to be an aunt of Roddy's, though I know of no such.

148

Yet she might well have been, for she knew enough of the family to persuade me she was. She wheedled and begged. She pressed me hard—near moved me—but in the end I could reveal nothing, urging her to apply to her nephew if she wished so heartily to know of his dealings. She did not like this; her look when she saw I stood firm was of such threatening malevolence that it made me blanch."

"Quimp," murmured Mr. Franklin to his chin.

"Eh?"

The gentleman pressed his glasses firmly upon his nose. "But a name. But a man. No matter." Rising with the aid of his bamboo, he shook Moses Trustwood's hand. "Thank you for confiding in me. You have helped indeed."

Out in the frigid air of Lombard Street Mr. Franklin grumbled and cursed and peered sharply up and down. "Our spy is not in sight, yet he no doubt hangs about. Quimp? Damn his effrontery!" He climbed into his coach. "New Bond Street, Peter. And drive smartly. I grow weary of ev'ry movement being known."

New Bond Street lay near. Peter turned our coach so quickly that I was thrown against the door and drove with such speed that my teeth clicked as we careered over cobbles.

In less than ten minutes we were at our destination.

In getting down I saw no coach which might be our pursuer. Glancing up, I glimpsed a smile of satisfaction on Peter's dark face, that he had displayed his mettle so well.

Mr. Franklin's gaze fixed on the modest, narrow brick building before us. "The office of Joseph de Medina. Come, Nick, to see what light this Portuguese Jew may shed on Roderick Fairbrass's dealings."

We mounted three stone steps to a white-painted door with a brass knocker, which Mr. Franklin rapped, and rapped

149

again. There was a spy hole. Did an an eye examine us? After a long a moment in biting wind, the door swung back, and Joseph de Medina himself stood there. "Mr. Benjamin Franklin," said he in his warm voice, yet with the dignified reserve which I remembered from Christmas day. "Come in, sir. And your young friend, Nicolas Handy. You are welcome."

We stepped into hardly less chill than had nipped at us outside, for the small, bare entranceway was cold, and I was grateful when de Medina led us at once through a door to the left, into a cozy room with fire hissing in the grate and an ornately-patterned carpet on the floor and tufted chairs before a broad mahogany desk. All the furnishings of this room were very rich, contrasting with the bareness of the entryway. Behind the desk sat a great iron safe the height of a man. Two velvet-hung windows marked the wall to the right, outside which I glimpsed a narrow alleyway. These windows were heavily barred.

De Medina drew the draperies over both and turned. He was tall in his black suit and gray waistcoat, over six feet. He wore no wig, his thick, dark brown hair tied back with a ribbon, as was mine, his broad, handsome face calm and still, his mouth seeming ready to smile, yet his eyes hooded, marked by a mixture of sufferance and fortitude. "I am pleased that you call on me, Mr. Franklin," said he. "I have often thought on our all-to-brief conversation. 'Tis not many Englishmen who grieve that the Jewish Naturalization Act was repealed."

"I grieve at all such prejudicial acts."

"You shall grieve long, then, I fear."

Mr. Franklin inclined his head. "Sad to say."

De Medina's deep, reflective eyes gazed a moment.

150

"Should you like a glass of Porto, a drink of my country?" asked he.

"On such a day, yes."

"And your boy? A glass too?"

"Indeed he shall have one. I teach him of the world, and as Porto is a part of't, he shall learn of Porto too."

De Medina nodded approval, and shortly Mr. Franklin and I sat before his desk in thick leather chairs, he behind it, all holding glasses. Examining the deep red color of his drink, Mr. Franklin sipped. "Warming, indeed. Would that Englishmen preferred this to gin or beer."

"Many do. Thus the trade grows, to Portugal's vantage."

"And are you in this trade?"

"No. Men may drink what I sell only with their eyes."

"I remember me: gemstones."

"Of the finest water."

"Thus the barred windows and sturdy safe?"

"And a pistol in my desk, which I hope never to be moved to fire."

"You are well protected."

"I have learnt to beware."

"'Tis necessary."

De Medina smiled thinly. "O, I am a great worshipper at necessity's shrine."

As the gentlemen spoke I too sipped my Porto, whose pungent sweetness tickled my tongue. The liquor spread to my bones, whispering of a warmer, gentler clime than England's winter, so that the more I sipped the more I took great, drowsy satisfaction in my company and surroundings and sank deeper in my chair.

"Should you wish to examine some of my goods?" inquired de Medina.

"Gladly," replied Mr. Franklin.

Rising, the Jew worked the lock of his safe and swung open its heavy door, near a foot thick. Inside were wooden shelves and drawers. Sliding out one, small, no more than six by six inches, he spilt its contents upon a dark cloth on his desktop: a dozen gleaming crystalline stones, cut in facets that sharply caught the light. They made me catch my breath—never had I seen such sparkling things. "Diamonds," murmured the Jew, "the finest you may find in London." Yet there was a strange dispassion in his voice.

Mr. Franklin poked his finger amongst the gems. "Pretty," said he. His gaze rose. "You do not care for 'em?"

"There are men would rob or murder to possess 'em, for the love of the things; but to me they are mere stones, useful because of the desire they inspire in men's—and women's—breasts. Are they food? No. May they shelter a man 'gainst adversity? Not in and of themselves. Yet I am pleased that other men want 'em and pay well for the privilege of making baubles of 'em. They have one more excellent quality: they are easily transportable. A man may carry a king's ransom in his waistcoat pocket, or hide it in a boot heel, yet appear poor as a beggar. We Jews have learnt the value of easily transported wealth."

"More necessity?"

De Medina smiled. "The way of the world." He next spilt out emeralds, green glowing things with a flaming life beneath their hard, icy skins. Sapphires. Opals. Bloodred garnets. But he was indifferent to all, and in the end scooped 'em up as if they were acorns and scattered 'em in their drawers like a squirrel storing for winter. Shutting the great safe door and settling in his chair, he gazed over the last of his Porto. "I prefer this to any gem," said he, lifting his glass. He cocked a brow. "But, sir, you are not come to buy gems."

152

"No. I wish to know what Roddy Fairbrass came to buy. He was here on the twenty-fourth of December, I believe."

De Medina coolly drained his glass. "He was. Why do you inquire after poor Roddy?"

"Murder," said Mr. Franklin, telling the story which he had less than an hour ago related to Moses Trustwood.

Joseph de Medina's deep-set eyes revealed little dismay, seeming to say he knew men would do violence if they might. "And you seek Roddy Fairbrass's murderer?" asked he.

"I do."

De Medina gazed silently over the rim of his glass, while some dispute seemed to go on behind his eyes. "Roddy bought emeralds," said he at last.

"How many?"

"But four. Yet the four finest in my possession."

"How did he pay?"

"In bank notes, from Nash's Bank."

"Many thousands of pounds?"

"Near thirty thousand."

Mr. Franklin was silent a moment. "Why did he buy these gems?"

"I do not know. Not for love of 'em, for he barely looked at 'em before I placed 'em in a pouch in his palm. He wished, it seemed, only to change his banknotes to gems as rapidly as he might, as if the money burned his hands. I gave him good value; one might easily sell the emeralds for more than thirty thousand in any capital in Europe."

"Or America?"

"I know little of America."

"Men are greedy there too, for gems and much else. Some have fortunes to buy 'em. What was the man's manner?"

"He shook, he trembled. I wondered if he was mad. Yet there was a light of triumph in his eyes as well. He gripped my sleeve and adjured me to speak to no one ever of our transaction. This I promised."

"Yet you speak to me."

De Medina pursed his lips. "You will do no harm by knowing. And may do good. I pray you prove my judgment sound."

"Thank you for your trust. No one else has arrived at your door to ask of his dealings?"

"No."

"Yet someone may. If so, keep silent—but stay by your pistol. Take note of such a person and inform me at once."

"There is peril? Never fear, I am an excellent shot."

"I believe it. The eve Roddy was poisoned you stood not six feet from where he lay whilst the mumming Doctor crouched over him. Did he display any reluctance to swallow the Opliss-Popliss drops?"

De Medina shook his head. "None that I saw. I could see his eyes through the holes in his visor; they stared trustingly. And he drank readily—almost eagerly, I may say."

"Eagerly? And spoke?"

"No. Yet it seemed the Doctor said something, a hissing word. 'Sorrow,' I believed at the time, yet it may've been some other."

"Sorrow," murmured Mr. Franklin. "Aye, there is sorrow in this. There lay a small sprig of rosemary upon the man's breast. Did you see how it came there?"

"No. Does it signify?"

"I do not yet see how."

"But you are determined. How far has your pursuit come? Was the poor man murdered to obtain the gems?"

"It is possible." The gentleman rose. "Thank you for your trust, Senor de Medina—and for your excellent Porto."

"Easily transported wealth. . . ." murmured Mr. Franklin

154

as our coach jounced westward through the rutted ways about St. Paul's. "And Roddy Fairbrass spoke of removing to America. Does not our mystery show as many facets as a gem? It does not yet shine out in perfect shape, but we shall chip and polish, Nick; we will bring all clear."

Gems, thought I, The soft green glow of emeralds—yet I preferred the red of Porto, which warmed me better than fire on this cold day.

🎝 11 🎝

IN WHICH I learn more of Hamlet,
*Mr. Franklin sums up, and we talk of
poison with learned men. . . .*

Aₙ astonishing figure, Nick: thirty thousand pounds, all
Roderick Fairbrass's fortune, which he spent in an
instant."

"He did not fling the money to the wind," said I.

"True—yet he changed it to uncertain goods, emeralds,
easily transported, but also easily stolen. What drove the man
to't?"

This question remained unanswered as we returned to
Craven Street. From its top, as we moved down, the Thames
appeared a surging mass of gray in which great chunks of ice
bobbed like huge, jostling fish. Chimneypots spewed a
steady, black fog into the frigid air. Christmastide was not yet
done. We had seen, along the Strand, mummers amongst the
crowd in despite of the cold, and New Year's celebrations
were to come, as well as Twelfth Night joy. Only then would
greenery be swept from houses and men's eyes begin to
search for spring.

Indoors Mr. Franklin writ more letters: to his only remaining brother, Peter; to his favorite sister, Jane Mecom; to his
friend, Catherine Ray, whom he called my Katy (women were

much taken with Mr. Franklin). He writ also, on business matters, to David Hall, with whom he had struck a partnership when he retired from his printing shop in Philadelphia. This shop, now run by Hall, earned Mr. Franklin near a thousand pounds a year, which kept his wife and daughter well and paid many of his expenses on these shores. "I thought, when I retired, to devote myself to Natural Philosophy," sighed he, waving this last letter, "but look you, I sit in London waiting on the whims of petty officials. Yet I do't willingly; 'tis best ever to serve man before Nature—though Nature be the more beguiling."

"You do not 'sit,' sir," reminded I where I frowned over John Locke beside the fire.

He laughed. "No, you are right. I gad about; I love the London clubs! But what a look, Nick; you shall crack your brow with squinting. Locke's *Treatises* trip your feet? Right yourself, lad, press on. Better eat salt with the philosophers of Greece than honey with the courtiers of Italy."

Mr. Locke was not Greek, but I took Mr. Franklin's meaning and licked my portion of salt and agreed I was the better for't.

Did I not eat a goodly portion of honey in Craven Street?

That evening Mr. Franklin went to a meeting of the Royal Society at Gresham College. He was much respected there. Indeed when I thought on his achievements I was in awe of my teacher, who was so admired by learned men of many countries that they called themselves Franklinists. After supper Polly read aloud some portions of *Hamlet* in the front parlor, with much rolling of eyes and flinging of hands and a tremulous voice. This was my first hearing of Shakespeare. As Mr. Franklin had said, a ghost walked in the play, and I stared when it intoned its terrible admonition, as did Mrs. Stevenson over her sewing. "Child, child!" cried she to her daughter. "Is

157

this a story for Nicolas's ears?" Yet she did not bid me go up nor Polly to cease, for which I gave thanks. I listened close. Hamlet proved a strange mixture of resolve and inaction. One line lodged in my head: "There are more things in Heaven and earth, Horatio, than are dreamt of in your philosophy." I felt disloyal dwelling on't as I went upstairs with my candle, but I could not help wondering if Mr. Franklin's philosophy, which denied ghosts, encompassed too little. The night was black, my candle weakly flickering, and I was but twelve, the son of a hard life of which terrors were as much a part as puddles were of rain. I shuddered on the creaking stairs. Might not evil spirits lurk in dark corners?

I was greatly relieved when Mr. Franklin returned betimes, near ten, as I was readying myself for bed in my small, cold chamber. As often he bid me in my nightshirt into his room, where Mrs. Stevenson had kept coals warm in the grate against his return. "Fothergill was at our gathering tonight," announced he as he settled, unbuttoned, before the fire. "We visit him tomorrow, at his botanical gardens at Upton, where he may help us in our quest."

I perched at the end of his bed. "How, sir?" asked I.

"Through his knowledge of poisons." The stout man massaged his balding brow. The white, powdered wig he had worn rested on its wig stand by the painting of his dead son, Francis. His boots dried by the fire. His brown hair fell lankly to his neck, and his small, squarish glasses were slid to the end of his nose. Though he had returned the false Doctor's costume to the mummers, he had kept the leering mask. This he now held up, poking his fingers through its eyeholes, like worms in a skull. "If we but knew who wore this. . . ."

I nodded.

"Pray, Nick, who may it be?"

"Cato Prince?" offered I.

"A possibility." Sighing, he set the mask aside. "Let us make what sense we can of what we know. Roddy Fairbrass was downcast, that is certain, no matter that his wife denies it. Why? His business was going well. Ill health? Yet, though he looked unhappy, he had good color and a sturdy stride. His wife says he had palpitations of the heart, but he saw no doctor. Some distrust of doctors, she says, yet his children know nothing of that. Nor do they know aught of these palpitations. He kept 'em a secret, then, from all save his wife? May be—but may be, too, that he had no palpitations. A convenient invention of Hannah Fairbrass? To disguise what?" His fingers drummed his chair. "A handsome woman, is she not, Nicolas? And admirable. Such fortitude! Yet she is frightened. And she lies, Nick, I am sure of't. Lying rides upon debt's back."

"Debt?"

"The Hazard. James Fairbrass visited there. His father too. As for damned Caddy Bracegirdle, I believe he ferreted his way into the gullible James's graces, lured him to the Hazard as a harmless diversion of the city, which all young men must see, and there left him to sharpers who trimmed him well. Bracegirdle has no family money; he is a Puff, the sort named by Mr. Principal Justice Fielding, given coin to lead fools to play. The father went there too. To game? Yet, why? The fever may run in the family. Cassandra Fairbrass spoke of some such penchant in her uncle. And, I have heard, Roddy Fairbrass was known for reckless moves in his rise. Both brothers, then, were given to cast their lot with chance. As for young James, can we deny he knows little of snares? The rattle of the dice box sings sweet music to many ears."

"How does this explain Mr. Fairbrass's murder?"

"It does not, though it takes us along. What more? Roddy

159

changed all his money to gems. Where are they now? I pray in Mrs. Fairbrass's hands, for if they are not, her family faces hard times. Yet I fear she may not have 'em."

"Why?"

"Because of the rumor the coachman carried, of difficulties with money. How soon will it be before she and her children are turned out, like many others before 'em, due to gaming?"

Coals sank upon the grate. "Gaming, then, is at the heart of the matter?" asked I.

"Near—though Quimp may be the very center, damn him. If so, I am determined he shall not triumph! Am I too late? Does he already possess the emeralds, won by cheating? Yet if so, why does that coach follow us? And why did mummers burst in, to search my chamber?"

This talk gave me chill. "If some villain seeks after the gems, why poison Mr. Fairbrass, who may be the only man who knew where they were?"

"Aye, why indeed?"

I took a breath. "And, sir, the ghost . . . ?"

The coals now gave but feeble warmth. Mr. Franklin pulled somberly at his lip. "Aye, the ghost. O, 'tis a deep mystery." Yet though the coals died, a steady light glowed in the gentleman's eyes as he turned over in his mind the nut whose husk he wished to crack. "There is more," said he. "The brother in the West Indies. And this Cato Prince and his flood of tears." Abruptly he rose. "To bed." He patted my shoulder. "Sleep well, Nick, for we must rise early for our journey to Upton."

Mr. Franklin had spoke true when he said we should be gone early, for by eight o'clock next morn we were passing London Bridge, heading east. The bridge was much changed from its state of but a year ago, which had been a wretched jumble of

160

shops upon one another's backs that made it creak and groan. These all had been torn down. I glanced back, west, to the hook of the river, but no small, black coach followed. Ahead I caught glimpse of the Tower. Mr. Franklin gazed across the grinding Thames. "Shall she freeze?" muttered he through the scarf that was wrapt to his nose. "O, she may, she may. . . ."

We were shortly past Whitechapel, upon Mile End Road. I had spent most of my life amongst a few dismal lanes in Moorfields and, this being my first time this way from London, I watched eagerly to see what the world beyond presented. How huge seemed the sky, spreading toward Colchester and Harwich to the sea, a vast, leaden dome! And how far wound the road toward distant low hills! It was rutted and would in rainy days have proved a vexing passage, but the tracks were filled with frozen mud; thus Peter was able to drive our coach smartly, the only danger being sliding, which he was skilled at avoiding. We passed many other conveyances: men on horseback; post chaises; city-bound stage-coaches, horses steaming; wagons laden with all manner of goods. Drovers, too, pressed pigs and geese to London markets. Our journey took two hours, past frost-rimed fields bounded by hedgerows. Sheep waded in snowdrifts. Huddled villages made Lilliputian contrast to the close-packed city we had left behind, tiny, composed of but one short street, half a dozen thatched roofs, and a stoic stone church rimmed by gravestones. Trees were dwarfed by land and sky, oaks black against the gray, and the little sticks of men laboring in fields seemed ants lost from their tribe, doomed, alone.

Yet Mr. Franklin took pleasure in all. "Winter's beauty is spare but beauty nonetheless," mused he, gazing out. "How Nature consoles a man, in all times o' year! Yet she is cruel too—damn frostbite." He rubbed his gloved hands. "What

161

think you: might not a coach be fitted out with a species of stove, to warm its passengers? I shall sketch out some such thing when we are back at Craven Street." He pulled the traveling rug tighter about his knees. "I too worship at necessity's shrine."

Upton was a small town of red brick and stone, with snowcapped rooftops. Rooks gazed down from elms like dour canons in their stalls. Dr. John Fothergill's house lay a quarter of a mile outside the town: no manse but a pleasant abode of time-mellowed plaster and sturdy beams, into which he welcomed Mr. Franklin and me warmly. Another man was present: Peter Collinson, the London mercer whose well-known shop lay by Westminster Bridge. Mr. Collinson was a friend of such powerful figures as Lord Bute and Lord Holland, and through them strove to help Mr. Franklin in Philadelphia's cause. Gray-wigged, he shook both the gentleman's hand and mine. Like Fothergill, he was a Quaker. He had visited Craven Street many times, but Mr. Franklin had first conversed with him by letter across the seas, when the newly established Philadelphia Library Company purchased books from him more than twenty years ago. They had since writ about scientific matters. All three gentlemen were Friends of the Royal Society and set at once, by the fire with noggins of a warming concoction, to discuss of various topics, from the motion of tides to the migration of birds. I loved listening. "By what mechanism do birds know to fly to warmer climes before winter comes on?" asked Fothergill.

"They must sense the change of seasons," said Collinson.

"Yet how?" interposed Mr. Franklin. "And more, by what means might one study of such a thing? There be a challenge to ingenuity."

A fourth gentlemen joined us, Mr. Hurly Eccles, a short, stout, busy-fingered man who arrived as snow began to fall.

162

He was a spice merchant but spent much time studying botany, Fothergill informed as he introduced him round. Mr. Eccles eagerly told that he had just come from America, where he had made drawings and gathered seeds which he hoped might take root on English soil. This gentleman completing our party, Dr. Fothergill took us out to his gardens, where were to be found many plants from round the world, some (which might endure the winter) outdoors, but a larger number kept in an ingenious many-windowed house that was warmed by continual coal fires whose temperature was carefully tended by servants who acted nursemaid to these plants. Here were palms and other such trees, the like of which I had not seen, and flowers called orchids which had been made to bloom in winter. Like Mr. Eccles, Fothergill and Collinson were both expert in botany, and when we were once more by the parlor fire Mr. Franklin drew forth from his waistcoat pocket the small glass vial which contained the remaining bit of Opliss-Popliss drops.

"What might this be?" inquired he, eyeglasses glinting.

All peered at what he held.

"'Tis blue water to my eye," pronounced Fothergill.

Collinson clucked his tongue. "If I know Ben, 'twill prove much more than that."

Mr. Franklin said neither aye nor nay but told the circumstances of its coming into his possession.

A stony silence followed. Fothergill shook his head. "Roddy Fairbrass, murdered? 'Tis hard to believe."

"You have heard the facts," said Mr. Franklin. "I have told you of the quick action of the liquid upon the rat. 'Twas no less quick when Roddy drank it." He handed the vial to Mr. Collinson. "From what flower or herb might this be derived?"

Collinson held up the vial. The liquid caught light as he swirled it before he turned to Fothergill, Fothergill to him, their grave, intelligent eyes exchanging thought. "From the blue color—and the deadly result of imbibing this," said Collinson with judiciously pursed lips, "—'tis likely the Malivel Plant, or Devil's Kiss, a native of America."

"Found in the West Indies?" asked Mr. Franklin.

"If I may," put in Mr. Eccles, his chair creaking as he leant forward, "—it is." All turned to him, at which his busy fingers laced and unlaced in his lap. "Indeed I have seen it grow, for the Indies were my last stop before I returned to these shores."

"A common plant?" asked Mr. Franklin.

"No, though persistence will discover it on the leaward side of some of the Antilles. In the smallest quantities an admixture of a distillation of its petals, which grow a vivid, ruffled violet, may quell palsy in men so afflicted, yet in larger quantities the stuff is swift and deadly poison. I agree it must be the Malivel."

"As do I," pronounced Dr. Fothergill. "The notable pale blue of the liquid, with—see it?—its faint tinct of purple, is said to be a mark of the poison."

Mr. Franklin's eyes glowed softly behind his spectacles. "And where might one obtain the stuff in London?"

"O, one may not, at present," said Fothergill. "'Tis new in our pharmacopeia and not yet to be found here, though it may be had in Paris, I have heard, where the demonstration of its efficacy 'gainst palsy was but recently made. I read of this last month."

Mr. Collinson returned the vial to Mr. Franklin who held it whilst the three remaining gentlemen sat in thought.

"Begging your pardon," put in Mr. Eccles with a frown as the fire sent up a shower of sparks, "the poisoned man's name, was . . . *Fairbrass?*"

164

His tone had a peculiar, troubled cast, which made Mr. Franklin peer sharply. "It was."

"By any chance related to Mr. Lemuel Fairbrass, who oversees sugar plantations in Jamaica?"

"His brother."

Eccles's frown deepened. "Roderick Fairbrass died o' Christmas day, you say?"

"He did."

"Hum . . . ah . . . then the paying of respects to his wife and children cannot be why Lemuel Fairbrass has come to England."

There was silence a moment. Mr. Franklin sat very still. "Lemuel Fairbrass is in England, you say?" asked he at last.

"I believe so, yet. . . ."

"You have some doubt? Come, Mr. Eccles."

Eccles squeezed the bridge of his nose. "You shall hear my story." He sat back. "I sailed on the *Hecuba*, on the third of September, from Port Royal, Jamaica, after gathering the last of my specimens. 'Twas not a passenger vessel but a sugar-laden ship, the Fairbrass's own, captained by one Jack Sparkum. Yet it allowed, as such ships do, some half dozen or so of passengers, I amongst 'em. The crossing was not easy, but Captain Sparkum, a dour, reticent fellow, knows his job and steered heavy seas well; I should wish to sail with him in any sort of storm. I became aware after some days of a small aft cabin always shut. A man lived within, ill we were informed, of some debilitating fever which seldom strikes the native but may lay the white man low. Doomed, he was said to be, and never showed his face. He was waited upon by a negro freedman, a tall, silent, watching young fellow, named Cato Prince. Some might call this blackamoor haughty, yet he was brave, for once in high seas he risked his life to save Miss Burford, a fellow passenger, from being snatched by a wave.

165

I believe this sick man, whose name was given out as Mr. Stiles, was really Lemuel Fairbrass."

"And how come you think this?"

"We had a doctor aboard, a German of Frankfurt, Herr Blick, who, as do I, took an interest in herbs. We formed a friendship. Herr Blick was kindly and offered many times to minister to the ailing Mr. Stiles but was always refused. Yet once, as he pressed Cato Prince on this head, the blackamoor let slip that Mr. Lemuel Fairbrass desired no help. At once the servant recovered himself—he meant Mr. Stiles, he said—yet so shaken was he by his error, as Herr Blick reported to me, that I believe it was Lemuel Fairbrass secreted in that cabin. It was, after all, the Fairbrass's ship on which he sailed."

"Yet why should he give out a false name?" put in Mr. Collinson.

"I do not know."

"Was the man truly ill?" asked Mr. Franklin.

Mr. Eccles's busy fingers wrestled in his lap. "I cannot say for certain—yet my one glimpse of him suggested he was."

"You saw him?"

A nod. "When we docked I hung back to see my notebooks and specimens unloaded with proper care. I saw the man taken off and put in a sedan chair. The curtain to this was quickly drawn, yet the fellow within looked truly wasted, though he walked from the ship with no aid from his blackamoor. You suggest he may've playacted his distemper?"

"There has been much playacting in this."

The men murmured over what this might mean but drew no certain conclusions. In these ruminations Mr. Franklin offered little, his features pale and still. At last the conversation moved on to other subjects, though its stop amongst a

166

dark grove where poison and murder lurked had stole all briskness from it.

Before we left Mr. Franklin took Fothergill aside. "May you test this, John, to discover what it may be?" He slipped into his friend's hand the stoppered bottle of sleeping draught which Cassandra Fairbrass had got of her father.

Fothergill's cool gray eyes regarded him. "More mystery, Ben?"

"Aplenty. Roddy's wife said he mistrusted doctors, yet he gave his daughter this when she said she saw a ghost. Did he obtain it of a doctor? I wish to know more of the stuff."

We departed near three. "So," sighed the gentleman as we passed snowy fields, "When the *Hecuba* docked Cato Prince came to Soho Square. But," he squinted at sparrows wheeling in the threatening sky, as if he took aim at 'em, "in what dark corner of London did Lemuel Fairbrass secret himself? Ah, Nick, what strange, new numbers are these, which we must add to our equation?"

🎔 12 🎔

IN WHICH I hear report of a night's work and we discover dismay in Soho Square. . . .

This day was December thirtieth, tomorrow being the eve of New Year. Returning at half past five, we found Mrs. Stevenson in a great bustle of baking and preparing tomorrow's supper. All such occasions gave her excuse to practice her arts. There came much rattling of pans from below, and her merry hum, and rich smells of a bubbling sauce. I helped her to trim three pies, she giving me leave to chew the pastry bits.

Mr. Franklin poked his head into the large, warm kitchen. "No red-haired Lord of Misrule has again broke in to set things topsy-turvy?" inquired he.

"No," said the housewife, drawing herself up and tapping the mole by her nose, "and if he should I would beat him with my broom!"

"See he do not beat you in turn. Take care, dear lady."

I set to my studies, which had been put aside for the day. As I went up I saw Mr. Franklin in quiet consultation with Peter by the front door, and shortly discovered that he was slipped out into the night, without a bite of food, which distressed Mrs. Stevenson, who fretted that the cold which

168

had plagued him in November—coughing and sneezing and lying abed of a fever—would besiege him once more. Also hoping this would not be, I worked by lamplight at Mr. Franklin's desk, as I had leave to do. Wind moaned about the eaves, the sound blending with King's sad crooning from the attic above, a song without words, which made me think of all which might go wrong with the world: homeless souls, dead mothers, murder.

Life was a peril.

William Franklin looked in at ten. Frowning to find me in place of his father, he strode out without a word. I struggled on. My lids grew heavy. The case clock struck eleven at the foot of the stairs, and, wondering where Mr. Franklin had gone, I went to my room to crawl between icy sheets.

Faint violin music woke me in muzzy dawn light, and, quickly dressing, I crossed the hallway to discover Mr. Franklin in his dressing gown playing a sprightly tune upon his fiddle. "Good morrow, Nick." Setting his fiddle aside, he proceeded, as he did his knee bends (up, down, huffing and puffing), to quiz me of mathematical matters, which had near daunted me last night. Yet I mustered right answers, and a pleased smiled grew upon his reddened face. "Excellent, Nick (puff)! Soon you shall be ready to peruse Mr. Isaac Newton's *Prinicpia* (puff). I do not say you will understand all (puff), but you may see the wonder of Nature's perfect balance—and of Mr. Newton's mind (puff, puff)." He began to dress. "Did you wonder where I had gone last night? To Deptford, to see Captain Sparkum. 'Twill not surprise you to learn that Mr. Eccles's news prompted me thither."

"You are convinced, then, that 'twas Lemuel Fairbrass aboard the *Hecuba*?"

The gentleman buttoned his waistcoat. "I am."

169

"But why should he travel in secret?"

"Ah!—if we but knew that we should know all. Damn me, what part does Sparkum play? He acts the role of family friend, yet he must have known the true name of the man in his aft cabin. Indeed he must have been in connivance with Lemuel Fairbrass, to keep his person concealed. Yet he denies all. I found him in a grog shop by the Deptford docks, a haven for seamen. He sat with his pint before him as if 'twere a book of law, with a look in his old seafarer's eyes as if he spied for rocks that might sink him. 'Nay, 'twas Mr. Stiles aboard,' asserted he with whitened knuckles on his knotted hands, and called Herr Doctor Blick and Hurley Eccles fools for what they told. 'Mr. Stiles had caught a disease of the tropics, which might be got by others; that was why he kept so to himself.' Might not the man, Cato Prince, catch this disease? asked I. Sparkum hemmed and hawed. 'Why, the negro race do not catch it,' grumbled he. Nor can pass it on to others? asked I. 'No.' asserted he. Why was Lemuel Fairbrass's man waiting upon Mr. Stiles? asked I. 'Mr. Stiles and Mr. Fairbrass were friends,' asserted he. 'As the man, Prince, was sailing to London, why should he not serve on the way?' And where is Stiles now? asked I. The sea dog sneered. 'I pay no mind to cargo once it leaves my ship.' I faced him square. Roddy Fairbrass was poisoned, has Mrs. Fairbrass told you so? At this Sparkum dashed his rum into the fire and thrust his face in mine. 'You, too, are a fool, Mr. Franklin. And a meddler. There wa'nt no poison, and there wa'nt no murder, and you had best leave off. Mrs. Fairbrass, bless her soul, has shed tears enough. She needs no one apokin' his nose into matters which had best be left be.' And with this the man scraped back his chair, gave me a look that might crack stone, and stalked out. Many unfriendly pairs of eyes followed as I too left (sailors stick together), and I was

170

glad to have Peter waiting with the coach just outside." Mr. Franklin slipped into his plain brown coat. "That was my evening, Nick. Write it in your journal, that you may reflect upon't. And now," he rubbed his hands, "to breakfast. The telling of this tale has given Benjamin Franklin an appetite."

Ten A.M. saw us once again on the road to Soho Square. There seemed some slight warming in the weather, and a small, rude stage had been built in Charing Cross. From our coach, over the heads of a murmuring, jostling crowd, Mr. Franklin and I watched *The Second Shepherd's Play*. It proved to be less about the Christ child's birth than a comic contrivance about a man who steals a sheep. To cover his crime, Mak, the thief, disguises the sheep as a baby and hides it in a cradle. When he is caught out, he is tossed in a blanket, at which the crowd laughed loud, I joining 'em. Mr. Franklin chuckled by my side, yet as we drove on his smile sank to quiet rumination. "Disguise," murmured he, plucking at his lip. "Disguise, so we know not who is whom. . . ."

Greek Street was packed with dirty snow. Ragged boys played Blindman's Buff in a mews. In Soho Square my gaze lifted to Josiah Skint's tall, narrow house. The curtain of the right-hand, second-story window was held back, showing that the old curmudgeon still kept vigil. I pitied Skint—what wasted life, spent spying out imagined sins.

Yet Mr. Skint had something to observe this morn, as did we, for when we were halfway across the square a figure came rapidly down the Fairbrass's steps toward a fine, sleek coach that waited in front. At first I thought 'twas a boy—yet it proved a man, tiny, one of the smallest I had seen, with a pinched, scowling face beneath a plumed, black hat. With his scuttling legs and black coat flying, he reminded me of nothing so much as a beetle. "Gideon Kite," breathed Mr.

171

Franklin. I caught my breath. The man's pale face bore an expression of fury; I should not wish those hate-filled eyes fixed upon me. He leapt into the coach, which at once set off, horses whinnying at the driver's lash—but not before I glimpsed a second man in its interior: Caddy Bracegirdle.

"See you?" said Mr. Franklin, gripping my wrist. He sank back. "One fact comes clear: Kite and Bracegirdle are in league. They can mean no good for the Fairbrasses."

Yet I was puzzled: some muffled shouts, an admonishing finger, and a cowed duck of Mr. Bracegirdle's head as they departed suggested that Gideon Kite chid him. For what? There was no time to think on this, for our coach at once took the place of theirs, we stepped briskly down, and Mr. Franklin rapped at the front door.

Inside, the maid, Mary, bore upstairs his wish to speak to Mrs. Fairbrass. As we waited I glanced into the large assembly room to the left, where the Christmas revels had took place and Roderick Fairbrass had lain cold in his bier. It was still hung with black, the curtains drawn, an air of desolate chill about it as if't might never know cheer again. I trembled. Had a ghost truly walked in this cursed house? Yet why had the thing showed the face of a man who was then living?

"She shall see you, sir," informed Mary after some moments, though some coolness in her manner said Hannah Fairbrass was not pleased with our intrusion.

A moment later the widow came down, presenting again her long, handsome face, tragic yet composed, the jaw large and firm, the blue eyes wary and alert, a pinched look at the corners of her mouth, her long fingers clasped by her waist. Mr. Franklin bowed his head. Wordlessly she led us to the side parlor, where the scarlet nightingales stirred on their perch. A fire was laid. Winter light seeped through the narrow

172

space between this house and Josiah Skint's not three feet away.

Mrs. Fairbrass settled stiffly on the sofa. "You are back, Mr. Franklin," pronounced she warily.

"To bring you news, ma'am, which I hope will not disconcert you. But perhaps you know: your brother-in-law, Lemuel Fairbrass, is in London and has been since early December. He sailed on the *Hecuba*, with your manservant, Cato Prince."

Mrs. Fairbrass's hands lifted and fell in her lap, though her expression remained immobile. "That is impossible," asserted she.

"I believe 'tis true." Mr. Franklin told why.

Mrs. Fairbrass's eyes grew round with contempt. "You credit the hearsay tale of this Mr. Eccles, got of some German doctor?"

"Not entirely hearsay. Mr. Eccles saw the sick man on the docks as he left the *Hecuba*. He had met your brother-in-law during a previous stay in Kingston, in connection with his spice importing ventures. This meeting was brief, but Mr. Eccles is a practiced observer; he remembers faces. The man who called himself Mr. Stiles looked ill, but he was clearly Lemuel Fairbrass."

Mrs. Fairbrass shook her head. "There is some mistake, I say. My brother-in-law is in Jamaica. I have just had a letter of him."

"If you please, one may write at any time. One may have a letter posted too."

"You suggest some trick on Lemuel's part?"

"How else explain the deception aboard the *Hecuba*?"

"There was no such deception, I tell you. Mr. Eccles was mistaken. I am sorry, Mr. Franklin, that you believe such tales."

173

"I listen. I draw conclusion. Wrongly? Forgive me if my speculations are not to your liking. I have no wish to urge my belief upon you, yet murder has occurred, though you deny it. I wish to discover who did the deed and why. If reported rightly, this strange appearance of your brother-in-law upon these shores stands very near the mystery. Tell me, were your husband and his brother such good friends? All differences, which you said caused friction between 'em when they were young, truly put by?"

Mrs. Fairbrass abruptly rose and paced from window to hearth. "I do not like these questions, Mr. Franklin! You try my hospitality. You call me liar."

"A mistaken belief is no lie. Perhaps 'tis I who am mistook." The gentleman stood humbly with his beaver hat in hands. "May I inquire, then, of Cato Prince? Your husband took him on willingly? There was no insistence from Lemuel?"

"We were happy to have the servant. Are still. He is thoroughly loyal."

"Loyal to whom?" murmured Mr. Franklin, as if to himself. "There is some rumor about, that your husband withdrew all his money from his bank shortly before Christmas. I hope and pray that money is safe?"

At this Mrs. Fairbrass's stern look faltered. Her hands fluttered. She turned to the window, turned back, walked to the sofa, sank down. "The money. . . ." A transformation took place: she gazed up with lost, desperate eyes, as if she had no strength to fight more, and we saw her as she truly was, vulnerable, with no husband to aid or protect her. She spoke in a revery, as if to herself: "So, people talk of the missing money . . . but of course they do . . . such things get about. Indeed, he did take it from Nash's, so Mr. Trustwood informed me when I told him three days ago that

174

I needed funds for household expenses. 'But your husband has withdrawn it all,' said he, 'did you not know?'" The woman smoothed her dress, over and over, in a pathetic gesture. "No, I did not know—and know not now where the money may be. And the creditors! Hearing of Roddy's death, they swooped down with their dunning demands. Even this house is in jeopardy, for the yearly rent is past due. I believed Roddy had paid it, but he had not, and Mr. Blackwood, the agent, says we must give it at once or remove within days."

"Dear lady!" exclaimed Mr. Franklin.

"What shall I do?"

"Your creditors will not let be for a time?"

"If my husband were alive, surely, for he was always trusted. But his death . . . the disappearance of all we have put by. . . ."

"And what amount, pray, might satisfy these creditors?"

The sum which she named, near three thousand pounds, lay far beyond even Mr. Franklin's means, and he fell silent and chafed his jaw, whilst Mrs. Fairbrass sat sunk in helplessness.

"I know what your husband did with the money from Nash's," said the gentleman at last.

She peered in startlement. "You know?"

He described our visit to Joseph de Medina.

She flared. "You have been investigating my husband's affairs?" But this anger quickly died. "Yet this resolves nothing," said she in a lost way. "Emeralds? Why should he purchase emeralds?"

"He did not speak of 'em to you?"

"He rarely spoke of business."

"You believe, then, this was some business?"

"I do not know. O, Roddy!"—this a quaking cry, which stabbed my heart.

175

"Your husband kept a strongbox?" asked Mr. Franklin.

"Why . . . yes."

"Have you searched there?"

"No."

"Pray, why?"

"I did not think to. Indeed I near forgot he had one, for he was not used to putting aught of value in't. Besides, 'twas ever locked."

"The keys?"

"To my knowledge there was but one. I do not know where it might be."

"Yet such a thing may be opened by force. Do it now, dear lady; relieve your mind. Your coachman will have a crow and mallet. If they do not suffice, a blacksmith may break the lock."

A feverish hope lit the woman's features. "You are right. The gems will be within, will they not? That is where Roddy placed 'em? Mary!" The maid came in. "Instruct Cato Prince to fetch my husband's strongbox from my chamber, at once. He will find it under the bed." Five minutes later the young blackamoor stood amongst us in his livery, carrying a sturdy metal box some eight or ten inches high and a foot square. His expression was brooding and as mistrustfully watchful as ever. "Shall we go below, to the coachman?" inquired Mrs. Fairbrass eagerly.

"Not at once." Mr. Franklin faced the blackamoor. "Place the box on the floor. I may be able to have some effect."

Indeed I believed Mr. Franklin might, for in the Ebeneezer Inch affair I had watched him force a door with the skill of any picklock. Cato Prince set down the box, and Mr. Franklin knelt with a soft creak of bones. I was amazed to see him lift the lid at once.

"What . . . ?" exclaimed Mrs. Fairbrass.

176

"'Twas not locked," murmured the gentleman, his bald brow creased as he peered within, as did we all—but nothing showed; the box was empty.

Mrs. Fairbrass moaned.

Mr. Franklin's eyes lifted. "Have you tried to open this, ma'am, since your husband died?"

"No," said she, her hands to her mouth. "'Twas always locked. I believed it was so still."

Mr. Franklin sniffed in displeasure. "No way, then, to say when 'twas last opened. Or who opened it." He examined the lock. "It has clearly not been forced. Damn me, who has the key? And your husband's diary—he kept it within, your daughter said. Do you know where it has gone?"

"No."

He stood. "Gideon Kite paid you a visit not half an hour past. For what purpose?"

Mrs. Fairbrass blinked. "Why . . . to say he was sorry for my husband's death."

"Truly? He is tardy, then. He wished no more?"

The familiar belligerence masked Hannah Fairbrass's eyes. "I have said why he was here," asserted she.

"So you have." Mr. Franklin made a gracious bow. "I thank you for your forebearance. I am sorry the emeralds are not in the box; they may yet be found. Think where else your husband may've secreted such things. Surely he would wish you to have 'em." With an under-the-brow glance at Cato Prince, who stood fiercely still, like a carved idol guarding some treasure, Mr. Franklin stepped to the door. "Come, Nick." I followed him into the corridor, where he muttered to himself as we made to depart. Mary brought our coats—yet we did not leave at once, for just then James Fairbrass came in from the cold, rubbing his hands and blowing frosty breath, his long face gaunt and old-looking for one so young. He started as he saw us.

Mr. Franklin fixed a magistrate's gaze upon him. "I must speak to you, sir. At once." His manner brooked no refusal.

James Fairbrass removed his greatcoat. Beneath, he wore what seemed the same black coat and breeches and somber gray waistcoat and stockings in which we had seen him four days ago. He struggled under Mr. Franklin's fixed gaze but found no courage to gainsay him. Uneasily he led us to the small room to the left, where we had spoke to him before. Mr. Franklin firmly shut the door. There was an agitation in the son's manner and a furtive darting of his anguished blue eyes, which stayed downcast and wavered from side to side, but Mr. Franklin was firm: he sat him down and plumped himself upon the spindle-legged chair before him, quite near, with his hands upon his bamboo as if 'twere a watchman's cudgel. "Now, sir," said he, "'tis time for truth, which serves an innocent man well. Are you innocent?"

"Of what?"

"Why, of your father's murder."

The young man blanched. "I would do nothing to harm father!"

Mr. Franklin peered hard. "Well, and I believe you." (Did he truly?) "Yet though your father is dead and there is no bringing him back, he may be helped still, by the discovery and prosecution of his murderer. This I mean to do. Tell of gambling at the Hazard."

James Fairbrass's Adam's apple bobbed. "But how may that bear upon—?"

Mr. Franklin thumped his stick. "Tell of it, sir!"

Anguish pinched the flesh about the young man's eyes. "I am so ashamed!" cried he. "I say I would do nothing to harm

178

father, yet I did him great harm, by my foolishness about business, for which I had no brain, so that when he would have me take some hand I spoilt all I touched; and my foolishness in going about with Caddy Bracegirdle. Why did I persist? Both mother and father warned me against him. Even my sister, who knows no more of the world than the faeries and spirits which she imagines, saw he led me a dance. But I . . . I believed he was my friend who only wished to introduce me to the pleasures all young fellows must know."

"Fools first, wise men after."

"How true." James Fairbrass drew back his shoulders. "Well, I wish to be a fool no more. I shall tell all, though I blush to do't. 'Twas Caddy Bracegirdle introduced me to the Hazard, to the dice cup, the billiard table, the shuffling and playing of cards. His manner was so smiling-brave, so easy at winning, so easy at losing; he was a very soldier at the tables, with his white teeth gleaming in that pocked, leering face. O, I thought him one to emulate! Too, what did some few guineas loss matter? Did I not find fortune there at first?— 'twas easy to win. And how solicitous were Gideon Kite and his crew, with a glass of spirits ever at my elbow and, when I lost more than I won, an oily willingness to take my name upon a paper promising I should pay. Was I not the son of Roderick Fairbrass, the merchant, who could make good any debts? I signed readily, believing I should never have to apply to father, for though I sometimes lost—indeed lost more and more frequently—I should win again; I had only to continue to play for the scales to tip in my favor, and then I should be free of debt. Yet I began to be uneasy. The click of dice rattled in my dreams; cards whispered there too, calling me to the tables. Secretly I vowed that when I earned back all losses I should cease playing. Alas, I never won back what I had lost, and fell deeper in debt, an ever larger stack of those damned

179

papers multiplying in Gideon Kite's locked desk while, ever smiling, he remained willing to add more to 'em as if they were mere air, nothing to him. So I sweated and twisted in my coils and threw more coins upon the green baize cloth to watch it swept away by other men. Yet I loved playing ('tis a madness, Mr. Franklin!), signing ever more of the promising notes—'til one day they came due, and Mr. Kite, with a wry twist to his painted lips, said he was very sorry but he must have his money, and would I obtain it for him at once? I was struck cold with fear. Pray, not at once, replied I. O, at once, said he. I trembled. May you not wait a little longer? said I. Impossible, said he. But I have not the money, said I. Those red lips pursed. Then I must prosecute you for't under the law, said he—a pity, for t'would be a great scandal to your father, who would not wish his name connected with default on debt, even his son's, which might cause some loss of faith amongst his creditors. May you not obtain the money of him, to prevent such a thing? Surely you come here with his knowledge? Surely he will back you?—this all put in an insidious way, with the adjuration that the thing must be settled by midnight of that day or proceedings would be begun at once. Kite even had his lawyer present, Mr. Jolley, a gross, fat man, who rubbed his hands and laughed and said in a rich, pleased voice, as if I were a capon ready for carving upon his table, that he loved to bring such cases to court for they were simple and always went his way, there being no doubt due to the signatures which men made of their free will, all well-witnessed. Free will, Mr. Franklin! At this Kite waved under my nose those many pieces of paper, amounting to five thousand and some pounds. I could hardly speak. So much? Aye, said the villain, and showed me my name and the amounts, which I could not deny."

"On what day did all become due?"

180

"On the twelfth of June, this year. I shall never forget that terrible date."

"Six months ago," mused Mr. Franklin. "You spoke to your father?"

"What else for it? I gathered courage, I faced him. He took it ill, as I knew he would, with great anger, asking if I knew how long he must labor to earn five thousand pounds, which I flung away at dice and cards. Did I not know they cheated at the Hazard? Did I not know that setting my foot in the doors of such a den was willfully walking into a snare? Yet he was not as angry as he might have been. He spoke of a time when he too had drunk much gin and lost at cards. There was a dismal darkening on his face, a gazing away, a remembering, which made me recall talk when I was young of father's drinking and gambling, and anger in our house, and mother's words: ''Tis the family curse!' Indeed my uncle Lemuel was given to gambling too, though both he and father conquered the disease long ago, I am told. Yet now I have inherited it from 'em."

"Which you may conquer too."

"I swear I shall, in my father's name!"

"A first step is to eschew Caddy Bracegirdle."

"I do that, from today."

"See you stick to your resolve. But what occurred after you told of your losses? Your father paid your debt?"

"I do not know. He swore not to pay it. I had been cheated, said he; that was the way of the Hazard. He would face up to Gideon Kite and force him to return the papers I had signed or he should have him before the law. Indeed he spoke of Kite as if he knew him."

Mr. Franklin rubbed the head of his stick. "Knew Kite?"

"So it seemed, but when or where I do not know."

"What then?"

181

"In a great rage father set out at once for the Hazard and was gone many hours. When he returned he was red of face and stomped upstairs, and I heard him moving about in his room, swearing. There was some blearing to his eyes and a weaving in his walk that said he may've tippled."

Mr. Franklin looked grave. "Gin clouds the judgment; it makes a man foolish-brave. Go on."

"Father went to the Hazard some few other times. He would not speak to me of what passed there but made me promise I should never more set foot in its doors, which I was happy to do in my gratitude to have him save me."

"Yet the debt—what of that?"

"Settled. It must have been, for I heard nothing from Gideon Kite or his lawyer. Either it was paid or father forced the papers from Kite's hands."

"Yet 'tis from that time that your father's downcast state began. Have you not thought on this?"

James Fairbrass hung his head. "I have, though I did not like to. I wished to believe my gaming had no part of it."

"Yet I fear it may. Learn your lesson." Mr. Franklin rose with a sigh. "Well, well . . . I must see what to make of this." He turned at the door. "Did you know that Gideon Kite was here an hour ago?"

James Fairbrass stared up. "Why?"

"To see your mother. To express regrets at your father's passing, she says."

"But he was here yesterday too."

"And spoke to her? In your hearing?"

"Behind closed doors. I heard raised voices and made to rush in, but Cato Prince was there before me, as if he waited. He burst in; the look he fixed upon Kite was terrible. Indeed the dwarf was wise to leave at once, to save being thrown down the stairs—though his loathsome expression said he

182

would not forgive such treatment. He hardly glanced at me."

"Because you are no longer a player in this game," murmured Mr. Franklin. He beckoned me to follow. "Take care of your mother, Mr. Fairbrass. Stay near home. Watch for Gideon Kite. Should he come, deny him entrance, no matter his threats. Cato Prince may help you in this; he is your ally. One last matter: you stood near your father when he was poisoned o' Christmas day; how came the sprig of rosemary upon his chest?"

"Rosemary?" The young man's gaze was all bewilderment. "I know nothing of rosemary."

"Nothing at all?" As Mr. Franklin shut the door behind us an unsettling scene greeted our eyes. From the entryway I glanced again into the dim-lit assembly room. Cassandra Fairbrass stood in its center, humming, plucking at her runic stone like Ophelia in madness, seeming to see or hear nothing in this world. Near her her small brother, Tim, knelt on the carpet, his lead soldiers ranged for war. Moving them about, he made soft sounds of gunfire, while his sweet, strange smile played about his lips. Next him stood his seven-year-old sister, Emily, cooing to her big doll. Their blended voices made a strange, sad harmony, which gave me a chill.

I turned to find Cato Prince gazing hostilely upon us.

Mr. Franklin smiled into his face. "So, 'twas Mr. Stiles you tended aboard the *Hecuba*, was't? Nay, 'twas Lemuel Fairbrass, and I shall have the truth of you. Come, sir, deliver."

No answer came. The young blackamoor clenched his fists. His guarded yellowish eyes flashed out that he should like to throttle Mr. Franklin, but he only turned and strode from the hall.

"Indeed. . . ." murmured Mr. Franklin.

I was glad to climb into our coach, pull up the travelling rug, and be gone.

The gentleman sat some moments deep in thought. "So," said he at last, "money was lost at the Hazard. By father as well as son? Well, I shall know—and know tonight, from Gideon Kite himself." A smile broke out. "Yet as prelude to this venture, I shall partake of Mrs. Stevenson's grand New Year's supper. Shall not we both partake of it, Nick, with a great, happy smacking of lips? I dearly love her puddings and pies."

❧ 13 ❧

IN WHICH the new year brings bloody blows and I hear more of red hair. . . .

I awoke with a start, to gray dawn light. 'Twas New Year's Day, 1758, yet it was the last hours of 1757 which I thought on: Mr. Franklin's second visit to the Hazard. He had departed after Mrs. Stevenson's good supper of roast goose and mince pies and cheerful toasts. "To the old friend, farewell!" we had cried at table—Mr. Franklin and his landlady and Polly and William, and I, and Peter and King too. Upholding his glass Mr. Franklin had proclaimed he should cherish 1757, for it had introduced him to the ministrations of the best landlady in London. Mrs. Stevenson flushed red. "By'r leave," put in I humbly, "I am grateful too, for 1757 delivered me from evil into good." Polly stroked my hair, and all toasted this, even William, whilst Mr. Franklin's soft brown gaze said that, though he did not openly acknowledge me his son, I should always be so in his heart.

Tears filled my eyes to think on this that frigid morn.

Yet these soon ceased. I was eager to learn what Mr. Franklin should tell of his evening, and so dressed quickly. Surely he was up, for he was always up betimes, it being a maxim of his (and of Poor Richard) that rising early profited a

185

man. Shivering, I crossed the hallway, thinking as I did so of the note which had come from Dr. Fothergill last night, just before Mr. Franklin set out: a report on the sleeping draught, which the gentleman had left him. Mr. Eccles had again been of value, for Dr. Fothergill's houseguest had been able to say with certainty, following a number of tests which both gentlemen carried out, that it too was derived of a plant which might be found in the West Indies, though this plant, the Sawyer's berry, grew in many climes, being very hearty and adaptable. ". . . an infusion of the leaves, dried, produces a great drowsiness, followed by deep, fast sleep," Mr. Franklin read, his spectacles glinting as his eyes lifted to mine. "Was Roderick Fairbrass, then, his own apothecary? How good of him to wish to spare his daughter the trouble of her ghost. Or was't he himself he spared? We must discover this, Nick."

I rapped softly on Mr. Franklin's door. I had struggled to stay awake last night, but when midnight struck and huzzahs rang out over London, first footers stepping in ev'rywhere, the gentleman still was not returned, so I had gone reluctantly to bed. There was no answer, no sound of the violin. Rapping louder, I received still no reply. Had the gentleman not returned? Did he sleep deeply? I hung fire for long moments, but at last the cold—and curiosity—made me bold, and I turned the latch, which proved unlocked. If I disturbed Mr. Franklin at his sleep I should softly withdraw. Creeping in, I found his chamber as chill as the hall outside, no fire in the grate, the curtains drawn when I was used to find 'em flung wide and a shutter open for his air bath. Yet the gentleman was here, for I made out his form under covers in the featherbed. Chiding myself for my rudeness, I was about to withdraw when I heard an alarming soft moan.

Stepping rapidly to the bed, I pulled back the comforter. Mr. Franklin's balding head lay upon his pillow. His eyelids fluttered. Seeing me, he raised a wavering hand in the dim light, though he seemed unable to speak. I gasped. A great cut and swelling bruise marked his left temple; there was blood about his nose and lips.

"Mrs. Stevenson!" cried I, rushing from the room. Shortly she was with him, a lamp and basin of warm water at her side, I standing nearby with Polly and William, wringing my hands. As the landlady washed away blood, she tutted and ralleyed the gentleman for not calling for help sooner, though she cast black looks over her shoulder that said she prayed his injuries were not grave.

I too prayed: spare my father!

I sat long by Mr. Franklin. Others, looking in often, went about their chores, but I remained rooted as he slept, gazing at the pale brow and brown hair limp around it. So kind a man! So wise! William had wished to call a doctor, but Mr. Franklin had said no, 'twas his dignity which was most injured, and there was no physic save humility for that. All protested, but he would not be gainsaid.

And so I waited. Mrs. Stevenson poked in her head and said, "Dear, dear," and Polly came and stroked his brow, and William gruffly adjured me to inform Mrs. Stevenson should any downturn show, for he must be off to lectures at the Inner Temple.

At ten the gentleman's eyelids fluttered. "Yes, sir?" said I, bending near. Stirring in fitful wakening, he roused himself and struggled to sit against two fat pillows, which I set behind him. A poultice of Mrs. Stevenson's was bandaged to his cut. Winking feebly, he touched the white swath about his head. "Do I not look a very Turk or Pasha?" He chuckled, at which I was heartened. He asked for *Shakespeare*, which I brought, but he let the heavy volume lie closed upon his lap. There

187

followed an increasing agitation—a muttering and fiddling of fingers and kicking of feet beneath the bedclothes. Abruptly he flung back the covers. "Pah, I cannot bear such confinement!" He lowered his voice. "Pray you, Nick, see the door is locked, for I would not have our good housewife discover my transgression. She would surely bind me to my prison bed. Never underestimate the tyranny of housewives! There," with the aid of his bamboo and my shoulder he groaned to his chair by the fire and sank down, "—better by far."

I noted that the tip of his bamboo was splintered.

His shrewd eyes observed my discovery. "Aye, Nick, more than Ben Franklin has suffered injury. Faithful stick! There is a story to tell. Shall you hear it? Shall you write it down? Is your pencil shaved sharp?"

At once I took up the book of blank pages which had been got of Mr. Tisdale. Mr. Franklin had spoke (with some vagueness) of being attacked by a gang of cutpurses in the Haymarket, yet I had all along suspected this was not whole truth. "I am ready, sir," said I.

"As ever. Then here is my tale. . . ."

. . . 'Twas this way, Nick: bitter cold, no stars in a black sky, and New Year's eve as well, which men might better wish to spend amongst family and friends, yet light spilled from the windows of the Hazard when Peter delivered me to Bury Street; and there pulsed a great heat within, of fires warming the rooms but of gaming too, by men aflame, who seemed not to know what day it was—indeed whether 'twas day or night—but only that the dice cup went round with their fortunes inside or that cards fanned about the tables ferrying hope or ruin. Aye, some men laugh there, but 'tis cruel laughter, or bitter, or a nickering to mask desperation. 'Tis a sad place, a hell, and Gideon Kite is its satan, lurking everywhere, scuttling, peering, smiling out of his hard, marble face which might be some old Roman head, chiseled in a leer of spite. I understand well why James Fairbrass's knees shook when Kite announced he must pay his debts.

Yet there is worse than Kite, as you shall hear.

But it was Kite I sought out after some survey of the rooms, which put my heart down. The young man whom I spared was there again, the fever heating his brow, the fear in his eyes. As I stood at his very shoulder he lost once more at ombre and cried out, but I could not stay to save him. Caddy Bracegirdle was there too, leading about a well-dressed young fellow as callow of face as James Fairbrass. A new lamb for slaughter? Bracegirdle showed this man the faro tables, yet he himself appeared diminished, a captain sent down to footsoldier. Indeed as I approached the master of the den, the little man fixed upon Bracegirdle a withering look that warned he must mind his step or find himself in the street. How has he displeased Kite? Somewhat to do with Soho Square?

Yet I had no time to think on this, for at that moment the painted dwarf spied my approach. "Mr. Franklin," greeted he in his soft, insinuating voice.

"You remember well."

Kite's white lace handkerchief dabbed his reddened lips. "I remember all who set foot in my house. You are come to dice? To play at cards?"

"I am come to speak to you. You desire, do you not, to obtain the thirty thousand pounds which Roderick Fairbrass lost at your tables?"

Kite wore a curled gray wig. His smile hardly altered, but his little eyes in his whited face, examined me with composed yet vicious speculation. His laugh was a high-pitched bark. "You are more than you seem, Mr. Franklin. I thought so, when first you came. This is not a man like other men, said I.

189

I judge of men well; you are no gamester—yet you play a game." He peered up. "What may it be?"

"Let us speak in private."

"Then in my chamber."

Whispering words to his brutish minion, Bumpp, he led me with his mincing walk to wide stairs, which we climbed to a hallway. From this we entered a long, thickly carpeted room. I was surprised still to hear sounds of gaming—until I discovered that there were narrow windows in one wall at the height of the little man's eyes. Through them I glimpsed by means of cunningly arrayed mirrors the floor below: dice tables and card tables, men in the fever of play. I turned to Kite. "You watch from your heaven, like a god," said I.

"Tut, no god, but a warder, who keeps close watch over his precincts."

"Which you police well."

"Mine is an orderly house. I want no trouble with the likes of John Fielding." He dabbed his lips. "Do you know the man?"

"We have met."

"Zealous, officious, troublesome!"

"He wishes to keep the same order in London streets as you do in the Hazard."

"I do not like his means."

"They are honest."

Kite's face twisted. "Perhaps that is why I do not like 'em."

"You are frank."

He came near. "Be frank with me, then. Come, why are you here?"

"As I told, to help obtain what is due you. Thirty thousand pounds, do I hit the mark?"

The little man's powdered face and red lips made him look

190

a bizarrely painted doll. "Nearer thirty-two thousand," said he after some rumination.

"Of which five thousand is money the son had lost."

A sly smile. "Have you been at my books?"

"Not all is writ in books."

"Yet debt is. How I hate the unfilled spaces which say owing, owing, owing." He crushed his little hands together. "I always fill those spaces, Mr. Franklin—one way or another." He face screwed itself up. "You may help me to obtain this money, you say? Why?"

"So that I may have some of't," lied I.

He gave his barking laugh. "And why should I give it you?"

"Because a share of something is greater than the whole of nothing, and nothing is what you have got now. Roderick Fairbrass withdrew all he could from Nash's Bank. It has vanished, as his widow told you. You apply to her often. You were there o' Wednesday; I saw you depart as I drove up yesterday. Well, prying and threats will avail you nothing. The money is not in her husband's strongbox; I myself saw it empty. Too, I observed Mrs. Fairbrass's dismay, which was real. Yet the money has gone somewhere. You may prosecute a man for debt, but there is no profit in prosecuting a dead man, and you would waste time in prosecuting his destitute widow or son—what profit in that when they do not own the house they live in or the ship that carried Fairbrass's goods? You are left with empty hands. But you may make use of a clever man. Tell all you know, and I promise that in the same wise that I learnt of Roderick Fairbrass's debt I shall discover where his money has gone. Then you may have what you deserve."

"And you may claim your share?"

"Only fools labor for love of't."

"And what part would you require?"

191

"I am not greedy. Twenty percent."

"Twenty . . . !" Kite dabbed his lips hard, yet a smile slowly grew, as if he found a man after his temper. "Very well, I consent—providing you deliver what you promise. Eighty percent will suffice me." He perched in a soft chair, his little feet dangling in the black buckled shoes. "Ask your questions, Mr. Franklin."

I sat in a chair opposite, the rattle of the dice cup rising from below. "Caddy Bracegirdle brought James Fairbrass to you?"

"O, brought. They happened round one evening, that is all."

"Bracegirdle is not in your employ?"

"As to that—" The little man fluttered his hand.

I let be. "Some few weeks thereafter young Fairbrass had signed notes amounting to five thousand pounds."

"The poor fellow lost. He must then pay."

"Yet he did not. He informed his father of his debt, and the father came round."

"Aye, in near apoplexy. He accused me of cheating his son; he demanded the promissory notes. I am no gull, I would not relinquish 'em. But I am a reasonable man. I gave Roddy Fairbrass gin. After all, were we not old friends?"

"When? How?"

"Twenty years ago I kept a small gaming house in Gill Lane where young Roddy sometime played, before he made his success. His brother played there too. Lemuel. As alike as peas in a pod—though sometimes they fought. I was a good host, yet the brothers and I had a falling out. 'Twas not my doing. They said I cheated and, though they paid their debts—modest sums—both swore to leave off liquor and cards, which to my knowledge they did 'til some months ago."

"Six months, to be exact, when Roderick Fairbrass came to you."

"Did I not offer friendship to his anger? Fairness too, over some glasses of gin—how as of old his anger drove him to drink! I said if his eye was so sharp at spying a cheat why did he not play for himself? To show I meant well, I said that to stake him I should give back half the money his son had lost. At this he grumbled and rubbed his jaw and struggled to hang back. 'Twas in this very room, with the sound of play below. I saw the old hunger in his eyes—a fellow with gaming in his blood ne'er washes it out!—and at last he said damned if he wouldn't, to show me and win back all and more."

"And so he went to the tables."

"With eager speed."

"Primed by gin."

Kite shrugged. "He had drunk some few glasses."

"He lost."

"Fortune did not favor him." Kite said this with great sanctimony, as if 'twas a pity mankind was so led astray.

"He came again."

"Two or three times, 'til I had his name on notes for near six times what his son had owed. Poor man. Yet it must be. Those notes were due today, the thirty-first of December. I said I should accept papers signing over all assets of his business in lieu of 'em, but as you say the damned fellow has sold all to Nash's Bank and took his profit and died."

"The profit did not die with him."

"I want it, Mr. Franklin! I am owed." Kite's hands gripped his chair arms hard. "Damn Fairbrass's sniveling widow! If I believed she trifled with me I should see her in prison."

"Believe me, she truly does not know where her husband's money has gone. She and her family are this week to be turned out of their home."

193

"I care not."

"Yet there are small children."

Kite's face empurpled beneath his powder and rouge. "A gentleman's bond before children. Else how should the world get on?"

I contained my dismay. "You would have taken Fairbrass's business in lieu of money?"

"I would."

"But the managing of't—?"

"O, there are men for that," murmured Kite. "And so, Mr. Franklin, when may I expect the result of your labors?"

"I give no date. But soon." Yet so angry was I at Kite's willingness to add to a family's distress that I let slip a rash boast: "Had it been *I* in place of Roderick Fairbrass you should have been the loser that night."

At this the tiny man sat straighter, a fervent glittering in his eyes. "A gamester after all? You boast of your skill—ha, you must try your hand, sir! Come, join some three at a table, do." Leaping from his chair, he plucked at my sleeve, and there showed such eagerness in his urging that I saw he too had a fever, not to game but to watch others lose at it. I understood him then: Nature cheated him of a full measure of height; thus he covers himself in paint and foppish clothes, practices a mincing swagger, and dotes on other men's ruination. What danger in his mania.

Yet did I heed? I am ashamed to say I was piqued by his challenge. His look said I had not the courage to act as he urged. Too, I was angered by his callousness. And so, in a wish to prove he might not trick ev'ry man of his purse, I said, yes, I believed I might try me with some willing fellows.

Thus I showed myself a fool like other men.

We went down, and I sat me in a chair which came vacant by a glance of Gideon Kite's sharp eye. "Welcome, sir," said

194

the other gentlemen. One was a thin, sad-looking fellow in a rumpled wig; the second a great, thick log of a man with many rings on fat fingers that were ever paddling the table; the third a hatchet-faced fellow with hangman's eyes that seemed to measure my neck for a string. There were, too, the usual watchers, some half dozen or so, who hung over the table like vultures and sometimes bet amongst themselves as to the next card or outcome of the game or e'en whether at the next hand a player would cry off in a black rage.

"A game of some skill," demanded Kite. "Mr. Franklin boasts of his skill. Shall't be ombre?"

All consented, and the cards were shuffled and dealt round. I saw Kite's quick look at hatchet face, which showed 'twas this man who played for the house, to help fill Kite's books with money owed. Bumpp's dour countenance loomed as play began. Hatchet face was more skillful than the jolly sharper I had beat before; he bided his time, losing even when he might have won. He had long nails, with which he marked the cards, subtly, at their edges, and when he dealt 'em—so fast they whispered as they flew round—he did not always draw the top card, but sometimes the bottom. Too he hid cards about his person, which he slyly plucked from sleeve or waistcoat. O, he was clever, and I pitied the fat fellow and the thin one, for they had no chance against him. He manipulated all, and to begin I let him manipulate me, the betting amongst the men who stood round turning in his favor once he began to win, as if fortune took him under her wing. Mr. Winks was his name, yet the glassy eyes in that murderous face seemed never to close. He won many pounds of me, near two hundred. He rooked even more from the others, who bet capriciously. (If all men who come to the Hazard are as they, Kite may fleece 'em as he pleases.)

And all the while the painted dwarf stood across the table

195

dabbing his reddened lips and smiling at my losses though now and then clucking his tongue as if he thought 'twas pity I went down. "Tut, sir," mocked he, "your skill has deserted you."

"May be," said I, bravely setting out a great sum to challenge Mr. Winks, who glanced at Kite. Quivering with glee the little man gave a sly nod, at which Winks coolly matched my sum, and added twice as much to boot. I met his challenge. Near six hundred pounds lay upon the table.

With great modesty I showed three kings.

Winks stared. His Adam's apple bobbed. His fingers tightened on his cards. He coughed and made a small move, as to stifle this cough, at which my hand reached out and gripped his wrist. "If you please, sir, your cards first upon the table."

"Why . . . !" cried he but could not 'scape. I forced down his hand, which held but two knaves and a trey.

"I have beat you," said I, collecting my coin. I looked at Kite. "I do not think I shall play more tonight."

A flush of fury rose beneath the dwarf's powder. I made to rise but felt a hand upon my shoulder. "Pray, do not go." The hand was strong. I turned. A tall, masked man stood next me, in a red cloak, a red wig too. I could not guess how long he had watched. "Mr. Mimm," pronounced he, with a small bow, his voice cool and even, yet burred, making me think of nettles, which appear harmless yet sting. "And you are Benjamin Franklin, from America. Your reputation proceeds you. Men in some circles hate you; you are thoroughly despised by the Penns. Yet I pay no heed to this. 'Tis a man's gaming interests me, and you play well. To put down so sharp a man as Mr. Winks bespeaks skill. I too have some skill. May I not persuade you, Mr. Winks, to allow me to sit in your place?"

Winks scraped back at once, and slunk off, and Mimm settled

196

in the chair opposite me, folding long-fingered hands upon the green baize cloth. He had a large, beaklike nose. The full lips below his black mask smiled. "Will you play awhile, Mr. Franklin? I assure you, I will give you a brisker canter than Mr. Winks."

The fat man and thin man swallowed hard and looked as if they wished to flee, yet so ominously persuasive was Mr. Mimm's slow gaze round that they made no demur but remained as if nailed to their chairs. I glanced at Kite, whose smile was back. Looming above his head, Bumpp's squarish features glowered as if he longed for a neck to wring, and the circle of vultures flapped their coats and hummed: might a new carcass be flayed for their devouring?

"You do not grace our tables often, Mr. Mimm," said Kite.

Behind the slits in his mask Mimm kept his glittering eyes on me. "I wish to play cards with Mr. Franklin."

I shrugged, though I felt ill ease. "I may try me some few more hands," assented I, to take the measure of this strange new player.

And so Mimm cut the cards and shuffled and sent 'em round.

And we played, and I lost, and lost again. And yet again. And more.

And I could not see how Mimm did it, for there were no tricks of dealing, nor did he have cards hid about him. Yet he cheated, I knew. Gideon Kite now rocked, beaming, on his heels. The vultures murmured, more men joining 'em, crowding, leaning in, 'til the air grew hot and close. Bumpp grunted now and again. Fat man and thin man bet little but ever folded their cards with hardly a glance, so they became no more than spectators. Through his narrow eyeholes Mimm watched me and appeared to laugh, his mouth set in a sardonic twist. Pit yourself against me, Franklin, do you? he

197

seemed to say—and I came to wonder if 'twas really Mimm I
played or another, and I grew sick at heart, for I knew not how
to defeat him, either at cards or in the Fairbrass affair, where
he might pull secret strings. I glanced at Gideon Kite. He
smiled, but I saw deep in his eyes that he feared the man who
called himself Mimm; and I saw too that as Caddy Bracegirdle
was Gideon Kite's minion, Kite was Mimm's. Had the aim all
along been to scoop Roderick Fairbrass's successful business
into the expanding net of power of which John Fielding told
us?

Quimp!

Yet I could not be sure. The man's coat was the finest dark
blue cloth, white lace at his throat and wrists. His jaw was pale
and lean. Something in his left hand caught candlelight,
which now and again flickered in my eyes, like the electric
spark. 'Twas a large ring—yet why (for Mimm held his left
hand palm down as he dealt) did the underside of this ring
shine so brightly?

And then I knew: a mirror, small, implanted in the under
curve of the ring, so that as Mimm dealt the cards he could
read the face of each one, thus knowing what ev'ry man held.
I had heard of such rings, trickster's tools. It was why, when
I had the best cards, Mimm bet only if he was assured his
hand would beat mine.

I lost again.

"That is a handsome ring, sir," said I as the fat man dourly
dealt the cards. (I saw that even when another man dealt
Mimm might glimpse the faces of some cards by holding his
hand just so.)

"'Tis," agreed he brusquely.

"May I examine it?"

The eyes behind the mask narrowed. "A strange request."

"Come." I held out my hand. "I have a friend who is expert

198

in gems. Joseph de Medina, have you heard the name? I should like to report to him of this ring. Diamond, is't not?"

"Yes." Still smiling, Mimm twisted it from his finger and dropped it in my palm as if 'twere no more than a hazelnut.

I paid no mind to the mirror but peered in great mock admiration at the stone, a large, bluish diamond, which must be worth many hundred pound.

And then I dropt the ring on the parquet floor, and stamped my heel hard upon't. "Lord!" cried I as if 'twere accident, and bent and lifted the thing, now twisted metal, the mirror broke, though the diamond was hard and bright in its setting. Handing it back, I made profuse apology.

Mimm gazed at me, at the ring. He slipped the twisted metal in his waistcoat pocket. "Mischances occur, Mr. Franklin," said he with a new, warning edge to his voice, "in which things are crushed beneath heels. I shall require no recompense from you—not now."

"I await your demand. Meantime shall we play on?"

"I think not."

"Do you fear to lose?"

The vultures grew alert at this; I heard their lips smack, their indrawn breath, an eager shuffling of feet. Mimm's expression hardly changed, yet an inky look suffused those hooded eyes, skin tightened about his mobile mouth (it might, Nick, have been the mouth of an artist), and his elegant, thin fingers twitched upon the table. "I shall play some few more hands," pronounced he darkly.

And so we did, and 'twas I who cheated now, using all the subtle tricks I had learnt when a boy—none so crude as Mr. Winks's but secreter strategems, and Mimm began to lose and lose again and more, and I saw a fury about him. He forfeited his coolness; he became reckless in his desire to beat me, and was thus even more a mark for my tricks, which placed court cards in my hands whilst he had mere deuces and treys, sixes and eights.

The upshot? I won back from him all I had lost, and near two thousand pounds as well, all in bank notes and coin in a pile before me. Gideon Kite ground his teeth to see it. Bumpp looked like murder.

At last Mimm pushed back his chair and stood, his red cloak furling. "You have me this time, Mr. Franklin," said he, "but we shall play again, on other grounds. Watch for me."

"I shall," replied I, "keenly."

His red cloak danced as he strode from the room.

Bumpp vanished amongst the fevered throng. Gideon Kite saw me to the door.

"Who is this Mimm?" asked I, about to leave.

Kite's tongue flicked over his lips. "I know little of him. A gentleman of some stamp, whose caprice is always to wear a mask."

"Did he play cards with Roderick Fairbrass?"

"I believe so, and won a deal of him."

"Yet you know him not?"

"Tut, Mr. Franklin, it does not do to enquire too closely of certain fellows. Congratulations on besting Mimm. So skillful a player as you may easily discover where Roddy Fairbrass hid his money. Your coach is near? I bid you good eve."

Bury Street is a narrow lane; Peter waited with my coach in Great Jermyn Street some distance apart. My winnings in a thick pouch beneath my greatcoat, I descended six marble steps and turned in this direction on cold, snowy cobbles. Soon the spilling lights of the Hazard were left behind, and black night gathered round me, my footsteps echoing in a ghostly way. Icy mist hung in air. There arose about London New Year's cries, yet I greeted her alone. But was I alone? I began to hear other footsteps than my own. Muffled voices?

Walking close against damp brick walls, I gripped my bamboo hard, for well I knew that cutpurses and cutthroats lurk ev'rywhere, and a solitary man must see to himself.

They attacked then, Nick, from an areaway, swarming up like rats, three of 'em, muffled and masked. They thought to finish old Ben Franklin, but I laid about 'em with my bamboo, and in short order one lay moaning upon the cobbles leaving but two to circle warily. These snarled and attacked with cudgels. I struck one across the eyes, and he cried off, staggering away with shrieks. The third, however, was quick. The money pouch had fallen upon the ground. This he scooped up as he struck at me, landing a sharp blow to my brow, which stunned me. I fell, and he stood above me, cudgel raised to crush my head, but I thrust my bamboo hard into his gut, at which he too shrieked and stumbled and made off, hobbling, along the dark way.

I lay there 'til I might catch breath and assure myself no bones were broke. Damn me, would I had rounded 'em up, all three, to deliver 'em by their collars to good John Fielding! Rising in some dizziness, I found my way to my coach. Peter wished to seek for help, but I said, no, Craven Street would minister to me best. Was I not right? Has not Mrs. Stevenson patched me up well?

This, then, is the history of my night. I shall rest me now. Let us think on all it means. . . .

❧ 14 ❧

*IN WHICH we make pilgrimage to a
grave and learn more of a ghost. . . .*

After telling his tale of gaming and midnight peril
(which I thought on with a mixture of awe and
trembling), Mr. Franklin crept abed saying he would
read him some Shakespeare. But he fell promptly asleep and
remained so for two hours more that first day of January, 1758.
Upon waking he appeared renewed, and roused himself and
moved with no need of my aid, pacing up and down. In
despite of the injury to his head he was dressed by two o' the
afternoon and eager to set out. "We must pay respect, Nick,"
said he as I slipped into my long coat at his urging. "Peter!"
his voice rose up the attic stairs. "The coach."

Mrs. Stevenson made a great, fluttering protest at the front
door but was forced to content herself with seeing her favored
lodger's scarf wound thrice about his neck and his beaver hat
set just so over the white bandage. "O, sir, sir," scolded she.
She waggled her finger at me. "See to him, Nicolas; see the
gentleman returns betimes."

I had thought the weather might grow warmer, yet it
seemed more bitingly cold as we stepped down the steps of
Number 7, Craven Street. Icicles hung from ev'ry eave, the

cobbles were treacherous (I slipped, but Mr. Franklin caught me), and the sturdy mare that pulled our coach puffed frosty breath. I looked toward the Thames. The bobbing chunks of ice from its frozen upper reaches showed more numerous than ever, a rushing swarm, meaning some danger for lighters and wherries. Above it the sky was as gray as an archdeacon's eyes.

We headed northeast, by way of St. Martin's Lane and Longacre. With a surge of feeling, I guessed our destination. "You writ all I told you of my adventure, Nick?" asked Mr. Franklin as we reached West Smithfield.

"I did. Please, sir, do as the masked fellow bid you: keep a sharp eye."

"Never fear, I shall. As for the attack last night, 'twas Mr. Bumpp, of the Hazard, who near bludgeoned me in Bury Street, I am sure, tho' he was masked. Damn him for making off with my purse! And I have strong suspicion 'twas Caddy Bracegirdle whom I struck across the eyes. The third was no doubt also some sneaking confederate of Kite's."

"Yet you believe this Kite works for Mimm?"

"I do."

"And that Mimm is Quimp?"

His lips made a grim line. "I cannot say for sure. Yet what make you of this plot? Quimp seeks power by wrongful means; he works his will in many ways: by robbery, extortion, pandering, gaming—all such vices; this much we know. His net spreads, a web growing strand by strand. One aim of this net is to entrap victims. Quimp uses Gideon Kite's gaming house to ensnare worthy men who might be fleeced to clothe Quimp's greed. Roddy Fairbrass was drawn in through his son."

"Caddy Bracegirdle befriended James Fairbrass to get at his father?"

"Aye, to lure him to game, for which Kite knew he had a passion."

I took breath. "'Tis a wicked plan, sir."

"But clever, if I describe it aright. It worked ruinously well. Poor Roddy! And damn Quimp and Kite and all their kind. 'Twas Fairbrass's business rather than mere money they sought, for Quimp aims to build an empire."

"But they did not get his business. Or his money."

"At which they gnash their teeth. O, I am glad they are foiled. Yet where are the emeralds, which Fairbrass bought of Joseph de Medina? I have no intention that any part be shared with Kite."

Our coach moved steadily northeast. Three P.M. bells rang out. "Was Quimp, then, the red-haired Lord of Misrule who did such mischief at Mrs. Stevenson's when we were away?" asked I.

"Can it be any other?"

"But, why?"

"He knew Cassandra Fairbrass had applied to me (recall that watching, waiting coach). Further he knew I was a friend of Roddy Fairbrass's, who visited Craven Street the day before Christmas. And I was at Soho Square to witness his death. As you know, Quimp's path and mine have crossed before, to his detriment. Surely he would wonder if I had discovered something of Fairbrass's money? Quimp ransacked my rooms to see."

Passing through Moorgate, Peter headed into country ways. "Sir . . . I still do not understand why Mr. Fairbrass was murdered."

Mr. Franklin squeezed his brow. "The question pesters like a blowfly. We watch a play, Nick, as if performed upon a stage. We see the first act clear: the entrapping of Roddy Fairbrass. But the second act, his murder—dark night is

204

drawn over this, so we may view it but dimly, in shifting light, where a ghost walks, and a mysterious mumming Doctor creeps in to do his awful work before rushing into the wings. Next door Josiah Skint rails, while within the Fairbrass house Cassandra Fairbrass is sunk in superstition, the weak-willed son hides shame, and the widow gives out but half the truth. I tell you, half the truth is often a great lie."

"Would Quimp have poisoned Mr. Fairbrass?"

"Why should he murder the one man who could pay him his due? Yet Quimp has his caprices. Might he have done so nonetheless? As punishment? A warning?"

"Warning to whom?"

Sighing, Mr. Franklin rubbed his gouty legs. "We stray far afield, into what-ifs and how-d'ye-knows." He gazed out the window. "But here is Finsbury, Nick—and your dear mother."

Indeed we had reached Finsbury Village and its church, a bleak, stone Norman structure with a stubby tower raised above open fields marked by creaking windmills and sheep huddled in snow. A sharp wind blew as we got down and crept with flapping coats to the graveyard, where amongst others a new stone rose. Writ on it was: ROSE ELIZABETH HANDY, BELOVED MOTHER OF NICOLAS, 1725–1749.

We stood there long, my father and I.

My mother, like Roddy Fairbrass, had been poisoned—though with slow-acting draughts which had taken many weeks to work their way.

We had come here before, to pay homage. I fought tears. Dear mother! Was not the world a vexing mixture of joy and cruel injustice?

We returned along Fleet Street. "'Tis a week since Fairbrass was done in," Mr. Franklin broke his brooding silence. "I fear we do not progress toward discovering his murderer. Will he go free?" His fingers flexed in his lap. "I am aweraied by my wound and must rest me, or I should go at once to Soho Square to wring more truth of the widow. Yet we shall make one stop before pleasing Mrs. Stevenson by our early return. To Porberry's, Peter."

This was the toyshop in the Strand, between Craven Street and Charing Cross. We hád passed it many times on our out-and-abouts, I gazing in wonder at the mullioned windows showing all manner of children's delights. I had never yet had the pleasure of stepping in its doors, so was pleased to hear Mr. Franklin's plan. It was five-thirty and near dark when our coachman reined in our mare. We got down. Mr. Porberry proved a round-bellied, rosy-cheeked man, bright-eyed, who with nimble fingers plucked at the dolls and puppets in his windows, tugging this way and that, arranging, as if he prepared children for bed before blowing out a candle. He spoke to 'em too: "Now, Ned, this way . . . dear Sally, so down? . . . this shall cheer you . . . come, a smile, my popinjay. . . ." He looked round brightly as his shop bell tinkled, and bobbed his white-haired head. "Good even to you, sir. And young gentleman. What may I show you?"

Mr. Franklin smiled. "Something for a boy of five and a girl of seven." To me he said, "Gifts for Tim and Emily."

Mr. Porberry's eyes grew round. "I have many delights." With this he proceeded to hop about, showing dolls, and little houses with tiny beds and tables and chairs, and small wheeled carts, and whistles and drums, and spyglasses that had colored lights within, and stuffed animals too: bears and lions. Mr. Franklin ended by choosing a marionette for Tim, a jiggling clown, and for Emily small twin cloth dolls in a cunningly painted crib.

"By the bye," said the gentleman as he took these, wrapt

206

in pretty packages, "Mr. Roderick Fairbrass sometime stopped by?"

"Why . . . how do you know that?"

"I have spoke with his coachman, who gave out that his master came here the day before Christmas."

"Indeed, he did, that very day, as often before, and bought lead soldiers for his boy and a handsome, great doll for his girl, a fashion baby just over form France, the latest thing."

"The last gifts to his children," murmured Mr. Franklin.

Mr. Porberry blinked. "Last gifts?"

"Forgive me. You do not know. The man is dead."

"Dear me! And when? And how?"

"His heart ceased to beat on Christmas day."

"Such a generous heart, too. How he doted on his children!"

Snow began to fall, wet flakes. Mrs. Stevenson was indeed happy to see us indoors in time for supper. To her great satisfaction Mr. Franklin went straight up and sat himself in bed with a lamp and his *Shakespeare* but had read little when he was visited by his friend William Strahan, the printer, who tutted at his injury and strove to cheer him with the latest news of London.

"And does London hail Ben Franklin the deliverer of Pennyslvania's right to tax the Penns?" inquired the gentleman.

"O, not yet," said Mr. Strahan.

Mr. Franklin thumped his coverlet. "Bring me that news, Straney! When the bells ring it out I shall grow immune to all injury and leap from bed to dance a jig in Craven Street!"

The second day of January dawned with more snow. "As troubled with rats as before, Mrs. Stevenson?" asked Mr. Franklin at breakfast.

"No, sir. Your traps are a wonder. Just yesterday I set out three with a bit o' suet in each. The rats go right to 'em and are caught; I then hang the little cages out o' doors, whence I obtain frozen rats. These King drops into the Thames."

Mr. Franklin laughed. "O, prodigious!"

At ten our coach drew up before the Fairbrass house in Soho Square, I carrying the gifts for Tim and Emily. Mr. Franklin rapped the brass knocker. A chill air of gloom seemed to blow through the entranceway as the maid, Mary, admitted us with a downcast look.

A man was just departing: Captain Jack Sparkum.

"Ye're here too, are ye, Franklin?" said the weathered old salt with a squinting stare from his lean, leathery face. "Ye sail in forbidden waters. Veer off."

"My course is fixed, I fear."

"Fear." With a grim smile Sparkum tugged his seaman's cap upon his weathered brow. "I see a bandage about yer head. Ye've reason to fear, right enow. The wonder is, ye do not act upon't." He strode out into driving snow.

"Are we threatened, Nick?" asked Mr. Franklin with a look of mock dismay. I did not answer, for at that moment Cato Prince appeared at the end of the entrance hall. He glared before he rose up the stairs, and I felt a strange mixture of trepidation and awe. The young blackamoor was insolent, yet for all his eighteen years wore dignity like regal robes. But six years older than I! Watching him go I doubted that even threescore and ten should deliver me of such defiant self-possession.

Mrs. Fairbrass consented to see us, and in five minutes we were once again in audience before her, in the little chamber with the nightingales. This time no fire blazed, and the room was as chill as her reception of us. She sat in her chair like a tragic queen and gazed stonily, her back straight, her shoul-

208

ders stiff, her mouth a thin line of displeasure. Yet her gray eyes watched and questioned (they seemed to stare out of a soul in fetters), and she looked poised to start, as a rabbit might at smell of a fox. Her brow furrowed at sight of Mr. Franklin's bandage, but she said no word.

The gentleman stood before her, hat in hand. "I come to you again, ma'am, humbly yet urgently. May I first ask: have you discovered the emeralds which your husband purchased?"

"No."

"A pity. I truly wished to hear otherwise. Then you are still to be driven into the street at week's end?"

"So it seems."

Mr. Franklin shook his head. "As ever I desire only to help. Will you not allow me? Will you not tell all? Gideon Kite's visit of two days ago was not to say he was sorry to hear of your husband's death."

"Again you call me liar?" The red birds fluttered.

"I spent an evening at the Hazard, a place your son knows well. Your husband knew it too. He lost all there; he owed more than thirty thousand pounds to Kite. He was inveigled, he was cheated—he is not to blame. But the debt he owed is why Kite continues to plague you. He cares not a fig for your husband's death but only for his money. Why do you say otherwise?"

The woman stirred in protest. She seemed girded for angry outburst, but her stiffness abruptly withered, her shoulders slumped, and she looked again lost, as when she saw the lid of the strongbox opened, to reveal it empty. There was terror on her face, which moved me, for, having been many years an orphan I well knew the pitiless degradation of lacking power or means. What would become of this woman's children?

"Come," urged Mr. Franklin gently. "You deny that your husband was downcast, yet everyone says that he was. You

209

knew of your son's folly; you know it was your husband's failed attempt to save him which put him in a dejected state. A weak heart? Nay. Your husband was poisoned. Do you know aught which might bring to light the poisoner? Do you know aught which might help to recover the emeralds?"

She roused herself. "Recover them so they might fall into the hands of Gideon Kite? That is what the law would demand. Do you not think, sir, that if could speak I should? I may not speak, I may not!" The woman's fingers flew to her lips, as if she wished to take back these words. She stood, all atremble. "Mr. Franklin, you must leave be. I believe you are of good heart, but you put me in great danger." She plucked desperately at his arm. "For the sake of my family—my children—ask no more, nor ever come again. I beg you, retire to your affairs and forget Fairbrasses."

Mr. Franklin bit his lip. "Danger? Retire? Forget?" With a grudging bob of head, he assented. "If you wish. But, pray, tell this, for I still take interest: whatever will you do?"

"Captain Sparkum has just been here. He is a good man, a loyal friend. He has offered to take us to America, where we may begin a new life."

"You have considered this well?"

"I do what I must."

"But when do you sail?"

"In four days. The creditors may then fight over the furnishings of the house."

"So soon? A winter crossing will be trying."

"Captain Sparkum is master of the sea. He will deliver us safely."

"And will help you to establish yourself on that far shore, I hope. You say he is your friend. May Cato Prince be equally trusted?"

210

She flared. "Will you not leave be? Cato Prince is loyal. He sails with us."

"Does he indeed?" Mr. Franklin made a small bow. "Since we shall not meet again, I wish you well. By the bye, I have brought some gifts for Tim and Emily. Might I have the pleasure of delivering 'em?"

"You may. Do not mistake me—I do not suspect your kind motive." She drew a shaking hand across her brow. "I am weary. I shall have the children brought down. Mary will then see you out. Farewell."

She withdrew with a rustling of her black widow's gown. Mr. Franklin kept his brown eyes a moment on the closed door. Turning to the nightingale cage, he thrust a finger through its wires. "Is Ben Franklin's nose too sharp?" came his voice, with a burred edge of doubt. "Does he truly do more harm than good?" He shook his head. "Indeed I may blunder—any fellow may, and even an old man must guard against arrogance." A bird pecked at his finger. "Yet the woman's fleeing is precipitous. Such rush to escape! What may it mean?"

"Shall we never know?"

He abruptly swiveled. "Never is the closing of a door. Yet doors have keys. If that most adamant dame, Nature, may be cajoled to unlock her secrets, Hannah Fairbrass may be persuaded to do the same." He pushed his spectacles firmly upon his nose. "We are not turned away so easily."

I was heartened by this renewed determination. In five minutes Tim and Emily were before us, delivered by thin, lame Miss Box, the governess, who stood rigidly behind 'em with reddened eyes. She sniffed. "I have just learnt of Mrs. Fairbrass's plan to sail to America. I am to lose my place. I shall never see the children again." Tears flooded her cheeks.

"There," said Mr. Franklin, patting her hand. "You will

211

find another place. And do not fear for the children; there is much to recommend in America." He turned. "Now, Tim, Emily, see what I have brought. Nick?"

I gave Tim his package, tied with red ribbon. From it he drew forth the clown on its strings. "O, thank you, sir!" said he with his fey smile and his eyes that did not quite look at us. As if we were not there—indeed as if he were all alone in the world—he began to make the clown strut and warble in a singsong. I went to Emily, who stood shyly by Miss Box's side. She carried her great doll with its cunningly sewn buttons. This she handed to her governess as I held out Mr. Franklin's gift. She took out the twin dolls in their painted crib, holding them as if she knew not what they were. "Very pretty, sir," said she, making a polite little curtsey. "I thank you greatly." Yet she at once set the gift aside as if 'twere nothing and took back her great French baby and hugged it tight.

"The doll was from her father," said the governess, stroking the child's hair. "Take no offense. She will play with your gift in time."

"I take no offense."

"Poor children," murmured Miss Box, "to've lost their beloved papa."

"Papa is not lost," came Tim's high, small voice as he went about with his marionette.

"Not lost?" echoed Mr. Franklin.

"Why, yes. I have seen him."

Mr. Franklin looked at me, at Tim. "Pray, where?" asked he.

The boy wore his odd little smile. "About the house."

"O, when?"

"At night."

"Child," chid Miss Box, "you are abed o' night."

212

"Not ev'ry moment."

Her eyes saucered. "What? You rise from bed?"

"Sometimes," confessed Tim blithely, "to play with my soldiers, which Papa gave me the day o' Christmas. I light a candle. I have seen him in the hall, passing by."

"You are certain?" pressed Mr. Franklin. "What nights?"

"Last night, for one," said Tim, jiggling his clown. "He did not speak to me. I told sister Cassie of't, but she said 'twas a ghost and not to fear. 'Twas the ghost of Papa, said she, and thus could be no danger. Papa would not harm me. He watches over me. I am sure to see him again."

"Fond, foolish child!" exclaimed Miss Box. "How it has affected him."

I heard a rustling at the door. "Tim has told you of what he saw?" Turning, I saw Cassandra Fairbrass in her long black mourning dress trimmed with black lace, her runic stone upon her breast. She came into the room like a wraith. "You see, Mr. Franklin? It is as I said. There *is* a ghost, and it is Papa's, and my spirit came to me as warning, which I did not heed. Thus Papa died. O, I am all to blame." She looked whiter and thinner than ever, and her gaunt, fixed stare, with gray smudges of weariness about the eyes, appalled me.

Mr. Franklin took her shoulders firmly in two hands. "It is time, Miss Fairbrass, to give over this idea of ghosts. There are none. 'Twas an imagining you saw—or 'twas flesh and blood—but it was no spirit."

The young woman paid him no mind. Her eyes looked past, fixed on the gift dolls we had brought, which Emily had placed upon the sofa. "Twins," murmured Cassandra, "like Papa and Lemuel."

Mr. Franklin started. "Your father and his brother were twins?"

Her eyes drifted to his face, as if she only now saw it.

213

"Why, yes. Did you not know? And looked quite the same, so I am told: mirror images."

The conclusion of our time at Fairbrasses was brief. The two young children were taken upstairs by Miss Box, but Mr. Franklin kept his gaze quietly on their older sister. "When I asked where your father had obtained the sleeping draught which he gave you," put he, "you said you did not know. Did he himself know of such things, roots and herbs and the medicines which might be got of 'em?"

"Somewhat," replied she in her bleak, despairing way. "A small part of his business was to import such palliatives from the Indies."

"Ah."

She saw us to the door. Peering out, she shivered at more than the cold. "O, I believe Caddy Bracegirdle is my punishment. I hate this badgering."

"He continues to plague you?"

She lifted an arm. "That is his coach."

Snow blew in flurries in Soho Square. At the farthest corner stood a small black conveyance, which I would not have noted amongst four other larger coaches had not the young woman pointed it out. "'Tis Bracegirdle's," said she. "He lurks about the house, he importunes me—or did, when I consented to see him—to help my family by (I blush to say it) giving myself to him. O, he is vile! Thank God James has at last seen him for what he is, and threatens to thrash him should he set foot on our steps. But still he hovers like an incubus; I see him often from my window. I have been foolish enough to speak to him. When I did, he wheedled, saying I must know where Papa's money is hid—or, if I did not, I must find out from Mama so he might obtain it for Gideon Kite."

"You know the truth of Kite?"

214

"Mama told me just this morning—gaming debts, which force us to sail to America." She shuddered. "Bracegirdle has placed his hands upon me, Mr. Franklin. Had it not been for Cato Prince, who drove him from the house, he would no doubt have taken liberties and thought himself my benefactor. I despise him."

"For good reason." Mr. Franklin's expression was dark.

For my part I felt both relief and ill ease. The small black coach was that which had followed us about London's streets; thus I knew who rid in't. Yet I was in no wise pleased to learn that this man was Bracegirdle, who ensnared innocents and treated Miss Fairbrass so ill, and was driven by a desperate need to win his way back into Gideon Kite's good graces. Was he indeed one of the three who had attacked Mr. Franklin? What more might he dare?

"Twins!" exclaimed Mr. Franklin as we rode back toward the Thames. "But think on it—twins! And looked quite the same!" His eyes glittered, a smile playing about his lips. "And the boy believes he sees his father's ghost."

"Aye, the ghost, sir," murmured I with my mind on other matters. Snow slanted past our windows. Glancing behind, I saw that indeed Caddy Bracegirdle's coach had chosen to follow us once more.

This I told to Mr. Franklin.

His smile fled, replaced by a mask of ire. "Enough! I have a sufficiency of this cur nipping at our heels." He thumped the roof with his bamboo. "Stop the coach, Peter!"

We were in Prince's Street. At once Peter drew up beneath the swaying sign of a milliner. With surprising alacrity for a man of his years, who had gouty feet and legs, Mr. Franklin leapt out. I too stepped down, alarmed at what might come. Breathing hard the gentleman astonished me by stepping straightway into the middle of the road directly before

215

Bracegirdle's oncoming mare. The driver attempted to urge his steed faster, to strike Mr. Franklin aside or trample him; but, flapping arms, swinging his bamboo, the gentleman faced down this attempt, the mare being frighted to a sudden, pawing stop. The coach skittered and yawed on icy cobbles, the driver cursed, a startled *yawp!* burst from within. "Here, sir!" cried out angry voices, for all traffic was brought to a halt by this unexpected interference, other coaches pulling aside, clashing wheels, chairs halting too, ladies lifting curtains to peer out, street boys gathering, shop keepers rushing out-doors into the blowing snow.

Mr. Franklin paid them no mind but strode to the coach and flung open its door. "Step down at once, sir!" cried he.

There was muffled protest from within.

At which Mr. Franklin reached and dragged Cadwallader Bracegirdle from his seat.

"I beg you . . . I say . . . but nay . . . you take un-wonted liberties," gasped the pocked, black-browed young man, writhing in Mr. Franklin's hard grasp. He was more than twenty years Mr. Franklin's junior, and taller, yet he seemed a mere puppet in the older man's hands, dancing and screeching.

And then I saw the coachman leap from his box. Brandish-ing the handle of his whip, he bore down upon Mr. Franklin's back, arm raised, moving with purposeful speed.

With no thought I rushed pell-mell and flung myself against this hulking fellow's legs.

His knees buckled, but he did not fall ('twas like butting a great tree), and I felt a hand grasp the back of my coat, my feet leave the ground—and in an instant I was flying in air, tossed as if I were a chip from a woodsman's axe. I fell, rolled unhurt in newfallen snow, and rushed at the brute again—yet this time he waited for me, and I was dealt a blow to my temple that knocked me, head ringing, upon the icy cobbles. "No boy says nay to Bumpp," came his growling voice. I sat up and shook my head, the world spinning. Slitted eyes in a glowering face emerged from a red fog. My heart beat hard. Bumpp? Who had near killed good Mr. Franklin, my father? With difficulty I found my feet and would have charged him once more but for a sudden sickening that near made me vomit.

A form interposed itself 'twixt me and the driver.

Peter, his whip in his hand.

"You struck the boy," accused he.

Bumpp only smiled. "As I shall strike you!" And, unfurling his whip, he lashed at Peter. Flinching I heard the whip crack and felt warm drops fly back into my face: our good coachman's blood. I saw him stagger, yet he righted himself at once. He crouched low, as did Bumpp, and the two men circled one another, Mr. Franklin and Caddy Bracegirdle now as still as statues, watching, Mr. Franklin's hands still gripping Bracegirdle's collar. The growing crowd watched too, and began to urge 'em on as if 'twere some bear baiting or other base sport, the men but animals. "Stop!" cried I, but they did not heed, striking at one another again and again, hard lashes, a raining of blows that cracked in the frigid air beneath the gray sky and creaking shop signs. "Huzzah!" cried the eager watchers. No one called for halt. No one sought a constable. The battling pair protected themselves with their arms, in thick woolen coatsleeves, so most blows did little harm, yet I saw that Peter was wounded, blood dripping into his eyes.

And then Peter's whip flicked out to catch Bumpp's whip and lift it from his hands, high in air, to drop by my feet in the snow.

I snatched it.

Bumpp rushed at me to grasp it, but Peter's arm stopped

217

him. He held Bumpp's coat in one fist, the other fist drawn back. This fist seemed to hang in air, and I felt a strange species of joy: never had I noted how big a hand had our good Peter.

And then the fist flew forward as if 'twere a rock shot by a sling.

Did Bumpp attempt to dodge it? He made a shuddering twitch. Yet his face had fate writ across it, mouth drooping. With a wet sound the taut black knuckles struck, and Bumpp's blood joined Peter's on the trampled snow. A great cheer went up from the crowd as the coachman flung himself about, hands to his ruined nose. He staggered, moaned. At last with a great groan he sank upon the ground, his head striking a wheel rim.

He lay as still as stone.

I looked toward Mr. Franklin. His eyes sent a question to Peter, to me, but when he saw that we were well enough to return his gaze, his look swiveled meaningly to Caddy Bracegirdle. "Who sends you? Kite? Mimm? Quimp? You shall follow me no more, sir, do you hear?" He shook the man so hard his jaw jiggled. "And you shall never again set foot in Soho Square whilst I am in London. Do you understand this?"

Bracegirdle's pocked face was ashen with fury. "You . . . you . . . !" He struck awkwardly at Mr. Franklin, landing a blow which set the gentleman's spectacles askew.

"Oho!" cried Mr. Franklin. Straightening his eyeglasses, he began to lay about Bracegirdle's shoulders with his bamboo, in loud thwacks—"That for you . . . and that!"— which the crowd cheered too.

Screeching protest, Bracegirdle turned and fled into Ironmonger's Row.

Brushing his coat, Mr. Franklin retrieved his beaver hat, which had fallen. Puffing, he knelt momentarily by the prostrate Bumpp, peered, stood, glared round. "He breathes

218

and will wake soon, a wiser man. Begone! Disperse!" At this, booted feet shifted uneasily in the drifts. The curtains of sedan chairs snapped closed, and the bearers moved on. Coaches disentangled themselves. Street boys dashed to discover new mischief. Shopkeepers shut their doors.

Mr. Franklin came to us. "I thank you, Peter. Good man. But you are injured."

"Not to speak on, sir."

"We must nonetheless drive home quickly, where Mrs. Stevenson will wrap your head in its bandage of honor. Thus we shall both show we have been in the wars." He squeezed my shoulder. "And you, Nicolas, equally brave—are you well?"

I nodded, "I need no bandage." Yet my smile took effort, for, if I had not shook before, I did so now, though I hid my trembling as best I could.

Mr. Franklin grasped both our arms. "Come, to coach, and home. Anger led me to this foolish impulse—yet the villains were overdue their drubbing."

15

IN WHICH we borrow fingerprints of a dead man and pursue a red-haired stranger. . . .

And yet I am filled with chagrin," said Mr. Franklin that evening as we sat in his chamber by warming flames. "John Fielding fights disorder in the streets, of which there is aplenty without Ben Franklin provoking more. Anger is never without a reason but seldom with a good one. The rule of law must be upheld. The world is lost if reasonable men resort to blows."

"You were provoked by Bracegirdle's actions," said I.

The gentleman paddled his fingers in his lap. "Well, and you are right." His eyes crinkled; he softly laughed. "I must rein in my temper—yet how I should like to give vent one more time, to beat the Penns with my faithful bamboo, driving 'em like sheep into the fold of justice—and all petty officialdom with 'em!"

I smiled from my perch upon his bed. "I should like to see that, sir." I had been moved by his solicitude over my struck head. A bruise had formed by my right ear, but there was no damage more, save a slight ache. I had been moved too by his solicitude for Peter, with whom he had spent more than an hour in his attic room, himself seeing to the fire and to the poultice applied to his servant's brow, where a dreadful welt stood out. "Such bravery. Such loyalty," he had said when he came down. "The color of a man's skin signifies nothing. Many of dark hue reveal sun-bright souls, whilst some white folk hide black hearts."

"Sir," said I as coals crumbled in the grate, "what of the news that Roderick and Lemuel Fairbrass are twins?"

"Ye think on't too?" His chin sank upon his chest. "Indeed, Nick, the fact may change all. Yet I did not guess it. When Cassandra Fairbrass first told me her father was the elder of two brothers, I assumed some years between 'em. But of twins one is always the elder, for he is first dropt from his dam, no matter that the second sees light mere minutes after."

"And so—?"

The gentleman gazed out at black night, where winds keened like spirits lost. "And so I fear, Nick, that we must rob a grave."

"We must proceed in great secrecy," said Mr. Franklin as we prepared to set out at one A.M. next night. The path for our doing so had been laid by Peter going out at noon, and then Mr. Franklin about two, followed by a stranger's arrival at five, just as Mr. Franklin returned with a mysterious air, which even Polly could not breach. I had stayed abed nursing my head, which throbbed 'til near three o' the afternoon. Mrs. Stevenson stopped by my little room often to gaze in sympathy—yet in some mistrust too, tapping the mole by her nose, as she did when suspicion stirred her.

"You say you struck your head upon a projecting window? In what street? By what building?"

Mr. Franklin taught me to worship truth, yet I discovered myself sinfully proficient at prevaricating, for a street name

221

came to my lips unbid, and a building of two stories, brown brick, which existed just in my mind. I added without being asked, like a forger embellishing his design, that a costermonger's barrow had interposed itself 'twixt me and the proper way, and I had stepped aside as a housewife, who could not be so fine a one as Mrs. Stevenson, nor bake so tasty a pie, had chanced to ope her shutter, which struck me.

The good woman's eyes narrowed. "And Peter too was injured in much the same way upon this journey?" She tapped her mole thrice as she turned to go. "I hope you do not learn of Mr. Franklin too well."

Alone, I pulled the covers to my chin, torn betwixt shame and pride that I had limned my forgery with such nicety. Was I a wicked boy? Even a worshipper of truth might hide it well.

Was't thus with Fairbrasses?

As for the stranger, Mr. Franklin saw him into his chamber just past five and closed the door. The man was raggedly dressed, with an odor of must and earth, and bowed in an odd, sidewise way, as if twisting himself into the floor. He proved to be Daggett. "Daggett only; just Daggett; always and ever Daggett, if you please, Mr. Franklin," said he, wheezing, as he sidled to the bow window and lifted the curtain to peer out, as if 'twere necessary always to keep watch. He let the curtain drop. "First names is baggage, sir, and I prefers to travel light, for there is other baggage I must carry, as you well knows." Winking, he fixed rheumy eyes on me. "The boy?"

Mr. Franklin introduced me. Black grime showed beneath Mr. Daggett's broken nails as I squeezed the dirty paw he held out like stolen goods. His hat was crushed and dusty. He sniffed. "To business, Mr. Franklin. 'Tis a body you want resurrected, for that is my profession, unofficial tho' it be."

"Not the whole body. But a part. The right hand. Then we shall replace things as they were found."

"The right hand . . ." Daggett thoughtfully rolled his eyes. "And should you require this appendage *severed*, sir? To take along? I merely asks, no judgment meant. In my experience, 'tis sometime what a loved one wishes. A widow once desired her dead husband's pizzle in a jar. Daggett was happy to oblige."

With a small smile Mr. Franklin shook his head. "No such severing will be required. I merely wish to examine the hand. Then the man may rest in peace."

"O, very fine. Very delicate. You understands that this must be done at night?"

"I do."

"Late."

"As late as you please—but *this* night."

"O, no question, sir; I shall sweep aside all other engagements. St. John's churchyard?"

"The very place."

"A recent interment, may I ask?"

"But days in the earth."

Daggett nodded, judicious as a judge. "That will make it much more pleasant for us all. The weather being wot it has been, the frozen ground may prove some difficulty, yet it shall not deter. Shall you meet me in Oxford Street, at two A.M.? By the Pick and Bones?"

"I shall."

"And now—" his open palm slid forth, "somewot in advance?"

Mr. Franklin counted twelve shillings into the grimy paw. These disappeared into ragged vestments. "You are indeed a gentleman! I shall await you at two. Good day." With another sidewise bow the man was gone.

I stared at Mr. Franklin. "A grave robber, sir?" asked I.

At his desk he picked up the pen with which he had been writing letters. "One may turn up anything one pleases in London—a grave robber or a grave." He gazed at me over the tops of his eyeglasses. "Never fear, we seek nothing of our corpse save his name."

I had gone to bed at ten, Mr. Franklin as well, to give no hint to Mrs. Stevenson of our intent, so as to forestall queries and protests. Yet I could not sleep but tossed, listening to the soft moan of winter wind and the lapping glide of the frigid Thames past London's shores. Yet I must have slept, for I cried out when a hand shook me in the blackness: Mr. Franklin's. Dressing quickly, I crept to his chamber to find him pulling on his long coat. By candlelight he motioned me to his workshop, where he tucked a cloth brayer, a pot of ink, and some rolled-up foolscap in a small leather bag, which he entrusted to me.

We went downstairs, the gentleman muttering curses at ev'ry creak of wood. Peter waited with the coach in Craven Street, which lay empty and dark.

Shivering with cold we started off.

The snow had ceased. A gleaming three-quarter moon shone brightly in the sky. "I do not like it," muttered Mr. Franklin. "Could we not have been favored with cloud?"

I liked it no better. I knew as well as he the harsh penalty for grave robbing and, though we had no intent to steal a body, was sure that any watchman or constable who might surprise us would hardly credit our protests.

Yet laughter rumbled in Mr. Franklin's chest. "What would the Pennsylvania Assembly say should they discover their trusted agent had been locked in Charing Cross stocks for robbing graves?"

I could not share his amusement. "Sir, why must we do this in such secrecy? If you believe this may lead to Mr. Fairbrass's murderer, why not apply to the magistrate to see it done?"

"Three reasons: One, t'would take too much time; and, two, they would not allow it. Dig up a body for the purpose of rubbing ink on its fingers to press 'em on a sheet of foolscap? Madness, they would charge. The third reason is that I wish no breath of my intent to escape. Mrs. Fairbrass protested that my persistence in this matter placed her and her family in danger. I am come to believe that it does, for there is a double plot in this, Nick, which neither Kite nor Quimp must be allowed to uncover. No, we must take this all upon ourselves." Lapsing to silence, he rode, swaying, to the clip-clop of our mare's echoing hooves. Leicester Fields gave way to Oxford Street. Lights gleamed dimly in few windows. Black forms moved in the road, furtively. Cut-purses? Bludgeoners? Poor souls without homes, who must walk or freeze?

Ah, London!

The Pick and Bones proved to be an alehouse frequented by gravediggers. Even at two A.M. some dusty fellows huddled at benches under its low ceiling, mugs of beer in their work-grimed hands whilst they chatted cheerily of their grisly trade as the clowns in *Hamlet* had: of the skulls they had dug up or whether a tanner's skin might truly hold off water and worms better than a mercer's. Daggett was there and sidled up, drawing us back outside into the dusky street—though first retrieving a mattock and spade from beside the door amongst many such, which the gravediggers left there as they entered. With him was a dull-eyed, madly grinning fellow whom he introduced as Bill Sinkum, who also carried a mattock and spade but never spoke word, only followed Daggett like a dog.

In a quarter of an hour we were past the litch gate of St. John's churchyard, amongst the stones, Peter waiting some way off in shadow with our coach. In swinging lamplight Mr. Franklin pointed out Roderick Fairbrass's grave.

Daggett scratched his stubbly jaw. "Newly dug, with earth not settled yet. 'Twill take no more than half a hour. You, sir, stand by the gate with the boy and keep watch whilst Bill and I does our work. Then you may have hand or foot or any part ye wish."

This we did, stamping our boots, the church tower behind us looming against the moon. I heard grunting, the chuck of the mattock, the slide of the shovel, the plop of earth. "All come to't," sighed Mr. Franklin. "Let us hope to have so blithe a one to dig our graves." He fairly danced in the cold. "Damn Mrs. Gout!"

I peered warily at strange, flickering shadows cast by the moon and was glad when the work was done and we called to the hole. Daggett showed his lamp in, to reveal the coffin. "They does not bury deep o' winter. Shall I lift the lid?"

Mr. Franklin was grim. "It must be done."

Stepping into the grave as if 'twere no more than stepping into some happy alehouse, Daggett raised the brass-handled mahogany lid. I did not like to look on this, yet I did. The body was in its shroud. "The brayer, Nick," said Mr. Franklin, and I ope'd the leather bag and handed him brayer and ink, which he took into the grave. With Daggett's help, Bill Sinkum holding the lamp, he unwrapt the shroud—and there lay Roderick Fairbrass's head upon linen, looking white and drawn, cheeks sunk, lips already drawing back from teeth to show the skull. And a smell too, in spite of the cold, which

226

made me sick though I suffered it as brave as I might. I did not envy Mr. Franklin his task. He lifted the right hand, inked it, pressed the five fingers carefully upon a sheet of foolscap.

Daggett watched and scratched his head. "O, ye're a whimsical fellow."

When Mr. Franklin was done he returned the brayer and ink and foolscap to my possession, I placing the paper carefully in the bag so as not to smear the ink. He and Daggett rewrapt the body and closed the lid; they climbed out.

Mr. Franklin handed Daggett a small purse of coin. "For work well done—and somewhat extra for Mr. Sinkum."

Daggett bobbed his head. "Sinkum thanks ye. I thank ye. Keep Daggett o' mind, sir, for I should be happy to serve again, if need arise."

"I shall do so."

A wind made tree limbs rattle and tick. My teeth chattered.

Daggett saluted like a soldier, and Mr. Franklin and I hurried off to the sound of earth falling once more—for eternity—on fine red mahogany.

"'Tis not Roderick Fairbrass in that grave," said Mr. Franklin an hour later, in his workroom. We had not took off our coats; it was too cold. Yet Mr. Franklin could not wait 'til morning— nor could I, to have results of our adventure. Thus we had crept upstairs and lit a lamp and now stood shivering by the workbench with the glass rods and iron filings. Open upon it lay the sheet of foolscap on which Mr. Franklin had pressed the dead man's fingerprints. Next this lay the sheet on which he had set the fingerprints of Roderick Fairbrass when Mr. Fairbrass was alive. Mr. Franklin bent near, drawing me with him, to show by the point of a glass rod how the tiny lines of the dead man's fingers made one pattern, the lines of Mr.

227

Fairbrass's another, with the scar of an old cut crossing 'em. "From when I was young and noted in my brother's printing shop in Boston how no two man's—or woman's—fingers displayed the same design, I have gathered many samples, and now may say with certainty that each person's fingerprints are as individual as his soul. Such diversity! Thus Nature helps to lead us to our murderer."

I gazed at him. "Is't, then, Lemuel, the twin brother, in that grave?"

"It must be."

"But how? Why?"

"I do not yet know—though I suspect. Give me the night to mull this, Nick. O, such a plan!"

I could not let be. "Then Tim Fairbrass truly saw his father pass by his chamber?" asked I.

"Aye, though surely was not meant to."

"Roderick Fairbrass is still alive?"

"I pray so."

"Was't, then, her uncle whom Cassandra Fairbrass believed was a ghost?"

"Your mind goes as mine."

"But what did he in the Fairbrass house, unknown, in dark of night?"

"If we but knew that, we should know all. To bed, Nick. The morrow may resolve this puzzle."

In truth 'twas nearly the morrow, with but two hours 'til first light.

So filled was my mind with whirling thoughts that I did not believe I could sleep, yet I sank almost at once into a dreamless void, black as ink, starting awake only at rooster's crow (a chickenhouse was kept next door by Miss Spinny, from whom Mrs. Stevenson sometimes bought eggs). Slip-

228

ping quickly into stockings, breeches and coat, throwing a woolen scarf about my neck, I crossed straight to Mr. Franklin's chamber to see if he was up.

I discovered him listening close to the sad-eyed King, who spoke hat in hand with his wonted downcast air. "There is someone acreepin' in o' night, sir, as you b'lieved," delivered he as Mr. Franklin admitted me.

"Oho. Listen close, Nick. Describe this person."

"I can say little," murmured King, "for he is muffled to the eyes and sneaks and peers about."

"Enters by the front door?"

"By the alley o' back, where the dustbins is."

"Is admitted legitimate?"

"Goes in. That be all I know."

"A housebreaker, then—or nearer and dearer of kin? What time did you see him enter?"

"Half past three."

"And he had not emerged, to your knowledge, when you left off watching at six?"

"No, sir."

Mr. Franklin wore his long, striped nightshirt. Brown eyes sparkling, he began to do his knee bends: down, up, down. "Excellent, King. Go and warm yourself; take well-deserved rest."

King crept gloomily out.

Mr. Franklin's joints creaked as he exercised his legs. "I am fifty-one, Nick, and may do one of these for ev'ry year of my life. How many men half my age may say the same?" At his basin he splashed water on his face, vigorously rubbed his cheeks, then quickly tied back his brown hair. "Your look asks volumes. Yes, 'twas I set King aspying in Soho Square." He winked. "'Tis not only our enemies who may make use of sharp eyes." He began to dress. "Go up and rouse Peter. I

229

dislike to wake the goodman, for he has been hard-pressed of late, yet I wish to be off at once, post haste, to try if we may discover who this sneaking visitor is."

Mr. Franklin had glanced back often last night as our coach moved through the blackened London streets, to assure we were not followed. He did so now, as we headed north from the Thames, toward Soho Square. "I misdoubt me if Caddy Bracegirdle would dare pursue us after yesterday's drubbing," said he, "—but Kite or Quimp might send some other spy. Yet I see no one at this seven A.M. Good." I looked too. In truth there were few conveyances about so early, Greek Street behind us lying empty save for a groaning dray whose horses blew white steam, and a smart chaise trotting south with jingling bells.

"Nay, Peter, let us out at Sutton Row," adjured the gentleman as we came near Soho Square. "Wait out of sight, round the corner." We got down where Mr. Franklin had said, Peter driving on toward Charing Cross Road. Our footfalls muffled by snow, I followed the gentleman, along the lane of three-story brick, to the narrow alley running behind the line of houses which numbered Fairbrasses' amongst 'em. In but short time the family departed for America. Where in that vast continent would they settle? Should I, some day, cross the seas to visit Mr. Franklin's home, to see Indians and wide, cold lakes and forests larger than England spreading to the west?

We halted. "Here is the back o' Josiah Skint's house," said the gentleman. "And here," he tapped it with his bamboo, "the bin wherein the mumming Doctor's costume was found. And, next it, the back o' Fairbrasses'." Gazing up, he pulled speculatively at his chin. "Did the ghost enter this way,

230

Nick—or had he no need to enter because he was all along hid in that room upstairs, where dust was recently disturbed, as I discovered when we visited the house's top floor. May we have answers soon. But, hark—look sharp!" He drew me quickly into the dark overhang of Josiah Skint's back doorway. A soft rattling of keys sounded once more, then the rear door of the Fairbrass house creaked open, and in a moment a man crept by in black boots and a long black coat and a hat pulled low so I could not see his face, though there was the briefest glimpse of red hair as he swept by. I glanced at Mr. Franklin to discover a smile upon his lips. "I see," breathed he, though I did not see at all, "—and furtive too. Come, Nick," he gripped my shoulder, "—but soft, for we do not wish to put the wind up our quarry."

Waiting 'til the man had rounded the corner, we followed, whilst all about us London wakened, the rattle of metal wheels echoing up from nearby streets. A cooper rolled out fresh-made barrels amidst pungent yellow shavings. "Apples!" cried a fat woman swinging a rush basket of pippins.

As we peered cautiously into Sutton Way, the mysterious man stepped into a waiting coach near Charing Cross Road.

The driver flicked his reins. The coach set off.

"Foot it, Nick!" barked Mr. Franklin, leaping so suddenly that I was hard pressed to keep at his heels. "Run!" His voice flew back like the wind.

"So, Nick, we head east," said Mr. Franklin from deep within his seat beside me. Indeed this was true. We had found Peter and at a discreet yet steady distance had pursued the coach to Holborn, along Newgate Street, through Cheapside, and from thence to Thames Street past London Bridge and the Tower.

The wide brown river flowed to our right, just over the enbankment, as we jounced along St. Catherine's toward Wapping Dock, where scores of masts stood out against the iron morning sky.

Chin sunk in the folds of his long coat, Mr. Franklin looked both eager and grave. "You expected the man to go this way?" asked I.

"I should have been surprised had he not." Digging deep, he pulled forth his gold watch on its chain. "'Tis another two hours before we reach our destination, I believe. Shall we leave the excellent Peter to follow as he may, whilst we steal some needed sleep?" At once he closed his eyes and in a moment snored.

Fidgeting, unable so to rest in the midst of this pursuit, I watched intently as we moved beyond the environs of London to muddy roads. East. Where? Who was the sneaking man we followed?

Cassandra Fairbrass's ghost? Lemuel Fairbrass's murderer?

Inbound stagecoaches passed us. Geese honked as they were driven in fat flocks toward London markets. We lost the Thames to our right, then gained it, the river growing in size as we moved toward the sea. I thought of countries across the channel, of which Mr. Franklin had told me. France. Might I see France some day, and Frenchmen in Paris? How astonishing that the fame of the man beside me, whose elbow rubbed mine, had reached to Paris, yet this same discoverer of electrical secrets was treated in England as a gnat to be swatted and cursed. Some redress must be made.

And then came a signpost: DEPTFORD; and I believed I too knew where the mysterious man led us.

I shook Mr. Franklin. "Deptford, sir," said I. "Wake you, please."

He started. "Um . . . ah . . . Deptford, as I expected."
Sitting straight, he rubbed his eyes. "A town of excellent
citizens, Captain Jack Sparkum amongst 'em. Do you think
we shall soon again meet the doughty captain?"

In a quarter of an hour we were within the town. Many
ships moored there. As they had in London, masts rose above
slate rooftops, and ship's chandlers and ropemakers and
sailmakers and all manner of shops supplying the seafaring
trade lined the high street. A sharp salt smell filled the air.
Poking out my head, I glanced before us. The coach we
followed moved purposefully, Peter maintaining his careful
distance. The coach turned off the main road. We followed,
into a rutted lane lined by shanties with smoke spinning up
from stumps of chimneys like snakes climbing the sky. The
coach drew up before one of these, near the Thames, and I
was astonished to view men walking upon the water, swinging
picks. Then I saw that the water near shore was froze,
entrapping the great hulls of many ships, and that the men
swung picks to break this ice. The sound of 'em—*snick,
snick*—came to us faintly, like the sound of pecking birds. The
horizon was a low, black line, the river a broad, coldly
shimmering expanse, somehow mournful beneath the
great, desolate sky, only the stolid masts and the curling
snakes of smoke standing out against it, and a few gulls
like bits of flotsam in the sharp breeze from the sea. Far
across the river the ruined shell of a windmill raised drooping
arms.

"Stop," commanded Mr. Franklin, who peered out from
his window, as I from mine. The man in black scurried
from his coach into the shanty by the Thames, a low,
mean structure, no smoke blowing from its chimney. The
door shut like a sotic mouth, and the coach moved off

233

sluggishly, turned parallel to the river, and was gone behind a long wooden shed.

"What now, sir?" asked I.

"Why, rap upon the door," said he. "We must put an end to sneaking."

I was took aback by such boldness; yet, trusting Mr. Franklin, I followed over dirty, frozen puddles to the creaking stoop of the shanty. Oiled paper filled its windows. With no hesitation the gentleman lifted his bamboo and rapped three times, loudly. There followed a long silence. "Captain Sparkum?" came a voice at last, faintly.

"Nay, 'tis Benjamin Franklin," responded Mr. Franklin in ringing tones.

There came more silence, in which I quaked in the biting wind off the Thames.

At last the door opened, slowly. The man we had followed stood in shadow, quite still. At last he reached up and pulled off his hat to reveal red hair—but the red hair of Mrs. Hannah Fairbrass. She stood before us in men's clothes, her lips drawn back hostilely from her teeth, which made me think of a tiger crouched to spring. "You would not leave off, would you, sir?" accused she, all atremble.

"I sought justice for murder," responded Mr. Franklin.

The crunch of boots on ice made me turn.

Mrs. Fairbrass's coachman stood quite near.

'Twas Cato Prince.

Mr. Franklin turned too, one eyebrow quizzing, a mild expression on his face in view of the blackamoor's determined stance and hard look and the pistol he pointed at Mr. Franklin's breast. "Shall I shoot him, ma'am?" asked the fellow, with clear intent of doing so. "I shall shoot him if you wish."

Yet there came reprieve: "One murder is enough," said

234

Roderick Fairbrass, stepping out of shadow to enfold his wife's trembling shoulders in his arm. He smiled wearily. "As we are found out, dear Hannah, let us invite the gentleman in."

Gulls screamed by water's edge as Cato Prince came behind with his pistol.

✤ 16 ✤

IN WHICH explanations enlighten but do not forestall danger. . . .

The shanty was but one poor room, with a tilting wooden floor and a musty stink of rot and age. Yet its many cracks had been well-stopped with daubs of clay, and once Roderick Fairbrass lit the tinder in the rude iron stove a blaze leapt up, which he fed with dry wood, and we grew tolerably warm, though the core of me stayed cold because of the pistol which Cato Prince scowled over in unblinking mistrust. An old settle stood to right of the stove. Roderick Fairbrass sat upon this next his handsome wife, clasping her hand so they seemed to make one being. She held her head high, with a harsh, accusing gaze for Mr. Franklin. As for the husband—how odd to see him living when I had believed the wasted corpse in its bier in Soho Square was he! His long, pleasant face with its large jaw looked as before, ready to smile, yet its light of cheer was thoroughly snuffed, and he sat quite solemn and stiff. At his nod Mr. Franklin and I took the two plain wooden chairs opposite him, whilst Cato Prince remained restlessly by the door like Cerberus of the Greeks, a forbidding preventer of escape.

I gazed about. The only other furnishings were a humble wooden stand holding a cracked, stained basin and ewer, and near it a straw pallet spread with some few rumpled bedclothes which testified it was but recently vacated.

Mr. Franklin's eyes looked about too. "Mean lodgings," observed he. "How long have you lived here?"

"Since the night of Christmas day," replied Roderick Fairbrass.

"When you poisoned your brother?"

The man blanched but made no denail. "Since our plan was effected," said he.

"So you were the mumming Doctor?"

"You have guessed much."

"Mercly made sense of strange matters. You dropped your mask and costume in Josiah Skint's dustbin as you fled?"

"I covered 'em with rubbish. I thought they should never be discovered."

"Much that is concealed is brought to light. Your hideout was prepared in advance?"

"As it must be."

"By Captain Sparkum?"

"Our loyal friend."

"Loyalty. I have heard much on this. The captain's loyalty. That of Cato Prince, of which many have spoke. The loyalty of wife to husband." Mr. Franklin peered sharply. "Of brother to brother?"

Fairbrass flared with strong feeling. "That above all!"

Mr. Franklin sighed. "Sacrificing one's life is loyalty indeed. But to last night: you visited your wife in early morn, at half past three o'clock. You were in habit of doing so?"

"I must see my dear Hannah." He gazed at her with feverish fondness.

"But always in dark of night, so you would not be discovered."

"No one must know I still lived."

"Especially Gideon Kite. You crept away before dawn's break, around five?"

"So 'twas you my wife spied watching?"

"No. A servant of mine. He saw you arrive but did not see you leave. Yet your wife spied him after you departed."

Hannah Fairbrass stirred angrily. "He watched the house! He might be one of Gideon Kite's vile sneaks!"

"How that must have frighted you. I beg pardon for being the cause. Yet, wondering if your plan was discovered, you determined to go to your husband to warn him; thus you led me here. Is this your first time at this place?"

"It is."

"And prudent to make it so, until you sail for America. You still mean to do so?"

"We do," replied Roderick Fairbrass firmly. "Nothing shall prevent." He gazed meaningly at Cato Prince, and I saw that though Mr. Franklin appeared calm we were in some danger.

The gentleman clapped his hands upon his knees. "You spoke of a plan—a means to 'scape Gideon Kite's coils, do I hit the mark?"

"Your aim is true."

"A bold plan, if I see it right. Clever. Cruel? I believe I know it, yet I should like to hear it from your lips."

Mrs. Fairbrass clutched her husband's arm. "You need not speak to him, Roddy. He has been aprying from the first, poking in his nose where 'tis not wanted. O, do not tell him all."

Fairbrass grimly met her gaze, struggle visible upon his long, pale face. At last he gently patted her hand. "Dear Hannah, we have great reason for caution. Yet I believe Mr.

238

Franklin is our friend. We may trust him. Perhaps he may help. He has come far. He shall hear our unfortunate story." Staring a moment at the rough wooden floor, he spoke: "It began long ago, when Lemuel and I were young. We had our disputes—we were but twenty minutes apart in age and thus great rivals—yet we loved one another and though we often fought always smoothed over our differences. We not only looked alike (people often mistook us; we used to make a fooling game of this); we shared a mad passion for drink and gaming, which led us frequently astray, causing us to find ourselves often near sunk by debt, though we always righted our little bark and sailed on no matter the roughness of the seas. Yet temptation ever beckoned, like a siren, beguiling: *come, tipple, game;* and so we went off course ever and again and near capsized our ship and sank forever. Eighteen years ago we fell into debt to Gideon Kite. We knew he had cheated us, but there was no proof. 'Twas the last straw. Scraping together all we might, we paid him and vowed never again to dice or sit at cards. I was married by then to my dear Hannah, whose love I near lost by my gaming. We had two children: James and Cassandra. I had no wish to blast their future hopes. So I left off drinking and gaming. Lemuel agreed to do the same. He would see to our affairs in Jamaica, whilst I managed 'em in London. And so he sailed from these shores and made a life in the Indies."

"Until a month ago."

"As you discovered. Lemuel and I had a dozen hard years, but we made a success. Work and my family's love kept me from temptation. Jamaica demanded strong labor of Lemuel, and forged of him an upright man. We exchanged many letters of love and congratulation.

"Yet blood will tell, and as I was a foolish, weak young man, so my son James proved weak too, easily led astray. He grew up into ease, expecting the life of a young gentleman. I tried to show him the ways of hard work, and its rewards, yet he displayed no aptitude for business, no interest, but wished only to be gadding about town with the likes of Caddy Bracegirdle. Thus was he led to Kite's evil den."

"Led deliberately."

"No doubt. Damn Kite! And I . . . I, Mr. Franklin (how it shames me to say it), I was drawn in. Knowing Kite of old, I was certain he had led my boy on and cheated him and laughed to do so. When I got the news from James I was mad with fury and rushed starightway to the Hazard to confront Kite. Ah, error! When I saw the smirking dwarf, with his twisted, painted features and his mincing walk and his smile that said he had me like a flea betwixt thumbnails, I took the gin he gave me to spite him, to show I could hold my drink and face him down. Yet I could not. The drink made me even more rash, and when he tempted me with gaming—said in sly mock fairness that I might have half the money my son owed to take to the tables—I believed in my gin-benumbed brain that I could show him up and win back all James had lost and more, that I might even ruin the wicked little man, to see him before the magistrate for debt instead of me. And so I went to the tables and lost and knew I was rooked but played on believing I had some power within me to defeat the vultures that ringed me round. Yet I had no such power—the madness of gaming!—and lost, and lost more before many witnesses, 'til I owed Gideon Kite all I had in Nash's Bank and all my holdings abroad, which I could not give over without plunging my family into poverty. At first I refused to pay. You cheated! cried I. But, no, said he, still smiling, and brought forth all his witnesses, one by one, near a dozen, who smiled too, mockingly, and said whate'er he wished and vowed to say more before the law, to ruin me.

240

"I was lost. Kite gave me until the first of the year to pay my debt, before he should have me in prison. I went home in sorrow and chagrin, desperate. What to do? I writ a letter to Lemuel, informing him of my disastrous straying. I moped about town. Dear Hannah saw my state. At last I must inform her. I did."

"And James and Cassandra?"

"Cassandra knew nothing. In my shame I let James believe I had settled his debt."

"And your wife?"

He gazed at her. "'Twas hard news. Yet she stuck by me. She said we must see it through, did you not, dear Hannah? Was there not something we might do to prevent? But, no, there seemed not, though we spent many a bleak evening, hands entwined, staring into shadow, seeking succor from phantoms.

"Then something happened which aroused a terrible hope.

"Weeks passed. I had awaited some reply from Lemuel, yet each packet from America brought no letter of him. Why? I writ again. And again. No answer came, and autumn was upon us, with the date when I must give over all creeping near. Then, one night, in the cold rains of late November which now have turned to ice, I was returning home at dusk when a face rose up out of a dark corner of Greek Street. I gaped to see it, for it seemed a mirror of mine, though wasted; yet it proved no mirror but my brother! He accosted me and drew me with much hard breathing into a dark mews, where we embraced. But how changed was he—frail and gaunt and drawn. 'I have come to save our fortune,' said he in a ragged, moaning voice. His shrunken fingers plucked my sleeve. 'Take me home with you—but secretly, so no one sees. My man will help.' At this a black fellow stepped out of darkness, tall and strong and likewise cloaked, to support him on his

241

shaking legs: Cato Prince, who has been as loyal as you have heard."

Ashen faced, Roderick Fairbrass fed another log into the fire. "And so I saw my brother home, secretly in the back way to my chamber upstairs, where all in wonder, yet with a strange fear, I sat him shivering before the fire with a warm rum and water. Bit by bit he came to life, 'til he seemed almost as of old, a jolly fellow, though I was still took aback by his sunken cheeks and hollow eyes. He saw my wondering look. ''Tis disease,' informed he wanly, 'a rare fungus of the tropics which gets into a man and wastes and kills him. I have meant to write you of this, but then came news of your foolish gaming—ah, Roddy, to've backslid so!—and I thought on it and remembered Gideon Kite's sly ways. I thought too how I should like to thwart the cheating devil, if t'were the last thing I should do. And then it came to me that it *should* be my last, to save brother and family, all I love in the world. And so I came under false name, Mr. Stiles, on the *Hecuba*, which docked yesterday, as you know. Captain Sparkum is sworn to secrecy; do not misdoubt him, for once the old salt has promised a thing not even Neptune may wrest it from him. Some German doctor may've got my real name, but no wind of't can blow from him to Gideon Kite, for this doctor is already sailed on. You may believe me, our secret is safe.'"

"Yet wind did blow," said Mr. Franklin.

"Which much alarmed me when Hannah told me of't. You were fortunate, sir."

"Fortune favors the prepared mind."

"You do not think Kite has heard of this?"

The gentleman looked grim. "I pray not. Go on."

"By then, all astonishment, my wife had joined us and made much over my brother's pitiful state. 'You really believe you may save our family and fortune from Gideon Kite?'

242

asked she. The servant, Cato Prince, stood near. 'I may,' replied Lemuel, 'by my death.' At this we made great protest, which he brushed aside with clawlike hand. 'Dear Roddy,' said he with a terrible smile, 'I suffer of this disease—how it aches in my bones and makes me aweary! I long to be rid of a life of such pain. In truth I could not speak to you without cries and grimaces did I not take opium, which I consume more and more frequently to prevent the agony from dropping me upon the floor. This Cato may testify to, for he has found me in a wretched state when I was foolish enough to stray too far from the poppy. Yet I did so, once, to gather this.' He drew from a leather pouch tied to his waistcoat some bits of dried, curled leaf, of brownish-purple tinge and held it out in firelight. ''Tis the Malivel Plant, or Devil's Kiss,' said he, 'native of the Antilles. In tiny amounts it may cure palsy, but in even moderate doses it kills instantly, painlessly, by stopping the heart. 'Tis by it that I mean to die, and might already have taken my life had your letter not stayed me. My end must come soon, whether by poison or no. Let me give that end meaning; allow me to die in your stead. Do you not see how fortunate it is that we are twins? I may then be easily mistook for you if we arrange it right.'

"Hannah and I protested more—'twas a mad, impossible plan—yet our protests grew feeble and at last were overcome when we thought on how our children might be spared by Lemuel's idea, and how he would derive great satisfaction from knowing he should breathe his last for us. And so that night, conspirators, we set about assembling our strategy, part by part. Cato Prince heard all. Captain Sparkum, too, was let in on the thing, but no others. Only when all were safe aboard ship to America would we reveal to Cassandra and James and Emily and Tim that I still lived."

243

"But to effect the thing on Christmas Day?" protested Mr. Franklin.

"We did not choose the season, it presented itself. 'Twas near the time Kite demanded his money. Too, it took weeks to arrange the hiding place you sit in now, and a plan for sailing, and how to take away all I had saved so Kite could not set hands on't. I am glad, for those weeks gave me many hours with my brother before he must go from me forever."

"He lived in the disused room upstairs?"

"Spared from pain by opium. For a time he was even able to take less than before, for living amongst us rallied him; it seemed to slow the disease. Restless even in his illness, he came out at night."

"To become your daughter's ghost."

"'Twas never intended. Poor Cassandra! I hope the truth about Lemuel may help to alter her superstitious course."

"But why did you fix upon so public a death?"

"'Twas Lemuel's idea. We feared Kite's mistrust. But a roomful of witnesses could not be denied, especially if one of 'em was Caddy Bracegirdle to testify he had seen me die before his eyes."

"And John Fothergill. Bold, indeed. Why did you yourself administer the poison?"

"Could we trust any other? Too, 'twas proper that I, my brother's twin, lift him from his world of pain—a fitting *adieu*."

"At which, moved, you dropt tears upon his breast."

"You saw the wetness?"

"You placed rosemary there as well."

"A sprig. For remembrance—such a small thing; I did not think 'twould be noted."

"I noted it—noted too how drawn the body looked as it lay still upon the floor. A man is always diminished by death, and at the time I set down the sudden, shrunken change to this effect—how could I know your brother was your twin?—yet the wasted appearance stuck in my brain. Nick said he heard the mumming Doctor whisper words as he gave the Opliss-Popliss drops."

"But one word," murmured Mr. Fairbrass bleakly. "Sorry. Many times: sorry. 'Twas my farewell to my brother. Ah, I miss him so!" At this, great, silent runnels coursed down the man's cheeks, and his wife wept with him. I glanced at Cato Prince, who also showed tears on his dusky face, his wide mouth taut with grief. I had seen such tears before, in the funeral line; the blackamoor had clearly loved his master. As for me, I fought a lump in my throat, whilst Mr. Franklin too was visibly moved.

For a long moment we remained thus in memory of a man I had never known, the fire spitting, the faint *snick, snick* of men chopping ice coming to us from the broad east reaches of the Thames, gulls crying out in mournful second, as to protest the unfair fates of men.

At last Roderick Fairbrass mastered himself. He wiped his cheeks. "And so you know all, Mr. Franklin. You see why my wife wished you to leave off. You were our greatest danger—your pursuit might all unknown have led Gideon Kite to know I still lived."

"I am heartily pleased it has not done so. Nick and I were watchful as we came. No coach followed."

"I pray not. You may put away your pistol," said Fairbrass to Cato Prince. "Mr. Franklin is our friend."

The blackamoor slid the pistol into a fold in his coat.

Mr. Franklin stood. "I have found the truth I sought. It shall remain secret. You may trust Nicolas too." He held out his hand. "It remains only to say good-bye and to wish you well. I smile to think how Gideon Kite must stamp his little feet at your escape. My only regret is that his gaming house remains to ensnare other lambs."

Mr. Fairbrass stood too. "My regret is that I must leave London, where Benjamin Franklin resides."

A smile. "Tut, I shall return to America some day. We may meet there. Mrs. Fairbrass?"

She rose to stand by her husband. "I do not hate you, sir. I thought I did, but now I see you meant no harm. You are a good, kind man. Go well." She gave him her hand, which he kissed.

At the door Mr. Franklin gazed into Cato Prince's stoic face. "May I shake your hand, sir?" asked he.

The young blackamoor said no word but held out his strong, broad hand, which Mr. Franklin heartily wrung.

And then we were out upon the muddy path beneath the great, gray sky, the shanty door closed behind us. I felt befuddled though all seemed to be known. Was the Fairbrass affair, then, truly over?

Mr. Franklin was thoughtful as we skirted puddles. "The blackamoor's lineaments. . . ." murmured he.

"His lineaments, sir?"

"Did you not note 'em? Is there not the look of Fairbrasses about him?" Our boots crunched on crusted snow. "His blood is not purely of the negro race. Born in Lemuel Fairbrass's household, Mrs. Fairbrass told us. Do you not think he is Lemuel's son? I wonder, does he know the truth of his birth? He may; it may be from that truth that his great loyalty springs. Ah, fathers and sons!" We trudged toward our waiting coach, Mr. Franklin's arm loosely about my shoulders. "Well, we are all sons of that old sinner, Adam, with a bit of apple still lodged betwixt our teeth. I grow peckish. Shall we stop us in town, to eat before the long ride back?"

246

Yet our stopping proved that all was not done. We went into a sailor's den, the Mizzen, a grog shop, bringing Peter with us. Weatherbeaten men who smelled of the sea and looked carved by salt air sat about at long plank tables. We sat too and were served fish stew with slabs of coarse bread and butter, warming on this raw day.

"You found what you sought, sir?" asked Peter between bites with his wooden spoon.

"I did, thanks to your coachman's skill. Yet you, as I, must forget we ever traveled to Deptford this morn."

"Easily, forgot, sir." Peter started. "But, sir . . . !" He ducked his head. "Look, you, sir, but beware they do not see!"

My heart thumped mightily. Turning with Mr. Franklin, I gazed across the low-ceilinged room, smoky from many clay pipes.

There in the door, peering suspiciously out of cruel, sly eyes stood the hulking mound of Mr. Bumpp, and at his shoulder: Caddy Bracegirdle, with his foppish clothes and mean, pocked visage.

I grew rigid with alarm.

We sat at the far end of the room, beside a great post. Arm round my shoulders, Mr. Franklin bent us quickly forward so this post hid our faces. "Damn me, you are certain they did not follow us from London?" hissed he to Peter across the table.

"No one followed, sir; you may trust in that."

"They must then have tracked Roddy Fairbrass as he returned from Soho Square. 'Twas dark; let us pray they do not know the true identity of the man they followed." Bumpp showed a great blackened bruise across his nose where Peter had struck him. Pulling our hats low, we peered round the post as the two men strode haughtily to the host, putting

247

brusque questions to him, though the man only shook his head. They then went rudely about the room, coming nearer and nearer, demanding as if they were constables who must be answered; but the seamen, close-mouthed, did not like to be so pressed by strangers and returned little save wary looks and tight lips. I thought they might come even to us, but after so many sullen stares balked 'em they left.

Mr. Franklin scraped up at once. "Pray, what did those pushing fellows seek?" asked he of the host.

"A man," replied this squinting fellow. "And a coach. Ha, there be thousands o' coaches and millions o' men. Let 'em search the world."

"Did they give the man a name?"

"They didna' know his name."

"Roddy's secret seems safe yet," murmured Mr. Franklin as we peered out to observe Bumpp and Bracegirdle push into yet another grog shop some doors down, "yet the man they saw sneak from Soho Square has put the wind up 'em. They inquire to see if something may be made of't. O, Kite is persistent."

"And Quimp," said I.

"And Quimp." Mr. Franklin's brow creased with worry. "The devils must not be let to triumph. We must warn Fairbrasses. The family must sail."

❦ 17 ❦

IN WHICH ice proves both enemy and friend. . . .

The hounds sniff the trail," said Mr. Franklin back in Craven Street. "Thank heaven they are dull-witted curs." It was the eve of January third. In but three days, on January sixth, Twelfth Day, the *Hecuba* would sail with Fairbrasses aboard. Surely that was little enough time to stay hid and keep plans close. Waiting 'til Bumpp and Bracegirdle poked their noses far down the high street, Mr. Franklin and I, eyes peeled, had crept back to the weather-beaten shanty near the Thames. Upon hearing what we had seen, Cato Prince's eyes had flashed, his powerful hands had opened and closed at his sides, and he swore himself ready at once to murder the two pursuers and sink 'em in the Thames. Mrs. Fairbrass had fallen into moaning despair, but Mr. Fairbrass had kept his head and listened to Mr. Franklin, who adjured that as Bumpp and Bracegirdle (and thus Kite too) still did not know Mr. Fairbrass was alive, nor that Mrs. Fairbrass was downriver with him, nor that Mr. Franklin stood in that same startling company, they must keep to their plan, long conceived. Mrs. Fairbrass with Cato Prince, and Mr. Franklin and I, must steal away before we were seen. As for

249

Mr. Fairbrass, he must lay low in Deptford—no more forays to Soho Square. "May Captain Sparkum find a way of ferreting you aboard his ship and secreting you there?" asked Mr. Franklin.

"I am sure he may," replied Mr. Fairbrass.

"The *Hecuba* is out of dock?"

"She rides in Deptford Reach."

"I advise you then to board today. Thus hid, there is little chance of being spied. Will you do this?"

"Without delay."

Mr. Franklin turned kindly to the wife. "Do not despair, dear lady. You shall see your family safe in America. And now you and I and Nick and your servant must flee Deptford, lest those two nosing fellows sniff us out. Come, bid your husband *adieu* 'til you may be together once and all."

And so we returned west.

'Twas very still in London that eve, as if the great cold sealed people's mouths and silenced coach wheels and muffled footfalls and cut off rats' squeaks and froze the tongues of even the church bells that pealed the hour. 'Twas a strange, evil stillness, a shivering, a cringing, the City submissive before Nature, as if the veriest quavering attempt to shake off her frigid hand might crack the streets and tumble houses. Mr. Franklin sat broodingly before his fire, pulling at his lip, his boots upon the fender, whilst at his desk I attempted to do sums; yet the little numbers standing upon one another's shoulders leapt and tumbled and mocked and would not be brought down to an answer.

At last I turned upon the stool. "Mr. Franklin, sir—the emeralds. You did not ask Mr. Fairbrass of those."

"Bold," replied he.

"Bold?"

250

He swiveled his head. "Fairbrasses. Bold. Do you not know where those gems may be found?"

"That is what I wonder, sir," said I.

"Come, think."

I thought. "I do not know, sir," said I.

"Why, upon Emily Fairbrass's doll! They are her great green buttons, four of 'em, sewn in netting, so that though their luster is diminished they are in plain view nonetheless."

"Bold indeed—but how may you be sure?"

"I surmise. From Roddy's visit to Mr. Porberry, the toymaker, the day before his false death. Too, from the theatrical nature of Fairbrasses' plan—they make public show to disguise private truth. Clever, do you not think? Come, are not the buttons emeralds?"

"You lead me to believe so—yet why should Mr. Fairbrass not keep 'em safe in his breeches pocket?"

"Because if he were took, so should be his breeches pocket and so should be the gems. 'Tis his family he most wishes to save. Count upon it, Mrs. Fairbrass will make certain Emily does not forget her doll when they depart." Brooding again, Mr. Franklin tapped the fingers of his left hand against the fingers of his right. "Yet I pray Fairbrasses' boldness may deliver 'em to safety."

Mr. Franklin had been Grand Master of St. John's Lodge of the Order of Freemasons in Philadelphia. That eve he went to a gathering of the London fellowship. The secret nature of this organization piqued me (living with Mr. Franklin made me wish to know much I had not thought on before), yet 'twas not Freemasons I fixed on but Fairbrasses. I played with the electrified rod and filings in Mr. Franklin's workshop, but that did not divert me, nor did Polly's reading aloud the tragic end of *Hamlet*, though she did it with much drama, lying supine upon the sofa (her mother was not present) as she played the dying Prince of Denmark whilst flights of angels sang him to his rest. My thoughts flew elsewhere. I saw that I was fond of Fairbrasses—of the innocent youngest whom I wisht not to suffer as I had once done, of superstitious Cassandra, even of foolish James; of good Mr. Fairbrass too, and of his suffering wife, who loved her family as my poor, dead mother had loved me; she wanted but to save 'em. Let all be safe!

Yet Mr. Franklin's news when he returned did nothing to settle my ill ease. He had stopped by Soho Square on his way to his meeting, to ask if Mrs. Fairbrass was still importuned by Gideon Kite. She was not. Or watched, to her knowledge? No, she had kept an eye out, as had Cato Prince, but no one spied, she believed. Good news, I thought, but Mr. Franklin was not heartened: "I mistrust an enemy who ceases to struggle."

I slept ill that night.

The freezing dawn was no better, bringing arrival of a note, delivered by a surly footman, which I received at the door and brought up to Mr. Franklin.

The gentleman opened it at once. "'Where is your promise to obtain for what is owed?'" read he. His pinched brown eyes met mine. "Nothing more. 'Tis signed Gideon Kite." He began solemnly to dress. "Fresh paper and a pen, Nick." This I set out. When he was attired in his usual plain breeches and waistcoat, he sat. "Patience, sir," he spoke as he writ. "I am near, and within days shall deliver to you all you deserve, I promise." This he signed and sealed and gave to me to give to King, who was to take it at once to Bury Street. "We must placate this Kite. Damned Quimp too, who pulls his strings. We must feed 'em scraps 'til they have their full meal—of nothing."

Yet King himself added to my agitation. I found him in the

252

attic room rocking by the glowing little stove, hands hanging betwixt his knees and staring slack-jawed whilst from his throat came the broken, tuneless dirge he sang on downcast days. Yet he took the note and put on his long coat and scarf and hat and trudged out into the biting chill.

Mr. Franklin went out too, at midday, after writing more letters to men he hoped might further Pennsylvania's cause. For myself, I did what I could for Mrs. Stevenson. There was but one rat trapped that night, yet it must be got rid of; so in King's absence I bundled warm and carried the frozen body past the timber yard at the foot of Craven Street to fling by the tail into the Thames. The sky was a broad, bowl fit tight over the city. A keen wind tugged with bitter fingers at my cap. The river flowed swiftly at my feet, yet I noted that against the shore a crust of ice built up. Might it thicken, widen? Might we soon be able to walk—or skate—to Lambeth?

I flung the rat, hideous, with bared, yellowish teeth. It broke through the ice and sank.

I was glad when Mr. Franklin returned at four, though he was chilled to the bone. "Dear God," chattered he, "I have seen bad winters in Pennsylvania but none so punishing as this. Yes, Madame Gout! I attend, Madame Gout! Ever your servant, Madame Gout!" He chafed his aching legs. "Tell Mrs. Stevenson to fetch up a warm toddy, at once." Anonymous abuses of Pennsylvania had appeared in the *Citizen* early in his stay in London. William had written a refutation at his father's request, Mr. Franklin paying of his own pocket to have it published. Now he worked on a larger project, "to answer all ill-natured, ill-informed boobies." This would be an *Historical Review of the Constitution and Government of Pennsylvania*. Warmed by the fire, he spent much of the remainder of the afternoon discussing this with William, who proved very knowledgable. He wrote too to the English lawyer, Richard Jackson, who had penned the *Review*—though, fearing he might lose a chance at Parliament, only on condition that he might do't anonymously. "Bit by bit," sighed Mr. Franklin. "Little strokes fell great oaks."

And then evening came, with whistling winds and flurries of snow about the windows. Tomorrow Fairbrasses would be safe on the seas, yet I was not cheered, for tomorrow was not come, and much might happen betwixt times. Huddled beneath bedclothes, I thought of Quimp. This put me down. If what Sir John Fielding said of the conniving man was true, he could not like being gulled of Roderick Fairbrass's fortune and business, which would have made a fine addition in his quest for power. What if he discovered Mr. Franklin aided Fairbrasses in their plan? Would he then seek revenge against the gentleman?

Father, take care!

Twelfth Day dawned the grayest and coldest we had seen. Miss Spinney's rooster did not wake me, I learning at breakfast that all in her chicken house had froze in the night. William said gravely that many poor homeless souls had been found stiff in the streets; indeed upon coming home last night he himself had stumbled upon one such at the top of our way. "A woman, young, with a pathetic raveled shawl about her shoulders, quite dead in the doorway where she sought refuge." He had done all he might: informed the watch.

"Ah, who will answer?" murmured Mr. Franklin, shaking his head.

I silently thanked God for Mrs. Stevenson's snug haven.

The gentleman and I left for Soho Square at ten. "No, do not look back," commanded he. "We do not care who watches or follows. Let who may. We are all openness. Fairbrasses depart? What of't?—'tis no secret. They sail from Deptford?

Again, no secret. What *is* secret is that husband and father waits aboard ship for 'em, and we may best conceal this by appearing not to know it. Bold! And so we go as friends to bid farewell to Hannah and James and Cassandra and Emily and Tim, bereaved souls who are forced to flee, penniless, to America, in hopes of some chance there. They sail on the *Hecuba*? No secret. Are we not pleased that their plan is about to find success?" Yet Mr. Franklin's gloved hands fidgeted in his lap, his mouth made a fretful line, and once I thought he near leant out to peer back against his own adjuration.

All was not so well in his mind as he made out.

And I? No consoling warmth beneath the traveling rug for me. Kite, Quimp, Bracegirdle, and Bumpp—wolves on the scent, and the trail was not cold yet.

In Soho Square the coach waited ready in front of the tall brick house which would be Fairbrasses' no more, Cato Prince in the box, a great mound of baggage fastened atop, a large metal trunk strapped on back. A thick-shouldered pair puffed white breath in the traces. Glancing round as we drew up, I felt easier: no other coaches seemed to watch and wait. The curtain of the second-story, right-hand window of Josiah Skint's house was pulled back, and I could just discern the sour old man, peering. Was he pleased to have Fairbrasses to rail at no more? No doubt he should find fault enough with new neighbors, whatever their stripe.

And then out the door stepped Hannah Fairbrass, chin lifted, her red hair gleaming at the edges of her close-fitting black bonnet. Admirable woman. Behind her, Cassandra Fairbrass looked pale as a wraith. James came next. Emily. Fey Tim. Emily clutched her doll—bold indeed, though she did not know her boldness. Would she be proud in future years to know she had acted as agent of the family fortune?

255

And the doll's buttons—emeralds? To my eyes they seemed to glint brighter than any mere glass.

At last after good-byes the family was in the coach, and the small crowd of friends who had come to see 'em off gathered round its windows. Mr. Franklin stood amongst these. Mrs. Fairbrass leant out to grasp the gentleman's hand. "Thank you, sir," said she, feelingly; and then Cato Prince had flicked the reins and called *Ho!* and the coach set off with friends waving and crying, "Be well! Find happiness!"

Happiness. Where better to seek it but America, where I hoped to go some day? Should I not feel happy now? Was not all well, Fairbrass wife and children to greet husband and father aboard the *Hecuba* in two hours?

Yet I was still wracked with doubts.

The friends dispersed, leaving the coachman, Mr. Marker, the governess, Miss Box, and the maidservant, Mary, in a close trio by the door, gazing at the last glimpse of them who 'til now had meant home. Yet Mr. Marker looked cheery, for he had a place with Lord Tilbury, starting today, said he to Mr. Franklin. "Mrs. Fairbrass found it for me." With this he jauntily bobbed his head, tipped his hat and pranced off to his new life.

Miss Box too had a place, she informed. "Good Mrs. Fairbrass made sure as many were seen to as she might." She sighed. "Though I shall miss dear Emily and dear Tim, my affections—and person—must soon lodge with Lord and Lady Beavers." Climbing into a small, waiting chaise, she was in a moment as vanished from Soho Square as Mr. Marker.

This left Mary, who also had a bag by her side, all she owned in the world.

Mr. Franklin bent to her. "And did Mrs. Fairbrass see to you, too?"

A curtsey: "O, no sir, I saw to myself—or, rather, Mr. Kite saw to me."

Mr. Franklin's expression froze upon his face. "What? Mr. Kite?"

"Yes, sir, the gentleman who came sometimes to see Mrs. Fairbrass. She did not like him, and I own he is a very odd sort of man, but he was kind to me and said I should have by his intervention an excellent position in his friend Mrs. Binder's house, which was to've gone to another girl. All I must do is be round with him about what I had done in the Fairbrass household, so he might assure Mrs. Binder she should not be disappointed in me."

"This you were willing to do?"

"Why . . . yes, to obtain the position, sir."

"But you were not to tell your mistress you spoke to him?"

"You guess aright. Mr. Kite was quite secretive, not wishing Mrs. Fairbrass to feel beholden to him in her hard time, he said."

"Such elaborate kindness. Secretly, then, he asked you much of Fairbrasses?"

"A great deal, some of which seemed to my mind to have little to do with my work. Yet I did not wish to disappoint and so told all."

"About Cassandra Fairbrass's ghost?"

"Should I not? When I chanced to speak of't, Mr. Kite showed great interest and pressed me hard on the matter."

"The ghost's resemblance to her father?"

"I told what I knew, sir. 'Twas hard to say nay to anything Mr. Kite asked. But how you peer. Have I done wrong?"

"Did you say that Tim Fairbrass had seen his father after he was dead?"

Mary began to look doubtful. "I did. O, Mr. Franklin, why do you stare so?"

257

"You overheard me tell your mistress that her husband had bought emeralds worth a great sum. Did you tell that too?"

Mary's lips began to tremble. "I did."

He grasped her hands. "You are not to blame, child. Yet you may've put your mistress in a very bad place. Yourself as well, for you may discover you have no position with Mrs. Binder—or any other. If this proves so, apply to Benjamin Franklin, in Craven Street." He turned. "Come, Nick! Quickly!" Trotting to our coach, I at his heels, he cried to Peter, "To Deptford, post haste!" We set off smartly as Mr. Franklin sank back mopping his brow. "Surely it is no great thing to catch a laden coach, when ours travels so light. All may not be lost." Yet he looked quite grave.

The Fairbrasses had set out no more than ten minutes before, yet after a quarter of an hour, then half, then three-quarters of hard riding, we had not caught up with 'em. "Damn me," muttered Mr. Franklin, "there is more than one road to Deptford. Have they taken another way? Nothing for't but to press on. Surely we shall arrive beforetimes and tell 'em what Kite has learnt. He cannot have surmised their full plan, yet he guesses some trick has been played him, I am sure. He is tenacious. So is Quimp. Above all they will wish to lay hands on those emeralds. I hope this puts the child, Emily, in no special danger." He thumped his stick. "If we may just see the family aboard the *Hecuba*. . . ."

I thought the same: they would be safe with Captain Sparkum.

And so we traveled on, Peter our excellent steersman. We were much jostled by the rutted road. Snow fell, quite thick for a time, yet Peter pressed ahead. Mr. Franklin did not sleep this time, but ruminated. "America," murmured he when the Thames, which had been lost for awhile, came into view round a bend amidst flurries. "I remember when I sailed back to her shores at twenty. From Deptford to Bugby's Hole; from thence to Gravesend, a cursed, biting place. And then to Margate and at last in sight of the Downs—town and castle of Dover. We saw France too, a hazy line. And then Portsmouth and Cowes. A westerly gale took us, and it was Albion, farewell. I thought then never to return, but here am I. Life takes surprising twists. O, let Fairbrasses escape!"

He sank into silence. The snow stopped, and shortly after came the pointing wooden sign for DEPTFORD. In ten minutes we were in the high street amidst the rope shops and sail shops and grog shops, with Fairbrasses nowhere in sight. It was a quarter past noon, the sky broad and gray over the river. Mr. Franklin stopped at the Mizzen and asked which ship of more than a dozen that stood out in the reach was the *Hecuba*.

The landlord took us to the street corner, where a long slope gave a sweeping view. He pointed to a handsome three master. "There be the *Hecuba*. Ye may walk to her this morn." Indeed the sheet of ice we had seen two days ago was wider now, stretching at least two hundred feet into the broad reach, so that it had entrapped the hulls of several ships, the *Hecuba* amongst 'em. Men stood out like ants on the ice, chipping with their picks, as if they had never left off. Might they free Captain Sparkum's vessel so she could sail with the tide? A long pier stretched out; from its end planks were laid to the *Hecuba*, across which men carried wooden crates and barrels, the last of the ship's cargo and stores before she should weigh anchor.

No Fairbrass coach was in sight. "Impossible they should have got here before us," muttered Mr. Franklin. "We must wait." Peter drove us near the pier, and we got down. Gulls hung overhead in the wind. On the far shore a gibbet stood out, as if to warn of evils nearby. *Snick, snick* came the sound of the picks.

We walked to the end of the pier, where Mr. Franklin paced in the wind, coattails flapping, his look as grave as ever I saw it. "Go you to the *Hecuba*, Nick," said he at last. "Assure yourself, of Captain Sparkum, that Roderick Fairbrass is truly aboard. Report to me."

"Yes, sir." Eagerly (I had never seen a great sailing vessel at close hand), I climbed down and set out across the planks. They were but two feet wide, and I had to lean precariously to one side, nearly toppling, when some ostlers rudely brushed by as they returned to obtain more goods to carry to the *Hecuba*. I had thought the ice solid, but saw beside my feet that some spots were quite thin, with runnels of water oozing through. At other spots the planks moved beneath me in a dizzying way, as the river beneath pressed up, down. This, and the gusting wind, capricious in the whistling place betwixt shore and ship, made the way more perilous than I had imagined. Yet clutching my coat, teeth chattering, I pressed on and came at last to the great hull and mounted the steep gangway with wooden crosspieces as footholds and found Captain Sparkum upon the quarter deck, men below stowing goods in the hold. He turned his rugged face from the gale to squint at me.

I put my question: "Please, sir, Mr. Franklin wishes to know, is Mr. Fairbrass aboard?"

He scowled. "Aye, aboard—but where are the rest o' Fairbrasses?"

I said simply that they came, leaving out all Mary had told Mr. Franklin. "Sir, shall you be free to sail today?" added I.

His scowl deepened. "Get Fairbrasses aboard, and we shall sail!"

Indeed I felt the ship curtsey to the sea, and looking down saw that she was free and that in their hobnailed boots the men with picks were already moving across the ice to aid other ships. Even so shod, they stepped carefully.

My heart lifted. Let Fairbrasses come!

And then they *were* come. I saw a sudden start in Captain Sparkum and peered where he peered, to shore, and saw that a coach stood beside ours, laden with baggage, Mrs. Fairbrass, tiny in the distance but Mrs. Fairbrass nonetheless, just stepping down with the aid of Cato Prince. Mr. Franklin, tiny too, went to her and spoke, and though I could not hear I guessed that he warned her, for she lifted a gloved hand to her mouth in alarm. And then the both of them were urging elder and younger children from the coach, to get to the ship at once, and I saw them hurry out as they were bid, Emily clutching her doll tight.

Captain Sparkum poked my arm. "Go to 'em. Tell 'em to board at once. I shall send men for their baggage when I can spare 'em."

I made haste to do so: down the gangway and out upon the shifting wooden bridge. Yet I was filled with dismay, for the final breaking of the ice near the *Hecuba* had made the planks even more unsteady. They rose and dipped in a way that buckled my knees, and I was barely gone from the ship when I stumbled, my right hand saving me but my left plunging through less than a quarter inch of ice into freezing water. I was filled with fear as I gained my feet, for I found myself on the back of a writhing snake, whose wicked desire was to toss me in the Thames. Yet I learnt to go careful and saw that one might defeat the snake by moving slow.

Slow I went.

261

And then I saw what filled me with worse dismay: Bumpp and Bracegirdle, bearing down hard upon Mr. Franklin.

The Fairbrass family were all upon the planks, moving toward me. Nearer shore the bridge was steady, and so they so far came with ease, James leading the way, followed by his mother, then Cassandra, then Emily, Cato Prince at the rear holding Tim's hand. Having delivered his message and bid them farewell, Mr. Franklin had remained at the end of the pier, gazing anxiously upon their progress. Bumpp and Bracegirdle's faces were disguised by black hoods, but I knew 'em nonetheless. They had emerged from round a shanty near shore. No doubt they had waited all along, watching the *Hecuba*; when they had seen Fairbrasses arrive they came to stop 'em. With some plan? To steal Fairbrasses' baggage? To wrest by force the truth of the emeralds from the mother? Or had they just bided their time and now acted on the impulse of their brains? They were sly but not clever. Far better to've waylaid Fairbrasses on the road, as masked highwaymen, and snatched all they had. They might then have got the doll.

But now?

I did not know. All I knew was that two proven scoundrels raced toward Mr. Franklin's back. I madly waved. I shouted. But the gentleman, no doubt believing I waved to share in the near triumph of a bold plan, merely waved back, smiling, as did James Fairbrass at the head of his party. In the keening wind my shouts were to no avail.

And then Bumpp and Bracegirdle were upon Mr. Franklin. There was a brief skirmish, in which he defended himself manfully with his stick, but surprise and numbers were on their side, and they beat him and pummeled him and drove him back, and I cried out as he was took to the very edge of the pier, where he leant and spun and toppled six feet upon the ice below and lay unmoving as a log.

O, father!

Fury and despair choked me, and I tried to run, but this only made me stumble on the treacherous footing, near thrown out again upon the ice, which creaked and groaned like some anguished beast. Fairbrasses, with eyes only for the *Hecuba*, had seen nothing of what happened to Mr. Franklin. James was now within thirty paces of me. Clearly he began to feel the unsteadiness of the planks, for his smile had fled to doubt, and he gripped his mother's hand, she Cassandra's, Cassandra Emily's, and so forth, so the family made a creeping chain, anchored by powerful Cato Prince, who held Tim in one arm.

Black-hooded Bumpp and Bracegirdle lost no time, leaping upon the planks and racing after Fairbrasses. Working my way forward, I made gestures to try to make one of the family glance back, but with frowns they thought only of their footing. I was filled with anguish. Was there no one who might help? I peered over my shoulder, but Captain Sparkum had vanished from the quarter deck. Ahead, on shore, the ostlers who had carried out the last of the *Hecuba*'s store were tucked into the warmth of grog shops, and the men with picks were far away chipping ice. If they had seen the still form by the pier would they have known it was a man? Would they have made danger of two dark figures racing after six others on the gleaming, pitching ice, whilst one small boy waved his arms?

And then the pursuers drew near Cato Prince's back. I was close enough to James to hear a *Halt!* above the keening wind. 'Twas Caddy Bracegirdle. Fairbrasses heard too. Hand-linked, they stopped, turned. "You have gems which by rights belong to Mr. Gideon Kite," screamed Bracegirdle into the keening wind. "Hand 'em over, and you may go free."

I could not see Cato Prince's face, but I saw him place Tim deliberately behind him, where Emily could grasp her brother's hand. I saw the rigid set of the man's broad back. I felt hope: might he stand as a wall against these desperate interlopers?

But a look of determination glinted through the eyeholes of Bracegirdle's hood, and he quickly drew from his coat a pistol and leveled it at Prince's breast. "The gems, I say! Move aside. The gems!"

There was a moment of inaction, all rocking upon the precarious bridge. Did Prince keep beneath his coat the pistol which he had pointed at Mr. Franklin? I longed for him to pull it out. Shoot Bracegirdle, shoot Bumpp! But no, it seemed Prince had no weapon, for he showed none. Yet he did not step aside.

"Move, I say," growled Bracegirdle, pistol steady, though a species of fear stood out in his manner when these commands produced no result. Yet he was not to be gainsaid. "I shall drop you on the spot, I say," warned he.

More keening wind. "I did not come from America to serve as slave to such as you," came Prince's low voice.

"What? How dare you, man? Obey or die." The pistol was resolutely leveled.

"No, no!" cried Mrs. Fairbrass. "You may have the gems. Here they are, upon the doll." Stepping past Cassandra, she snatched the doll from Emily. The wind tore her bonnet from her head, and her red hair streamed out wildly as she proffered it. "See you? The buttons. Take them and leave us be."

"Buttons?" muttered Bracegirdle. "Why—" A light in his hooded eyes showed he understood.

But Cato Prince lifted an arm. "No!" said he, halting Mrs. Fairbrass. He took a purposeful step toward Bracegirdle.

He would have took more, but Bracegirdle fired.

There was a *pop* and a puff of smoke flew out from the pistol. Hannah Fairbrass cried out and dropped the doll, which the wind began at once to tumble across the ice, its little arms and legs flying. My dismayed eyes watched it go: the gems, all Fairbrasses had fought to keep! I looked back. Cato Prince still stood. Had Bracegirdle's shot gone wild due to the swaying planks? In any case his pistol had but one ball, and, the weapon now useless, he gaped at the stolid black man.

Yet Prince shuddered. With a strange, pitiful sigh he dropt upon one knee.

"Damn you, Caddy!" cried James Fairbrass, pressing his way past mother and sisters and his small brother, Tim. "Damn you, man!"

He flung himself at Bracegirdle, and they toppled upon the ice, struggling with grunts and blows.

Mrs. Fairbrass grasped Tim. "James, O, James," moaned she, as did Cassandra, clutching the runic stone pinned to her coat.

Terrible as was the struggle upon the ice, a movement drew my eye to Bumpp. He had lurked behind Bracegirdle but made no attempt to help his confederate. His dark gaze was fixed upon the doll, which lay on its back on the opposite side of the planks, some twenty or so paces from their rise and dip. The hulking man squinted at the ice between. Would it hold?

Cautiously he edged his way upon it and began to creep toward the doll.

I near scrambled out myself, to snatch the toy before the slow-moving Bumpp might reach it—but I was stopped, for Cato Prince shuddered and stirred. He had strength and will. With gargantuan effort he drew himself to his feet. As he

265

turned toward Bumpp an awful agony twisted his noble face. (Aye, there were Fairbrass lineaments; Prince too was of the family.) I was wrenched to see that blood stained his left shoulder, dripping from his left hand, which he seemed unable to raise. He shook his head, a man struggling to waken.

And then his eyes spied Bumpp moving toward the doll, and his gaze resolved to a terrible fixity.

Lurching, with great, painful effort which I seemed to feel in my bones, he came behind Bumpp, raised his right hand, and delivered a blow which felled Bumpp as if he were a sack of grain.

Yet that was not all his intent. Lifting his hand once more, he began to move toward the doll as if 'twere all in the world, whilst James Fairbrass and Caddy Bracegirdle struggled on the other side of the shifting planks. On the blackamoor went, the fierce wind teasing, tumbling the doll further toward the most dangerous part of the ice, where it met the liquid, stirring Thames.

Indeed the wind battered us all. I looked back at James and Caddy Bracegirdle. Hampered by their heavy coats, they fought ineffectually on the slippery ice, though James delivered one or two telling blows, Bracegirdle yelping at these, cowardly. My fists bunched. Strike harder! I myself longed to pummel the man for what he had done to Mr. Franklin.

Mr. Franklin. I squinted toward the pier but could no longer discern his form beside its wooden poles. My heart sank. Had he gone beneath the ice?

Yet there was no time to think on this, for a furious cry sent my attention once more toward Cato Prince. Bumpp had pulled himself to his feet, and the two giants now clashed and fell, Prince upon his left side, an agonized moan lifting from his lips.

The ice beneath 'em cracked.

A great, jagged circle of't moved and dipped and slid, and, crying "No!" I watched Cato Prince roll into the frigid water. He struggled, but Bumpp had pulled free, and stood at water's edge, and laughed cruelly to see how the blackamoor splashed to save his life. Yet Bumpp's laugh was short-lived, turning to startlement, then terror; for in a last great effort Prince's good right arm lifted from the water and stretched and grasped Bumpp's ankle. Bumpp swayed, he fought to right himself, to pull free, but the blackamoor's hand fastened like a convict's leg iron, and Bumpp was lost. With a shout he too fell into the water. There was a wet flurry. I saw Prince's body close over Bumpp's, to hold him down, the powerful back like the back of a whale before sounding. Then the back sank with a great bubbling, and freezing water closed over it.

"Dear God, dear God!" cried Hannah Fairbrass.

I too cried out.

But the men were gone.

From the corner of my eye I saw Caddy Bracegirdle pull free of James Fairbrass, scramble across the ice, gain the planks. With a great awkward windmilling he dashed toward shore. James, spent, dragged himself to his family.

But the doll.

The family huddled about James and lamented him and Cato Prince, Emily and Tim sobbing. Only I still noted the doll. Might I retrieve it? I was small, the ice would hold me. All Fairbrasses had planned might be saved. Cato Prince would not have given his life in vain.

Mr. Franklin would not have given his life in vain.

Yes.

Cautiously I stepped upon the ice. Go careful, Nick, foot before foot. I crouched against the wind, which wished to

267

blow me down. Yet strong as was this wind it no longer tumbled the doll, which lay face up, the green buttons tantalizing. I crept five paces, ten, twenty. Nearer ice's edge the lift and fall beneath my feet grew greater, slow, steady, dizzying; yet gritting my teeth I persisted. How pleased would be Fairbrasses to have their fortune in their hands.

And then I was near. Ten paces, five, three. The wind ripped my cap from my head. A wetness sloshed about my boots as Thames water lapped over the ice, yet the ice held. The doll's glass eyes stared up, roses blushing in its smooth porcelain cheeks. The thing seemed to smile just for me. I could bend down, reach. This I did, stretching my arm—and I had the doll! My fingers held it firmly. Joy filled my breast.

The ice gave beneath me.

I slid into a shocking cold, which made me gasp. This must not happen! Yet it did; my whole body went under, and so cold was the water, colder than anything I might imagine, that it seemed at first to burn. Too it sucked away my strength, as if in an instant I began to freeze, my blood to congeal. I could not even cry out, for my mouth was filled with water. Too, I had never learnt to swim—a Moorfields boy of work had had no time to practice swimming—and so I thrashed in blind terror. This brought me to the surface, and I opened my eyes and saw the sky overhead and the *Hecuba*'s masts like twigs, sails like shrouds, and near at hand—too near—the shelf of ice under which I must soon roll and bob in death with Cato Prince.

Odd, but I never let go the doll. 'Twas what I had come for; I clung to that.

And then 'twas time to die. I ceased to feel the cold, nor had I strength nor will to fight the water more. "Mr. Franklin," breathed I. What other name might I evoke at death?

268

And yet strangely a man was in the water with me: a round face, a fringe of wet brown hair, searching eyes I knew so well. "I shall save you, Nick," said this man, reaching out. "Let me save you, lad."

His good, strong arms buoyed me.

❧ 18 ❧

IN WHICH murder shows what wicked men may do, yet much turns out well. . . .

At first there was stinging pain in fingers and toes as the heat from the iron stove in Captain Sparkum's low-ceilinged cabin took off the chill. The ship's doctor, Mr. Burgess, had instructed two seamen to help strip us of our clothes. When we were naked they chafed our limbs by his direction whilst Mr. Franklin and I stood helpless as babes, knock-kneed, before the fire, Captain Sparkum by the door watching from crinkled, narrowed eyes. I was shaken and benumbed. How I had got here, saved from death, seemed a dream: lifted from the icy water to James Fairbrass's waiting hands, James then helping Mr. Franklin to climb free, followed by the terrible, windy trek to the *Hecuba* with a great wish to sleep or die crying from my bones.

I had not let go the doll; aboard ship they had had to pry it from my grasp.

Now I knew only shivering as my body waked, my teeth chattered, my skin screamed at prickles of pain worse than any nettles. I sobbed. Sorrow at Cato Prince's death? At my own narrow escape? Joy that Mr. Franklin had risked his life to save mine? I did not know. All I knew was that I could not keep still, the sound welling from my soul as a seaman's strong hands rubbed life into my arms and legs, so that after a time I could stand without falling and might speak to Mr. Franklin, whose skin was as prickled with gooseflesh as mine. "Th-thank you, sir," said I between gulps of air. "O, thank you."

He smiled kindly. "Tut, speak not of't, lad. I wanted a brisk swim; you gave me good reason for't. I am no stranger to Thames waters; indeed I once swam from near Chelsea to Blackfriars, practicing Thevenot's motions. True, I was younger by some thirty years, yet I fancy I have not lost my skill." He gently clapped my shoulder. "Do you not think I swim as well as at twenty?"

At this I laughed, betwixt chattering teeth. "O, yes, sir, quite as well!"

Mr. Franklin laughed too.

At which Dr. Burgess's grave look turned hopeful. "O, I think you shall both recover, for you were in the water but short time. Too you found warmth at once. Rum, Captain, if you please—that is what is called for now. And dry clothes and another hour by this hot fire. Then a day or two abed, to prevent distemper. That shall make drowned pussies purr."

I felt the ship move beneath my feet. "Fairbrasses are aboard?" asked I in sudden alarm.

"Where else might they be?" snapped Captain Sparkum, who had pulled a bottle of rum from a cupboard.

"Do we sail, sir?"

"D'ye suppose the tide waits upon men? We weighed anchor a quarter of an hour ago." With a crooked smile, he poured two noggins. "No Kite or Bracegirdle shall stay us now."

271

At my back Fairbrasses' nightingales fluttered in their cage. In borrowed clothes Mr. Franklin and I were rowed ashore at Gravesend in the bleak light of dawn, January 7, 1758. It had been another year when Cassandra Fairbrass arrived at Craven Street to tell of a ghost. Less than a fortnight ago? I had not met Fairbrasses then; my brief acquaintance was done. Farewell. The wan light of the rising sun made the Thames seem a thick, viscous soup, Gravesend a gray agglomeration of wharves, masts, and shanties lifting like another world from the wavering morning mist. Oars dipped and splashed. Though my body seemed undamaged by yesterday's near drowning (a night's sleep in a bosun's hammock had renewed me) I was still not at ease. I scanned the shore. Had Caddy Bracegirdle warned Kite and Quimp? Did they wait to intercept the *Hecuba*? Yet no enemy met us as we were let onto a deserted bar.

Our oarsmen made silently back for the ship, and, the mist lifting, we saw the *Hecuba* weigh anchor. From a copse of withered trees we watched for near three-quarters of an hour 'til her sails were tiny shreds against a clearing horizon. Mr. Franklin stretched and flapped his arms. "Methinks the weather turns warmer than it has been," said he. "Come."

The stagecoach for London departed Gravesend at nine. He and I were aboard it.

A dour parson and a fat corn chandler and a plump, red-faced woman with two small boys who pinched and poked one another and made demon faces were our traveling companions. I felt strangely wounded leaning against Mr. Franklin's shoulder whilst we rattled west. Was it ever thus when death brushed near? Not only my own. I had never met Lemuel Fairbrass, yet his brave passing moved me. So did Cato Prince's end. Admirable son! Yet I was consoled by reflecting on the scene I had witnessed in Captain Sparkum's cabin when Mr. Franklin and I were dressed and sipping our rum: the reunion of the Fairbrass children with their father—the embraces, the tears, the smiles, and the long silence as they sat and gazed long into one another's faces, as to say: can it be true you really are here? Tim and Emily were held close on either knee of their father, the elder brother and sister at his shoulders, Mrs. Fairbrass beside her husband stroking his hair. Captain Sparkum had placed the emerald-buttoned doll near me. Rising, I handed it to Mr. Fairbrass, who looked amazed and thanked me and, when he heard what I had done to save it, embraced me and said to Mr. Franklin how fortunate he was to have such a servant.

"Servant?" Mr. Franklin sputtered. "Why, Nick is more than a servant—much more, as Cato Prince was more to your brother."

This moved me deeper than all.

And so to London. In six hours Mrs. Stevenson's lace-fringed cap was flapping, her eyes flashing, and her flour-dusted finger waggling in admonition as she scolded us severely by the front door of Number 7, Craven Street.

I near sobbed again to hear her.

She thrust her round face into Mr. Franklin's. "No word, sir! No word! You may've been dead, and how should Mrs. Margaret Stevenson have known?"

He blithely stood his ground. "Indeed, 'tis hard for dead men to send news. Yet we are not dead, dear lady, but alive and hungry and longing for some of your good mince pie. Have you perchance set some by, that you have not fed to the rats?"

"Mercy, how I hate talk of rats!" Yet she led us to the pie

273

and in five minutes was humming to know her Mr. Franklin was returned and filling his belly in her warm kitchen.

Epiphany was past, and all decorations had been taken down: holly, mistletoe, yew. Mr. Franklin had been right, the days did grow warmer, so that after a time no chunks of ice were to be seen in the Thames. Eaves dripped, making musical splashes, and there was for some few days a false Spring. Mr. Franklin and I vowed to spend some days abed as Dr. Burgess had admonished, yet the gentleman could not bear it, and as the only result of his brief swim was a sniffing nose, he threw by the covers in six hours and was up and about, I with him, for I hated bed as well as he. Thus Craven Street settled into its customary ways, which I had come to know, Mr. Franklin rising early and taking his air bath, and then after some letter writing off to one of his clubs or to see some sight of London, to which he sometimes took me. Polly aided her mother with housework and continued to study the books which Mr. Franklin lent her. Mrs. Stevenson fretted that these books did not do for a girl of marriagable age. "A man is better pleased to have a good dinner upon his table than to have a wife who speaks Greek," asserted she, but Mr. Franklin chid that no man of sense wished to marry a dolt: "Was not Greek good enough for Socrates?" William was much occupied by his studies of law, yet found time for gadding, which frequently returned him late to his rooms. To me he stayed cool. I continued to think he liked Polly more than he let on, yet she persisted in tweaking him, to his consternation. Peter remained the steady, loyal servant. King was sunk in gloom.

Polly and Mrs. Stevenson, who missed little (each however interpreting in her way), had noted that their lodger's favored bamboo stick was splintered. Thus they presented him with a sturdy new bamboo at a little ceremony one supper. Rising with much pleasure, he practiced a stroll about the table, twirled the stick, thrust it like a sword and pronounced it perfect, after which he gathered mother and daughter to him, kissing each so firmly upon the cheek that I could not tell who flushed redder. The very next day he began to compose *The Craven Street Gazette*, a newspaper in which he reported the doings of Her Majesty's Court at Craven Street with mock solemnity. He also attended meetings of the Royal Society and spent many hours in his workshop, speculating on matters ranging from the earthworm to the fires of the sun.

He read me this, from the *Gentleman's Magazine:* "On Twelfth Day His Majesty, King George II, attended by the principal officers at court, heralds, pursuivants at arms, etcetera, went to the Chapel Royal at St. James's and offered gold, myrrh, and frankincense. In the evening His Majesty played at Hazard, according to annual custom." He peered wryly over his glasses. "Gaming is in the hearts of men, Nick; 'twill not be expunged. 'Tis in the King's heart. Does God game, I wonder?"

"Perhaps He does, sir, with men as counters. How goes your business with the Penns?"

The paper rattled angrily. "Pah, you may conjecture what reception a petition concerning privileges for the colonies may meet with from those who think that even the people of England have too many!"

Yet all concerning Fairbrasses was not done. I frequently imagined 'em at sea, the *Hecuba* riding the long winter swells toward America, the family tucked happily aboard like grubs in a nut. Mr. Franklin had given warning: "Caddy Bracegirdle is free; he will surely rush straight to Gideon Kite with news of the emeralds." This he had told Roderick Fairbrass in Captain Sparkum's cabin. "You may not be prevented leaving

275

England, but what of America—might Kite send emissaries there?"

Quimp he meant, I knew.

But Mr. Fairbrass had planned well. "The *Hecuba*'s recorded destination is Kingston," replied he, "and Captain Sparkum will surely put in there to unload goods—but only after a first stop in Virginia, where we plan our new life to begin. I do not think Kite or anyone will find us." He sighed. "I have thought me of staying, and facing down the villain to see the worst he might do. But I must think of my family. Too, I long to see America." He shook Mr. Franklin's hand. "We may meet there some day."

Why had no one attempted to intercept the *Hecuba* at Gravesend? This we learnt when we returned to Craven Street. Peter, waiting, had espied Caddy Bracegirdle fleeing along the Deptford high street. Seeing that we did not come back from the *Hecuba*, indeed that she sailed, he followed Bracegirdle and, as he put it, "detained the gentleman, sir, begging your pardon if I took more upon me than was my place," at which Mr. Franklin only laughed and commended his servant for knowing his place so well.

We heard too, and soon, from the maidservant, Mary, who had gone to the Hazard, Bury Street, to apply to Gideon Kite for the position he had promised with Mrs. Binder. The maid huddled in Mrs. Stevenson's front parlor in wretched floods of tears. "O, you were right, Mr. Franklin," moaned she, hands aflutter. "Mrs. Binder is a whoremistress—Gideon Kite wished me to turn whore!"

"Which does not surprise me." The gentleman patted her hand. "There, child, leave off your tears. You are a good girl, and I shall find you a respectable place. Lord Bottom, I believe. Do you not think my lord a good choice, Nick?"

We had met him in the adventure which found me my father. "He is a fine gentleman, sir," agreed I.

This arrangement was soon settled.

There also arrived, from Gideon Kite, a letter:

Mr. Franklin:

You have been unable to obtain for me the money owed by Mr. Roderick Fairbrass. Further I have reason to believe you never had any intention of seeking to do so. Why I do not know, for you would have profitted handsomely. Have you also played some part in the disappearance of my man, Bumpp? He is strangely absent, with no word.

Yet I hold no grudge. Come, game at the Hazard! I should be pleased to see you at Faro or dice. I should be most happy to have you within my doors.

Yours in All Sincerity, etc., etc,
Gideon Kite

Mr. Franklin snorted at this letter. "Within his doors? In his grasp, he means." He tossed the paper into the fire. "I think I must decline this invitation."

Yet I feared for Mr. Franklin. Was the red-haired masked man with whom he had gamed at the Hazard truly the dangerous Mr. Quimp? Twice Mr. Franklin had gone some way toward thwarting Quimp in his plans. Might Quimp then seek to do him harm? My fears were in no way allayed by a visit of Dr. Fothergill on the blustery afternoon of January 10. Mr. Franklin was showing his friend about his workshop, pointing out improvements he had made in his armonica, and playing on the spinning glass disks some air of Monteverdi with wetted fingers, when Dr. Fothergill's gray brows leapt as if he had just remembered something, and he interrupted gravely, "By the by, do you recall that young friend of James Fairbrass, Cadwallader Bracegirdle—a pocked face and a pushing manner? Unmannerly brute! He was at the Christmas party where Roddy Fairbrass died."

Mr. Franklin peered up warily. "I recollect the fellow."

"He is dead."

Mr. Franklin slowly rose from his seat. "Dead?"

Fothergill soberly nodded. "The wretched man was found two mornings ago in a mews off Bury Street, in the door of a stables, where he had froze to death."

Mr. Franklin stared. "Seeking shelter in a mews? But why?"

"Not seeking shelter. His hands and feet were bound. His mouth was stuffed with rags, so he might not cry out."

For a moment my own breath stopped. "O, Mr. Franklin," murmured I.

Fothergill's gray eyes glanced at me, then sharply back at his friend. "What do you know of this, Ben?" asked he.

"I know that Bracegirdle was not what he seemed. He lured young men to a place called the Hazard, where they were fleeced of their fortunes—or their father's fortunes. Gideon Kite runs this place. In turn he is run by a man named Quimp. Kite and Quimp play a vicious game; they do not forgive those who disappoint 'em."

"Barbarous!" exclaimed Dr. Fothergill.

"Indeed, barbarity seems ever to outweigh reason in the mass of men. Poor Bracegirdle. I pity him, in spite of the evil he did."

Yet no harm came to Mr. Franklin as the winter wore on, and I grew to breathe easier. Craven Street was our fortress, unassailable, the Thames at its back, good Mrs. Stevenson at its portal, Peter and I watchful, ready soldiers. Not that no more was heard of Quimp, for a man so good as Mr. Franklin was destined to cross him again. But for now we were at peace, and in April, when the first warm showers uncurled fresh shoots from Mrs. Stevenson's back garden, we received at last a letter from Virginia. 'Twas signed Samuel Weatherbee, yet it was surely from Roderick Fairbrass and told in disguised terms of the plantation which he had bought and intended to farm.

"I predict this Weatherbee shall prosper," said Mr. Franklin, "—though under a false name. How much falsity has there been in this! How much dissembling in the world! We must fight it, Nick." Setting the letter aside, he turned to his open casement, giving upon blue skies. "I love the spring. Mrs. Gout has took a holiday from Craven Street—perhaps she plagues the Esquimaux. Methinks I shall pay Mr. Tisdale a visit, to smell the honest smell of printer's ink, with which only truth ought to be set down." Humming gaily, he departed.

As for Nick Handy, he felt a bruising about the heart. Yet the bruised heart heals under tender care, and I had that in Craven Street. So for the meanwhile I bent to my books. Time enough for the day when the world again beckoned with her hard lessons, which would be learnt by the side of Mr. Benjamin Franklin, the best and wisest man whom I have known.